ALSO BY ISSY BROOKE

The Lady C Investigates Series
An Unmourned Man
Riots and Revelations
In The House of Secrets and Lies
Daughters of Disguise
The Continental Gentleman

THE WILLING GAME

The Scientific Investigations of Marianne Starr
Book One

ISSY BROOKE

LONDON, 1890

One

"If the tube fills with a brown gas, you must wake me up without delay," Russell Starr had insisted with the most ferocious look on his craggy face. He was an old man now, surviving on spite, laudanum and the memories of his past glories as one of the pillars of the Royal Society. It was said that even his reflection was terrified of him.

Marianne, his daughter, knew him better, and did not bother to be scared of him. "Only brown? If it is orange, or yellow, or red, do I let you sleep on?"

He glowered at her as if the answer was obvious, and said, "If any other colour should form, then you will not have time to wake me before the explosion does. Good night."

He retired to his bedchamber which lay next to the laboratory, and she knew that the pills and potions that he would take to help him sleep through his pain would prevent anyone from waking him until at least midday.

Marianne settled, as well as anyone could settle, on a tall stool by the long bench. Her father's experiment was a simple-looking one, with some lump of yellow stuff resting in a large round flask. A tube came off the top of it and passed through a condenser. She had no idea what it was designed to prove, disprove or reveal. Chemistry had never been her thing.

No, Marianne's interest lay in electricity. She was writing her letters by the light of a home-made Geisler tube, though the uranium glass gave the darkened laboratory an unhealthy green glow. Far off in other rooms of the house, her cousin Phoebe would be going to bed after a late evening of entertaining wealthy guests. There would have been laughter, wine, and even a little song. Now it was past midnight, and the guests would have rolled home, full of contentment at their secure places in life.

Marianne refilled her pen and stabbed at the letter, causing a splodge of ink to threaten her carefully chosen words. Her place in life was far less secure, and according to Price Claverdon – Phoebe's doting husband – she was making it less secure by her irritating insistence on trying to change the world.

I don't want to change the world, she thought as she blotted up the excess ink. *I just want to be able to access it.* Her letter was one in a series of tirades she had been sending, on a weekly basis, to all the major London newspapers, deploring the backward state of affairs concerning women's university education. She herself had gained her degree at Newnham, one of the newest Cambridge colleges. But she had not been awarded it there. She could study at Cambridge but sit no final examinations. For that, she had had to return to London and undertake the University of London's external exams. The system, she scrawled out angrily, was a patchwork quilt of hasty reactions and idle ignorance. She stared at that last sentence. Did it make sense? She was not sure. She slid off her stool and began to pace around, reading her whole letter aloud to get a better feel for it.

"If one were to spend many hours making a hearty meal, and then before serving this repast, one should simply fling it into a bucket and feed it to the pigs; why then, sir, is this not exactly what –"

The door handle clicked.

She stopped speaking, and froze. She stared at the circular handle, but it did not move again. It was as if someone had begun to turn it, heard her voice, and thought better of it.

Mr Barrington was the house steward and butler. He was the last man to be awake at night, as it was his duty to secure the house and check the windows and doors. He even patrolled the garden wing where Phoebe and her father lodged, so it could be him, but she was sure he had already done his rounds.

She put the letter on the bench and glanced at the bubbling experiment. No brown gases. She was wearing her indoor slippers and she could walk silently to the door. She pressed her ear to it but heard nothing.

She gripped the handle, took a deep breath, and dragged the door open towards her, dramatically jumping out into the corridor.

It was lit by one solitary gas lamp at the far end where the corridor joined the main house. Was that the flicker of a shadow on the opposite wall? It disappeared as soon as she looked at it. She could not be sure what she had seen.

Well, she might live here in Woodfurlong on sufferance and at the generous discretion of her cousin's husband, but while she *did* live here, it was at least partly her house. She inflated herself with some righteous indignation and set off down the corridor towards the shadow that she might or might not have seen. If it was one of the dozens of staff, they could only be up to no good. Not that Marianne had any spite in her nature – but if there was a problem, she would be the one to sort it out.

She was that kind of woman.

In fact she had more knowledge of the secret liaisons and troubles of the maids and the menservants that Phoebe did. She got to the junction of the garden wing and the main part of the house, and looked to the right. The door that led into the back corridor of Woodfurlong stood partly open.

And it should not be standing open at all.

The servants were bright enough to hide their night time trysts better than this, she knew. She approached the door with caution. The gas lamp was behind her now, and she knew that she was throwing her own shadow ahead of herself as a warning. She pressed to the wall but it wasn't enough to disguise her approach.

She heard a noise like a shoe knocking against something it did not expect to be there – so Phoebe's mad attachment to collecting furniture had a purpose, after all. It waylaid the unwary. Marianne reached the door and peeped through the gap but she could see nothing until she took the step to open it fully.

She flung it open. It startled someone who did not cry out, but she heard them hiss. They were halfway up the back staircase but they turned around, and ran back down, vaulting over the bannister a few steps from the bottom so that they did not have to come close to Marianne. It was a man, dressed all in black, with a scarf over his face. He landed on the tiled floor with hardly a sound and she knew, from that, that his soles were covered in felt or some such. He ran away from her, down the service corridor and through the baize door at the end.

She called out – she could not stop herself. "You there! You! Stop!"

She ran the same way, not to pursue him, but to alert Mr Barrington whose room was on the ground floor near to the wine stores and other vital repositories. She banged on his door, and hopped from foot to foot until he appeared in his night clothes, shortly followed by the housekeeper from her room close by. The other servants were variously in the attic or the space over the stables, and it was Price Claverdon who emerged from the upper rooms before the other servants did.

All was now chaos.

The intruder, of course, had fled. It takes time to rouse a house. Mr Barrington threw an overcoat over his long white nightshirt and he looked like a little round snowman in a jacket as he accompanied Mr Claverdon on a tour of the house while the women clustered around Mrs Kenwigs the housekeeper. Phoebe came down, pursued by her maid who insisted that she return to her room and be locked in; they quickly disappeared again, though Phoebe looked backwards at Marianne and tried to mouth something that she did not catch.

Marianne stayed downstairs, but the conversation was irritatingly circular – *who was it? Did anyone see them? What happened?*

When Mr Barrington and Mr Claverdon reappeared, they were mobbed by the half-hysterical maids. They were all told to go straight to bed and reassured that they were quite safe. Marianne remained in the shadows and pounced on Mr Barrington as Mr Claverdon left the corridor.

"Who was it?" she demanded. "I raised the alarm; I know

that Mr Claverdon will tell me in the morning, but you can surely tell me now."

Mr Barrington, small and round and as precise as a billiard ball, wanted to prevaricate but he also wanted to get back to bed. And Marianne spoke the truth, and they had a good working relationship. Marianne was a handy conduit between the servants and the Claverdons. He said, in a low rush, "There was a man, Miss Starr, who seemed to have gained entry by force, through the scullery. He had not got into any other room, as far as we can tell. He was pursued out to the gates but he has disappeared. I have instructed Wright and Ted to patrol the grounds tonight."

Marianne made a mental note to tell the cook, in the morning, that the groom and the boy would welcome a special hot breakfast. To Mr Barrington, she said, "I saw him start to go upstairs, and then he came back down."

"No doubt he realised that he would be trapped upstairs. You must not worry, Miss Starr. I have fixed the door and you will be quite safe."

"I never worry," she replied. "But thank you all the same."

But she did worry a little, though her concerns were about gases – brown or otherwise. She ran rather quickly back to the laboratory, but did not manage to settle to her letter-writing again. Instead, she pulled out her notebooks and perused her accounts.

If she could earn more money, she could provide for her father in a house of their own.

There was a great deal of pleasing possibility if she were to be successful in tomorrow night's séance.

Two

Things went wrong when the luminous glowing head floated out of the darkness.

Up until that point, Marianne had felt confident in her abilities to expose one more fraudulent medium. The séance itself had been lively, entertaining, and totally by the book. Marianne had been asked to attend by the heir of Mrs Silver, an elderly rich widow. The heir, a lank and limp young man who liked to count money rather than spend it, was worried that Mrs Silver was wasting all of her money on trying to contact her dead husband; and she had a great deal of money, and therefore a great many mediums of fame and reputation keen to help her. Marianne knew all about magnetism but could have stated a good case for money having a particular attraction of its own.

Marianne had attended the small circle in disguise, of course. She was getting too well known to be able to get invited as herself; who would want *Marianne Starr, Scientific Investigator*, ruining all their tricks? Only last month, an illustration had appeared in *Punch* that had looked suspiciously like Marianne, at least according to her cousin Phoebe. "I am getting well known!" Marianne had exclaimed in triumph, snatching it from Phoebe at the breakfast table, and poring over it with glee.

"You say that as if it were a good thing. Look closely, and you see they have pictured you in rational dress," Phoebe had retorted. "So unflattering. These women look positively deflated."

"Oh, marvellous, so they have. It is better than being over-inflated, surely!"

"That's true. I saw Mrs Wilson last week and her corset had pushed her unfortunate bosoms so high that she could rest her chin on them."

"It saves on scarves," Marianne said.

Price Claverdon snorted and coughed and Phoebe fluttered a hand at him. "Sorry, dear; I forget you're there when you're reading so quietly."

He forgave his beautiful young wife instantly, and resumed his perusal of the more respectable papers.

"Do you think it is really me?" Marianne said. "I am not the only woman in this field. There is no name. This could be Mrs Sidgwick."

"Hardly. She is ancient and you are ... tall."

Price sighed heavily. He did not like his breakfasts to be so full of chatter. They had lapsed into silence.

Marianne was in two minds about her increasing notoriety but it could not be ignored. So, at tonight's séance, she had arrived in the guise of one Miss Lily Bowman, bereaved of her dear brother just five months ago, and hence handily hidden behind a veil and a white-powdered face as she was still technically in the late stages of mourning. It was six months for siblings, so the manuals and aged aunts advised.

They had assembled in a nicely-furnished room, the guests

8

of Mrs Silver herself. There was a crowd of eight persons, plus the medium, who was a stout rough woman with an accent of the streets. Her gifts had brought her up in the ranks of society, at least into the presence of her betters, even if she were never going to be accepted by them in any other situation.

The medium had flabby cheeks and a tendency to look one directly in the eye when she spoke, which Marianne liked, and a secondary habit of wiping her nose on her sleeve every few minutes, which Marianne tried to politely overlook. She was called *The Great Italiano,* despite being thoroughly London and also thoroughly female.

The Great Italiano – or Mabel Frink, as Marianne had discovered prior to this evening's antics – was only nominally in charge of proceedings. As they were gathered at the house and behest of Mrs Silver, it was Mrs Silver who directed things. First, they dined very lightly on a selection of foods, the sort one might take before going to the theatre. Then watered-down alcohol – mostly sweet wine – was passed around but no one was to get inebriated. Marianne would have taken a little brandy and hot water, but none was offered. By this time, the gathering was talking most amiably and even strangers were feeling as if they were friends.

Usually they would then move into the room set aside for the real business of the night, but Mrs Silver seemed to crave the games of her past, for she clapped her hands together and suggested they "explore the hidden strengths of the human mind, and see whether we can collectively bend our will to propel another to act, telepathically."

9

Or, to Marianne, "play some parlour games."

The Great Italiano had protested, suggested that the spirits were waiting for them, hovering around impatiently in the ether, and that there was a danger they might float off to another séance. But the other people in the gathering – a mixture of couples and friends, a solitary gentleman and one other single lady – were pleased to go along with Mrs Silver's suggestion. The solitary gentleman was apparently a guest who was invited very late, to replace someone who could not make it at short notice. No one seemed to know him but he inserted himself into other people's conversations with persistence, charm and a little vulgarity. Marianne ignored the other people, and focussed her attention on The Great Italiano. The medium stood to one side of the room, twisting a rope of fake pearls with her fingers, glaring at everyone in turn. At first Marianne thought that she was simply eager to get her séance over and done.

However, the lively gathering grew even more animated and Marianne realised that their gaiety meant that they weren't going to approach the séance with the solemnity and edge of fear that the fake medium needed them to feel. Tricks were far more effective when people took them seriously and believed them to be true.

Marianne excused herself from the games, citing her state of mourning. She stood on the opposite side of the room to The Great Italiano. Mrs Silver directed the other single lady, an old spinster called Miss Henderson, to leave the room. Everyone else was to choose an object in the room, just one between them all, and a sparky young man, a dashing dandy called Timothy, alighted upon the ornamental silver snuff mull that was in the middle of a sideboard. "She will not think of that," he claimed. "Will she not naturally cleave to things of a feminine nature?"

"How clever, Timmy!" said his companion, a woman of simpering words and looks. "Yes, let us all concentrate our will upon that. Oh, someone call her back in, and we shall see!" Everyone put on very serious faces to indicate that they were imagining, very hard, Miss Henderson touching the selected object. They would *will* her to do so, and demonstrate the power of the mind.

Miss Henderson slipped back into the room and everyone affected great nonchalance, though there was a lot of lip-twitching and narrowed eyes as people sought to show how hard they were willing Miss Henderson to approach the ram's head snuff mull. No one looked anywhere near it, and it made the thing even more obvious; they stared anywhere but the silver snuff mull.

Miss Henderson looked at them all, and inched towards the object. The simpering woman could not contain herself, and her hand jerked. Marianne rolled her eyes. It was too easy.

Miss Henderson took another step towards the sideboard. Everyone had grown very still, holding their breaths. *Could they make it any more plain,* thought Marianne in disgust.

As Miss Henderson reached out towards the sideboard – and her hand might have as easily being heading for a nearby vase as the mull – everyone burst out into applause.

"Now might we begin?" The Great Italiano demanded. She looked as unimpressed as Marianne felt. Mrs Silver acquiesced and they left the "Willing-Game" and filed through to the room which had been set up for the séance.

"Set up" was entirely the right phrase. The lighting was low, and the air smoky. They were placed around a heavy table with one central pillar for a leg. A curtain had been hung across one corner of the room, and beyond that, Marianne knew, would be the "spirit cabinet" harbouring all manner of tricks and fakery.

They began in the usual way, with their hands resting on the table, their fingers lightly touching. The Great Italiano shuddered her breath in and out, and the gas lighting flickered; the lamps had been turned down so low that one went out. A man jumped up to attend to it, before they were all poisoned, but The Great Italiano ordered him to sit down again. She got up herself and went to the door, and called in a small thin girl. "My assistant," the older woman said with no more explanation than that, and Mrs Silver nodded, evidently already acquainted with her.

So they settled back down at the table while the thin girl fiddled with the lamps, but she was a clumsy sort and for a brief moment they were all plunged into darkness. The girl said something about the lamps, and instead lit a candle, which was woefully inadequate and now Marianne could not see anything but dark shapes in a dark room. The candle was put far from the table, deliberately so, at the opposite end of the room to the cabinet. The wick needed trimming and of course, this was deliberate, as the sides of the glass grew smoky and let even less light pass through.

That short spell of blackness had given The Great Italiano

12

enough time to extract her hands and join the hands of the neighbours to either side, so that each person thought that they still touched the person they were supposed to touch. With the weak candle guttering so far away, it was impossible to see one's own hands at all. Now she would be free to indulge in her trickery, Marianne knew. But Marianne could not expose this fraud yet. Everything rested on choosing the best moment for the maximum impact. Everyone had to *know* that The Great Italiano was a fake. It had to be demonstrated clearly and unequivocally.

Otherwise, people would continue to believe what they wanted to believe.

The séance progressed with the usual mixture of cold-reading, fishing, and shocking revelations of "facts" that The Great Italiano probably already knew from her research. One woman was told that her uncle did love her and was sorry about what happened to the carriage, and she gave a stifled sob. A man was assured that "she is always watching over you" but that could have easily been a threat as any kind of a reassurance. At one point, a flurry of rapping came from below the table top, which made everyone gasp but didn't seem to serve any real purpose – except perhaps to exercise The Great Italiano's toe joints.

And then it was time for the main event. This is what Mrs Silver wanted, and what Marianne was waiting for.

The Great Italiano, with much pomp and ceremony, retreated to the spirit cabinet, where she said that she would channel her spirit guides. They would announce their presence by music and drums, and everyone was to remain seated, whatever happened.

The Great Italiano called for two strong and honest men to come into the cabinet and tie her up. There was a veritable fight between the gentlemen to be allowed to perform this office; the victors proudly slipped into the cabinet and soon returned, announcing to everyone that the medium's bonds were secure.

The candle blew out.

That surprised Marianne; she hadn't seen anyone near to it, though at least one of the participants around the table was bound to be one of The Great Italiano's stooges. She filed the event away for further investigation.

Silence descended in the pitch-black room.

They waited, and even Marianne, who knew – or thought she knew – what was coming felt a tension rising. It was so very easy to let oneself be drawn into the atmosphere. She clenched and unclenched her toes, and concentrated on her breathing.

Finally a cacophony of sounds erupted from the cabinet – a drum was beaten, and a trumpet played, albeit badly. A young lady squealed but it was cut off, strangled and swallowed back down. A man laughed nervously and turned it into a cough.

Marianne remained calm. There would be more. She had to pick her moment. She could leap up now and fling the cabinet open to reveal The Great Italiano, free of her bonds, blowing on the trumpet, but that was a small revelation.

Suddenly there was a rustling and a puff of air touched Marianne's cheek. She shuddered. She blinked furiously as if she would be able to clear the darkness from her eyes and see what was happening.

It was at this point that the glowing head appeared.

No one had been expecting that.

14

The curtains billowed to each side, only noticeable by the impression they made around the rounded object as it loomed forward in the darkness. It had a wide and domed forehead, two sunken cheeks and a thick chin.

It was, Marianne thought, clearly a balloon painted with some sort of phosphorus. It was a common enough trick, but one that was unexpected here: it was a low kind of game. Nevertheless, this was her moment. She pulled a long hatpin free and leaped forward, and jabbed it viciously into the balloon's side.

The balloon shrieked.

Hands flapped at her, and someone else grabbed her from behind. Everyone was yelling and shouting, and a door was flung open and light flooded the room. It froze everyone to the spot.

Only Marianne moved, fighting her way free of the man who had gripped her around the waist. He harrumphed with an apologetic awkwardness.

The thin girl, the assistant of The Great Italiano, was holding her cheek and sobbing.

"Untie me!" called the medium from within her cabinet. "What is going on?"

Mrs Silver shot Marianne a look of pure venom. "How dare you launch such an attack! Who are you?"

"It matters not who I am. What is going on here, my dear lady, is fraud, pure and simple. I am sorry to tell you that you are a victim of dreadful duplicity."

"Absolutely not!" cried Mrs Silver. "How can you even say so?"

"Er – well, this girl here has been painted to glow in the

dark, and scare us, for a start," Marianne said, still waving the hatpin. "Look at her skin!"

"I was channelling a spirit!" the girl sobbed. "Madam, tell her." By now The Great Italiano had been freed from her ropes, and she had emerged, looking as furious as Mrs Silver.

In fact, everyone was looking angrily at Marianne. She had spoiled the fun for those who did not believe, and utterly ruined the night for those that did.

"Get out!" Mrs Silver said. "Don't you dare come back in this house again, Miss Bowman. Never."

"But she is a fake," Marianne insisted.

"You have no evidence, just bitter spite. The spirits will not reveal themselves again until you are gone!"

Marianne tilted her chin and stalked out of the room. She was followed by someone, and she assumed it was Mrs Silver or a servant, ensuring that she left the premises. Her heart was pounding now, partly in annoyance and a great deal in embarrassment.

She reached the ground floor hallway, and found her outdoor wear in a small room just off to the side of the main door. She glanced behind to tell the servant that she was only going to retrieve her things, but stopped in surprise when she saw she was being followed by one of the other séance participants.

It was the late-added guest whom nobody knew. She wondered how he had managed to get added to the party. He was a tall man in his thirties, with a well-built air, and a grin that spoke of whisky and song. He had shaggy dark hair, and pale brown eyes, and a dandyish love of colourful clothing. He spoke

16

with a smoked edge to his cut-glass accent. "Miss Starr, what an unfortunate turn of events for you."

"I am Miss Lily Bowman…"

"Balderdash. Or I am the King of China."

"I don't believe China has a king, actually. They have an Emperor."

"How clever of you. Tragically you were not clever enough to spot that girl was not going to pop like a balloon."

"It was dark," Marianne said scornfully. "If you will excuse me, I have business to attend to."

"No, you don't, actually. You have just been thrown out of a private house. Come, get your things, and let me escort you home. I would very much like to get to know you."

"Thank you, but there is no need for any escorting, sir." She slipped into her long travelling coat and pulled her gloves on. She adjusted her hat, and sailed out of the house onto the narrow London street. It was dark outside, but there were streetlamps casting light from afar, where they ranged along the main carriageway at the end of the side street.

She walked towards the main road, but the man followed. "Sir," she said, very sternly, "This area is frequented by policemen and I still carry the hair pin. It is very sharp." She often walked the streets alone, even at night, though she picked her routes with care, and knew most of the policemen and their regular beats. And she had more than one type of weapon about her person, which made her walk with a confidence that most footpads could recognise.

"A pin! Such a weapon hardly strikes me with any great fear," he said. "Though you nearly had that poor girl's eye out of her socket. So close. Pop! Like a winkle on a stick. Wouldn't that have made a tale for the papers?"

"Sir!" she said, with fear and caution now creeping along her spine. She picked up her pace. She wanted to be in a busier place. "I am afraid I do not know you."

"But I know you, and that is something."

He had used her name. "Well, you have the advantage of me. Jolly good for you. Ah! A cab. Thank you sir, and good night." She didn't have much money, and would not have usually indulged in a cab, but this man was a pest of the highest order and she had to get away from him.

"Wait." He put out a hand to the cabbie, who nodded, nestled in his greatcoat up on the step of the cab. The horse lowered its head, grateful for a moment's rest. "Then let me give you my card. I am Jack Monahan, and you know, I fancy that we should find much in common, were we to talk. You are a modern woman and don't need introductions and arrangements, do you? Let us become known to one another, naturally. I do believe that we shall be friends!"

"We shall be no such thing!" She took the card out of habit and pulled herself up into the cab. But the infuriating man still stood there. She did not want to give her real address, so she instructed the cabbie to take her to an address in Cavendish Square.

Jack Monahan laughed as if she had made a great joke. He grabbed hold of the brass rail that held the cab's lamp, and pulled himself up towards the cabbie's seat, one leg dangling in the air. "She's trying to throw me off the scent, my friend," he said with a conspiratorial air. "She actually lives at Woodfurlong, out at

Deenhampton. Bit of a trek for you, this time of night, mind."
He jumped back down to the road. "Off you go now! I shall call
upon you soon, Miss Starr. We shall discuss many things."

The cab lurched forward and she shrank back in the seat,
cursing.

How did this strange man know so much about her?
And why?

Three

Mr Barrington let Marianne into the house. Woodfurlong was just to the north-west of London on the edge of a large town that liked to think that it was nestled in countryside and rural peaceful bliss. However due to Deenhampton's regular train service, most residents of the town worked in the capital, and brought their city ways back home with them. It was but a short journey into London.

"Is Mrs Claverdon still downstairs?" she asked, but before the rotund man could answer, her cousin Phoebe had burst out of the drawing room to the left of the main hallway.

"Marianne! You wayward woman! Come in and tell me everything!" Phoebe said. "You are earlier back than I'd expected."

"Good, that means there will be some wine left for me. Let me sort my dress."

"No, nonsense to that, there is no one here, and I shan't mind. I am used to you looking a fright, anyway. Price is off smoking cigars in his study and pretending to work." Phoebe dropped her voice. "I want to ask you something about him. Come in, come in."

What her cousin meant was, *come away from the servants who will be listening.* Marianne followed Phoebe into the drawing room and left Mr Barrington to do his usual night time routine; likely counting wine bottles in the cellar before locking all the doors and windows.

Marianne had never lived on her own, and she had never run her own household, but she had a very good idea of the roles of staff in a large house like Woodfurlong, even though Phoebe Claverdon was the mistress here. She was the daughter of Marianne's mother's half-sister – so Marianne and Phoebe were cousins, but only loosely so. They had grown up very close, after Marianne's mother's early death, and had remained very good friends into adulthood. Now Phoebe was married to the old, rich and grumpy businessman, Price Claverdon. He had a certain amount of old money as well as new, and occupied a comfortable position in life. He worked in the city, he drank in his study, and he was altogether a very proper upper-middling-sort of gentleman.

It was a testament to Price Claverdon's devotion to Phoebe that he had accepted she came as a package – not only bringing Marianne to their new marital household, but her ailing father, too.

In spite of the roof over her head, Marianne rested in a far less comfortable position than Phoebe and her husband. She was an unmarried woman with the added encumbrance of a very good and thoroughly modern education. Worse than that, the education had been gained at the recently-founded Newnham College – hence her letters – and was in the Natural Sciences. Now Marianne had qualifications, a business, and of course no suitors at all.

The rugged face of Jack Monahan swam into Marianne's mind. She dropped her gloves and hat onto a small side table – one of dozens that seemed to breed in the corners of the house – and headed to the wine bottle.

Phoebe perched on an elegant couch. She leaned forward. "Is it cold out? You look pinched. Did you walk? You must not! Oh, will you stir up the fire?" It was not an action that Phoebe would do herself.

Marianne took up a winged chair by the fire, and sipped at the wine with one hand while jabbing the poker into the fire with the other. "It is not too cold, but I have had a trying evening." She sighed. "I fear I have made a fool of myself."

Phoebe laughed. "How so? Do tell. I have had a dull day today. I tried to read with Gertie again. That girl is so hard to teach."

Marianne shook her head and sighed. The daughter was eight years old and certainly not ready for *Clarissa* yet.

"Well, I stabbed that Mabel Frink's girl in the face."

Phoebe half-closed her eyes for a second and exhaled slowly. "Of course you did. Care to explain?"

Marianne drained the wine. "Is this watered? I hope not." She got up and refilled the glass, and when she sat down again, she told Phoebe everything that had happened, up to and including the unsettling meeting with the stranger.

"I have never heard of him," Phoebe said. "That is strange. I am sure that I know everyone. Jack Monahan; hmm."

This was true. She did know everyone, but only those in a certain social class. "It might not be his real name," Marianne

23

warned. "I thought he was a pickpocket, with a charming patter, but I did not let him get close enough."

"How thrilling. He might be a soldier of fortune or an adventurer, do you think? Did he have a dangerous air? How did he sit? I am sure you can tell an adventurer from their seated attitude. Show me how he arranged his legs."

"I shall do no such thing. But anyway, he still might be nothing more than a low-down street thief and card shark with a talent for acting and accents."

"Oh, you do attract them, don't you? The strange sort of people."

Marianne shuddered. The previous year, an elderly retired Brigadier had developed what could only be described as a young man's crush upon her, and had sent roses every day for seven weeks, until he had had an aneurysm in Bournemouth. She might lack for suitors, but she didn't lack for nutters. "It is the nature of being a public woman," she said. "I am sure the actresses have the same problem. Now tell me; what did you want to ask me about your husband?"

Phoebe's casual attitude tightened up. She played with the stem of her glass and looked into the fire, staring past Marianne. "Oh, this is all too silly."

"What is?"

"It is nothing."

"Is it really nothing?" Marianne asked. "Or is this something you are saying because you want me to ask you more questions about it? Please be straightforward with me."

"Oh, no, I am not playing a game – not with you, dear Marianne. No. It is only that sometime I think that something is not quite right with Price, but when I try to examine it, I can find no real reason for my feeling. I am wrong to cast suspicions on him."

"Suspicions? Gut feelings might often be right, if we trust them. We perceive more about the outward world than we are readily conscious of, after all. What is it that bothers you?"

Phoebe shook her head and smiled limply. "There is nothing. Poor Price, being married to a silly paranoid woman such as myself!"

"You are no such thing. But you know that." Marianne got to her feet. "It is late, and my father will be … well, who knows. Unconscious, raving, or inventing a new way of detecting acids. I shall bid you goodnight, and see what awaits me in the garden wing."

"Good night. Don't worry about what I've said. I'm imagining things. And don't worry about the incident at Mrs Silver's! No one will give her any sympathy when the story gets out."

Marianne left the room grimly. She did not care to be reminded that soon she would be the talk of the town. Again.

***

She threw herself into the usual run of things the next morning. She would let Phoebe peruse the newspapers – all of the major ones were delivered to the house before breakfast. Price would read most of them at the morning meal, and afterwards Phoebe took them with her. Then Phoebe would be busy writing letters, organising the household, planning meals,

25

and avoiding her children as much as possible, who were still at home with nurses and a governess, haunting the upper floors like giggling ghosts. Gertrude was eight years old now, and obsessed with horses and fairy tales, but showed remarkably little interest in complicated epistolary novels. Charlie was six, and already reading simple books that mostly seemed to have heavy-handed Christian morals as the main plot. He rarely spoke, but he did like to follow people around and show them pages from his latest story. Marianne liked the children, now that they were getting more interesting, but Phoebe seemed determined to have them at arm's length until Gertrude was ready for her first season of balls and Charlie was going up to Cambridge, as everyone already expected that he must. She did the minimum that anyone expected of a good mother and lady, but she was hardly the mirror of how the good Queen Victoria had been in her early years.

Russell had already warned anyone who'd listen that the silent Charlie should not be sent away to school too early. He knew a man who'd lost an eye at Westminster School, and had nothing good to say about it.

Luckily, Marianne's father, Russell, was not well, and so he didn't share his unwelcome views in public, nor even in private family dinners. His illness ebbed and flowed, much like malaria but it was a far less socially acceptable malady. The once-great scientist and esteemed Fellow of the Royal Society now kept to himself in the suite of rooms set aside for them in the garden wing of Woodfurlong. He had a nurse from the town, Mrs Olive Crouch, but there were no servants dedicated to the ease of Marianne and Russell. He had scared everyone away, except Mrs

Crouch, who claimed to have nursed in the Crimea. That would have made her either a childhood prodigy or about sixty years old; but such was her demeanour that Marianne didn't challenge her. One might as well have an argument with a plank of wood. She had probably survived the Crimea out of sheer traditional British bloody-mindedness.

Russell was having a bad day, so Marianne assisted Mrs Crouch to calm him and force some laudanum into him, and then she went to the kitchens in the main part of the house to hunt for some food. She had missed breakfast, but she often did. It was generally the most silent and painful meal of the day. Price read his correspondence and the papers, and conversation was frowned upon. If anyone began it, it would be Phoebe, and Price would indulge her a little, but it was rare. He would eat rapidly in a flurry of crumbs and spills, and the servants at the edges would look over everyone's heads and stare at the opposite walls. The click of knives on crockery would seem to grow steadily louder until Marianne would want to stuff a napkin in her ears to blot it out.

She found the kitchen to be a warm place of sanctuary, and Mrs Cogwell, the cook, welcomed her in. She welcomed anyone in. She would feed sparrows, and stray cats, and Marianne, and waifs from the street with equal generosity. The butcher's boy from town would have fought anyone off to retain the privilege of delivering to Mrs Cogwell. As soon as Marianne stepped into the kitchen, she was hustled to a chair at the table and presented with new fresh bread and a selection of offcuts of ham.

In return, Marianne promised to fetch some fresh fruit from the markets on her errands that morning.

Such was daily life, Marianne reflected. She walked briskly to the railway station and rode in the second class carriage to London. Her income was small, although she was proud to say that it was all earned by herself alone. It did not quite run to travelling first-class, unless she was with Phoebe, who would have been horrified to learn that Marianne went in the lower coaches. And a dent had been made in it from the previous night's unnecessary cab ride all the way home.

She would have to address the Mrs Silver issue. She'd write to her, Marianne decided, and no doubt the letter would do nothing, but it would be the polite thing to do. She'd ignore The Great Italiano's inevitable crying about the incident. To be fair, the medium and her girl had every right to be affronted, so Marianne could hardly argue back. Marianne *had* stabbed her, albeit lightly.

Marianne sorted all her duties in her head as she worked her way through the markets. She visited greengrocers' stalls and a chemist, and paid a bill at another shop. As the sun hit midday, and the streets teemed with food-sellers and office clerks snatching a break, she paused.

Her basket was full and her purse empty. It was time to go home.

But her feet took her another way entirely.

***

This part of town was a vibrant and exciting one. Which also meant that it was a pit of iniquity teeming with pickpockets, ladies with painted faces, rakish gentlemen, and frowning policemen. Depending on the time of day – or night – all social classes could be seen here, though when the moon rose, the posh ones were male and if you saw a woman alone, you could make a very good guess as to her occupation.

In daylight hours, though, it was merely a rough, loud thoroughfare on the edges of the theatre district. Phoebe would not come here, not alone like Marianne did, but Marianne had very little reputation to be lost. She walked briskly, partly to dislodge the hopes of any chancers hanging around, but mostly because she knew exactly where she was going.

She kept her eyes open and she nearly stumbled when she caught sight of a dark mop of hair under a midnight-blue top hat. The man was tall and had large curling sideburns, and when he turned his face to look into a shop window, she knew it was Jack Monahan.

It was a coincidence.

Except that it wasn't, because he clearly had no interest in a display of ladies' ribbons, and was instead looking straight at her through the reflection in the glass.

She jutted her chin in the opposite direction and walked away as if she had not seen him, and when she chanced to look behind at a street corner, she could not see him at all.

By the time she reached Simeon Stainwright's workshops, up above a tailor's rooms down a narrow side street, she was feeling flustered and a little anxious.

She ran up the rickety wooden steps and hammered on his door. From here she could see the whole street, though it was dark and gloomy. There were a few dozen people moving through it, but none were in blue top hats.

Even so, she breathed a sigh of relief when she fell through the opened door and into the comforting and familiar rooms belonging to the earnest and currently very annoyed stage magician.

"What?" he blurted out. "Kick down my door, will you?"

"I am being followed."

His eyes widened and he slammed the door closed. "Here? To me? *They know?*"

"Who knows?"

"The thieves! Oh, they must know where I live already."

"Have you been burgled?" she asked. "It is hard to tell, to be fair. Anyway if you have, they will already know where you live, and do not need to follow me. Do think, Simeon. Have you not eaten today?" She gestured at the mess and disorder. He had two rooms, both large, and both full of tools and wood and glass and metal. Furniture was not what it seemed here. You might think that you were sitting upon a perfectly ordinary chair, but if you accidentally twisted a dowel or pressed your heel against a spar, you would find yourself folded into it, or ejected from it, or possibly covered in doves.

Simeon pressed himself against the door. He had a pink face with red blotches; he was dreadfully allergic to the make-up he needed to apply for his act. He looked somewhat panicked.

"Oh, Simeon, come away from there. The man was following me, and it is nothing to do with you at all. What has made you so afraid today?" Last week she remembered he had been quite worried about oysters. She couldn't recall exactly why.

"They have stolen one of my designs," he told her. "Again. They watched my show, and stole it."

She persuaded him to give up his post at the door, and they

moved through into the middle of the first workshop. He told her about his latest upset.

The problem was that Simeon was an excellent, indeed a gifted, inventor of machinery and tricks for stage magicians. His designs could conjure butterflies out of handkerchiefs and women out of rocks. He was in high demand, and could have made his fortune without leaving his rooms.

Unfortunately, his desires did not match his talents. He longed for fame and success as a stage performer himself. Every night, he was either giving a show at a tin-pot theatre or low dive, or he was watching someone else's. And while his shows were brilliant in their complexity, his utter lack of showmanship made them dry and dull.

A good performer could make a crowd gasp with nothing more than a bunch of flowers.

Simeon could send them to sleep with a herd of elephants dancing through a ring of fire.

And no amount of greasepaint could make him into a more charismatic presence on the stage.

He was currently convinced that his latest development, a travelling chest with a set of hidden slatted rollers or "scruto" in the base, had been copied by a far more flamboyantly successful double act called Ali Rey and the Blind Boy. Ali Rey was a copper-coloured man from Paris and the boy was not remotely blind.

It happened all the time. She thought that they probably knew exactly where he lived, but she didn't mention that. She talked Simeon down from his pinnacle of paranoid fury, and then asked him if he had heard of a man called Jack Monahan.

31

"No, not at all," he said. "Should I? Will I?" He looked at her with sudden curiosity. "Are you planning on leaving your bluestocking life at last? Marriage, is it? Do not make me attend. I cannot stand the speeches."

"Good heavens, no. This is the name of the man that has been following me. He has made threats."

"What manner of threats?"

"He said we were to talk together and become friends."

"Well, that is a threat indeed, but I think it is more to his detriment. Poor man. So he really does not know you. What has led him into this delusion?"

"I don't know," she snapped at him. "And who are you to talk of other people's delusions? I see that I shall have no sense from you."

"No, wait, don't go," Simeon said as she got to her feet. "I need your help. I intend to expose these two fraudsters, these thieves, and this is very much your area of expertise."

"Lately I find my expertise is lacking," she said.

"Stay. I need to tell you all about them."

"I cannot. Phoebe is inflicting a dinner party on us tonight, and there are preparations to be made."

"It is barely past lunch! How much time does one need to put a dress on?"

"And there speaks a very bachelor man," she retorted. But she softened as she reached the door. "Simeon, don't worry about those so-called thieves."

"Actual thieves."

"Well, actual thieves. You know you are safe here; no one could come in without your knowledge."

"They might, at night, while I am out."

"Then get a dog. Or a servant. A boy with a stout stick would do it."

"He would be a thief too, and the dog would chew all my work. I am working on some traps," he added.

She rolled her eyes. Simeon was a man utterly lacking in trust. "I will help you," she said, stalling for time, "but I really must go now." She would not help him. He would have forgotten this and be on with a new obsession within the week.

He huffed, and turned away, and she left him, feeling ill at ease.

Four

She kept her senses alert as she made her way back to Woodfurlong but there was no sign of the strange man, this Jack Monahan. She couldn't imagine what he might really want with her. He had claimed he wanted to simply talk: it seemed unlikely. No one was without motive. And his actions were not without precedent; her previous obsessives had proposed marriage, or simple devotion. Nevertheless, he was clearly unhinged. She thought that she ought to alert the household staff to be aware of him – after all, he said he'd call on her, and she wanted to be absolutely sure that he did not find her "at home."

Although if she did not receive him, she'd never discover what he wanted.

What did it matter what he wanted? He was a lunatic, she reminded herself. If he needed her opinion on something – yet why would he? – he could write to her.

Perhaps she ought to receive him, if he called, she thought, but only in the hallway, and with Mr Barrington to hand close by, armed with something sharp.

She shook her head. Her own curiosity would be the death of her, she knew.

As soon as she got home, she was swallowed up by the flurry and fluster of the household's preparation for the dinner party. Everyone was having some sort of minor crisis of one kind or another, and the servants tended to come to Marianne with their woes as much as they approached Phoebe or the housekeeper, Mrs Kenwigs. Marianne, they knew, would set things right without judgment or fuss.

The problem with being such a reliable safe pair of hands, Marianne reflected as she helped the nurse to dose one of the children with chocolate worm cakes, was that everyone grew to rely on you rather than tend to things themselves.

Still, at least if Marianne did things herself, she knew they were being done right.

And soon it was time for the dinner party.

**

She had the strange and illogical fear that Jack Monahan would reveal himself as one of the guests.

She was relieved to find that this was not the case, and then felt faintly embarrassed that she'd even worried about it. She was going to end up as bad as Simeon at that rate, worrying about someone who might, or might not, have looked at her strangely and building some huge paranoid story as to why that might be.

Instead there was only one person there that was unfamiliar to her, and he was a business associate of Price Claverdon. He was a hearty man of early middle age called George Bartholomew. Though his face was gaining lines and his rich dark hair was flecked with early grey, his manner was youthful and loud, making him seem like a much younger man.

She guessed, from his enthusiasm for life, that he was not yet married.

As he was a solitary man, and her father had cried off from the dinner – to everyone's relief – it was Mr Bartholomew who escorted her into the dining room. Russell had been invited out of politeness. It was expected that he would refuse but there was always the fear that the mercurial man might one day turn up, and then there would be awkwardness. Price and Phoebe took the lead into the dining room, of course, Phoebe hanging on her husband's arm with a proud and proprietary air.

Also present were another local couple, of the minor gentry, called Mr and Mrs Jenkins. Both were pale grey sorts of people that were the very thing if you were struggling to get to sleep. A short conversation with Mrs Jenkins was much the same as reading Pilgrim's Progress, to Marianne's mind. But Phoebe liked Mrs Jenkins, because she hung on Phoebe's declarations about fashion and agreed with everything that she said, and Price went hunting with Mr Jenkins, and therefore the dinner table was complete. And the good thing about Mrs Jenkins was that she did not gossip, so Marianne was not going to have to listen to the latest scandals. She appreciated that in a person.

Phoebe unfortunately didn't feel the same about gossip, and they had barely started upon the second course when Marianne was informed by her cousin, in great detail, what was being said about her antics at Mrs Silver's séance. Phoebe was full of glee.

Price was unamused. He would not ever criticise her in front of guests, but he harrumphed and coughed and tried to talk, instead, about Portugal and Mozambique and Angola. Eventually his wife took the hint, and asked Mr Jenkins politely about his new dog.

Phoebe could get away with far too much due to her age and beauty, Marianne thought.

All throughout the meal, George Bartholomew was an attentive and respectful partner to Marianne. He spoke equally to everyone around the table, and did not mention business. Marianne asked him if he had been abroad for some time, due to his demeanour and faint accent, and he smiled.

"They warned me that you were an observant and uncanny woman."

"Who are *they*?"

"Oh – a few fellows in my club."

"Why am I the topic of conversation in your club?"

Phoebe overheard Marianne's rising voice. She interrupted. "Come now, Marianne, don't be spiky. They may as well discuss you as horseflesh."

"That is most rude. I am on a level with horses now?"

"Oh, you know what I meant to say."

Marianne did know, and would not have tolerated the slur from anyone but her cousin.

Mr Bartholomew coughed awkwardly. "Well, I can assure you that it was all in perfect innocence. Indeed we were admiring your talents. You have a reputation as an astute scientist and a great scourge of fakes and frauds, and we were speaking of you with much warmth."

He seemed genuine. So she thanked him.

Conversation moved on, and he told her a little of his travels. He had been working across Europe and spent much time in Prussia, which sounded fascinating. There was great upheaval in the region, he told her, and many opportunities for a hard-working man of trade. She would have asked him more about the trade and the politics now that Bismarck had gone, and who had filled that man's void, but Price coughed again and the subject was changed. Then the ladies withdrew, and the men took just enough time to smoke one cigar and down a large amount of alcohol before joining them in the drawing room for cards, a warm fire, and merriment. Price had just had a pianola installed, and was keen to show off the automatic music.

"None of us have any skill at playing," Phoebe confessed to Mr Bartholomew, who was admiring it. "So it seemed better to have this sort of machine. It can be played normally, too, if you would like…?"

Mr Bartholomew backed away, his hands upraised. "Oh, not I! They call the county police on me if I step near any instrument. I shall be content to listen." He caught Marianne's eye as he moved. He dropped his voice. "And you, Miss Starr? Do you play?"

"Good heavens, no. I understand your own reluctance; it is the same for me. I do not play music; I slaughter it."

"That is somewhat strong!" he said with a smile.

"It is the only adequate way to describe what remains after I have wrought myself upon a piano."

"Miss Starr," he said, his voice taking on a gravelly tone, "please, will you sit with me for a moment?" He indicated a pair of chairs tucked in a corner behind a table that sported a bust of the young Victoria and a selection of greyish photographs of the family posed against painted backdrops, scattered about in elaborate frames. "I have something that I must discuss with you."

Marianne smoothed her skirts and sat down. Phoebe had moved towards a card table with Mrs Jenkins, and the other two men were still apparently talking about dogs. Although with all the references to curly hair, pert attention and eagerness, perhaps it was simply code for mistresses.

"…forever squatting under bushes!" Price said and Mr Jenkins guffawed.

Mr Bartholomew leaned in a little too close. She leaned back pointedly but he didn't notice. He kept his voice down, and for all the world looked as if he was going to speak of love. She wondered if he was going to reveal himself to be yet another obsessed admirer. She ought to keep a list in her notebook, she thought, dedicated to men who pestered her.

"Sir, please," she said. "A lady must have air."

He looked confused, as if he were going to argue that she was not a lady. He said, "We could walk outside. Have you any gardens here? Of course you do. It might be best, actually, for what I need to say."

"Absolutely not." She would endure his pressing proximity, for at least they were in sight of other people. "We shall stay here. Please, sir, speak on. What is the matter that you wish to discuss?"

"I need your help."

"I see. Of course. I thought for a minute you were about to throw yourself down on one knee."

"Do men usually do that to you?" he said, and then blushed slightly. "Forgive me, of course they must, as you are a comely and…"

"Yes, yes, thank you. It was your earnest and secretive

40

manner, that is all. Now, Mr Bartholomew, please. You do not have to discuss it here and now, then," she said. "Why not write to me – that is the usual method – or we can arrange a meeting, formally."

He shook his head while saying "Yes, yes," in a contradictory way. "I will do that, all of that, of course, but time is of the essence. I did not know that you were to be here until I entered the house and heard your name, and realised that I had heard it before. It is a marvellous opportunity that I cannot miss. As soon as I saw you, I knew. I feel that any delay now will cost me. Things have happened, and I am unexpectedly back in London, and something will soon catch up with me. I must act now."

"Then what is the issue?"

He spoke now in a whisper. "Miss Starr, my father is not my father."

"Er … oh." This wasn't the time for a biology lesson, but she smiled kindly. "Paternity is such a difficult thing. However, I suspect you mistake my branch of science, sir."

"No, no, that's just it. You are an investigator of quite a modern mould, and that is exactly what I need. I need you to prove that he is lying. He is not who he says he is!"

"Have you spoken to the police?"

"They will think I am mad."

"Sir, I am inclined to agree with them."

He looked startled. He obviously hadn't expected plain speaking.

She took pity on him. Once again, she was attracting strange men and lunatics. He was a little unhinged. Perhaps travel had done that to him. "When did you come home?" she asked. "And what leads you to suspect foul play? Does your father look different to how you knew him?"

"That's just it," he said with some reluctance. "I have not known my father for many years. I was sent away to school at a young age, and my father and mother became estranged. I then went up to university, and after that I began to work for the importing company, and have only recently re-established contact with the man. He looks how I expected him to look. And yet, he is not my father."

"You must give me more evidence than this."

"You know of the Tichbourne claimant?"

"I do, and he was proved false, yes. Well then – that was a police matter, and I think perhaps if you can lay out the evidence to them, they will not treat you as a lunatic. But without facts, they cannot do anything. And I am sorry to say, sir, that nor can I."

"You are an investigator! Please, come to our house."

"You are living with him?"

"Yes, if you can call it living. I arrived back here in England not two weeks ago, and as my mother is sadly now dead, I went to the family home that I have not seen in decades. He received me coldly, and assigned me a small room not fit for a coachman. Since then I have barely seen him." Mr Bartholomew drew out an envelope from a pocket and scribbled an address in pencil for her. "Take this, please."

"Sir, I appreciate your faith in me, but my practise is to expose fraudulent mediums, not fraudulent fathers."

He grabbed her hands and held on. She was startled but

could not make a scene. He peered intently into her eyes and she saw nothing but desperation and fear there. "He does not look as he should, he does not talk as he should, and he does not act as he should."

"Nor does my father, but that is … illness. Perhaps he needs a doctor. Some kind of alienist?"

"No," Mr Bartholomew said. "You must visit us and then you will fully understand why it is you, and only you, that can help me in this matter. He spends all of his time closeted in a room that I am not allowed access to, and the strangest people come and go."

"What manner of people?"

"Mediums, of course! You see there is a reason why it must be you."

They were interrupted by Phoebe, and Marianne was glad of it. She dragged her hands out of Mr Bartholomew's grasp and stood up. "Oh, Phoebe, Mrs Kenwig's new recipe for the beef was superb, wasn't it!"

Phoebe looked pointedly at Marianne's hands, as if there were traces of Mr Bartholomew all over them. Marianne folded them behind her back. Mr Bartholomew realised his error and muttered various apologies as he retreated towards a card table, but he shot Marianne many meaningful glances.

Phoebe hauled Marianne back down to the seat that she had just risen from, and hissed, half in humour and half in shock, "What were you doing with that man, Marianne? What game are you playing here?"

Five

"It's not at all what it looks like," Marianne said hastily, trying to sound calm. "He wants my help."

"Oh, you poor innocent lamb," Phoebe said. "He does not. It's a ruse. He wants his wicked way with you. Have you read none of the novels that I have given you? And besides, you can do much better than give yourself up to a rugged old traveller."

"He is not old."

"You have only just met him – don't defend him! If you wish to marry, dear cuz, then simply say the word and I shall mobilise my considerable forces in society all on your behalf. We shall find you the perfect husband."

"Do not dare."

"Well, then, come and join the game. I am winning. You must let that continue, of course. Don't get mathematical with the cards, or we shall never find you a husband."

***

Marianne stayed out of Mr Bartholomew's grasp for the rest of the evening. Mr and Mrs Jenkins, being sober types, did not outstay their welcome, and when they left, so did Mr

Bartholomew. It was then an early night, relatively speaking, for the household. Price claimed to have an attack of dyspepsia, and retired to his bedroom. Marianne and Phoebe stood by the fire for a little while, letting it die down while they finished the wine. Marianne told Phoebe everything that Mr Bartholomew had said and how he had begged for her help.

"But that is nonsense," Phoebe cried. "You are right – it is no business of yours. This is not at all what you do – no, not your type of investigation at all. Why, I don't think it is his father that needs a doctor. The son needs an alienist, you were correct! He is not well in the head."

"I quite agree."

"I shall have words with Price. He ought not to have invited an unstable man into the house. He shall not be admitted again. I knew he was too ... unpolished."

"Indeed."

Phoebe looked at her sideways. "You're curious, aren't you?"

"Yes. Of course I am. Aren't you?"

"Yes. Will you visit him, then, as he asked? You must not. Except ..."

"Absolutely not! I am curious but not a fool."

And she meant it, too.

***

The beef, while lovely, had been the best part of the meal; Marianne had picked at the rest of the vegetables, and now she felt hungry. Mrs Cogwell was an excellent cook so she could only imagine that one of the maids had been left in charge of the carrots and potatoes. She went to her room, but jumped up again as soon as she had sat down at her dressing table. It was no use. If she went to bed with a grumbling belly, she'd wake in the morning with a headache. She took up a stout candlestick, lit the candle, and made her way through the silent dark corridors, heading for the kitchen. Only the hallway was still lit by the gas lamp, and Mr Barrington would be along to turn it off very soon.

The problem with the gas was the way the companies cut the flow of the stuff at night; often the lights would go out, but the gas would continue to seep into the room. More than one housemaid in England had blown her eyebrows off – or worse – when lighting the fire in the morning. Marianne had read all about Swan's lights in the marvellous house of Cragside, and she longed for such electrical wonders to be available more widely. Anything would surely be better than dirty candles and smelly gas.

The candle's light sent up huge guttering shadows to the walls of the corridor on either side. She slipped along the back way, and the bare red tiles struck cold even through the soles of her slippers. She knew she would find the kitchen empty, and still warm. It was a little haven, and she smiled as she entered. At night, it was made strange by new reflections and shadows. The rows of copper-bottomed pans shone like small suns, and her slightest movement made them shimmer. She moved quickly through the kitchen and into a much colder storeroom, hunting for some discarded piece of pie or a hunk of yesterday's bread. Who knew what delights lingered under the muslin cloths or overturned bowls.

She managed to pilfer two boiled eggs, some bread and a wedge of sweet, crumbly cheese. She wrapped them in a scrap of fabric and scurried in triumph back into the main kitchen.

It was lucky that she'd wrapped it all up, because it didn't make a mess on the floor when she dropped it in surprise.

"Mr Claverdon!" she said. She had never seen her cousin-in-law in the kitchen. Nor had she ever yet brought herself to call him Price to his face, though she could manage it sometimes in her own private thoughts. She maintained strict politeness when she encountered him in day to day life. She knew that he wasn't exactly devoted to her, and he only barely tolerated the presence of her father too.

He was as shocked as she was. He was wearing a greatcoat, and had his hat on, and he froze. He had been creeping through the unlit kitchen towards the door to the inner hall, and he blinked as she lifted the candlestick higher.

"Ah! Miss Starr. Oh."

She said, "Is everything all right, sir?"

"Yes. No. Yes, most certainly. Your things? You seem to have dropped something."

She slid the candlestick onto the long scrubbed table and bent to retrieve her stolen midnight feast. "Nothing is damaged," she said as she scooped up the now-smashed eggs which were mingling with the broken cheese. It was still food. It would now take less effort to chew.

"Miss Starr, please don't mention this trifling aberration to my dear wife."

That gave her pause. "I would not have; until you said that," she said sternly. She had thought he might have been taking the air or checking the security. But "aberration" made everything different. Her first loyalty was to Phoebe, always. What was it that she had wanted to talk to Marianne about, earlier? She had hinted at some trouble in the marriage. "Sir, if you are indulging your basest tastes, like some young man about town, that ought to be your own business but if you are to bring shame upon my cousin, why then, no, I shall not be silent."

He sighed heavily. "You do me a disservice. I may have faults, but straying from my dear wife's side is not one of them. You may rescind your attack."

Marianne had to concede that the idea of Price having an affair was barely credible. In spite of the age gap, they doted on one another. Price adored his vivacious young wife and in the first few years of marriage had been positively puppyish, even in public. More than one lady had been scandalised by their sweet talk.

"Then may I ask what the trouble is?" she asked.

"Trouble? Who says there is trouble? Have you heard something? Has there been talk? I will not stand for talk."

"I think that I am the talk of the moment," Marianne said. "No. But trouble is written on your face, your manner, and the fact that you are creeping through the kitchen and speaking of *aberrations*. You have been out. You do not have dyspepsia at all, as you earlier claimed."

"I do now, with all the stress and alarms. Well, then, I shall tell you under strictest confidence. Indeed, you might be able to help me. I had thought of telling you, recently, more than once. You are trustworthy. And God knows, someone needs to know."

Oh for heaven's sake, she thought crossly. *Everyone wants me. That Jack Monahan, then Simeon, then Mr Bartholomew and now this! Can people not organise their own lives?* She thinned her lips and nodded for him to go on.

"I have been unwise," Mr Claverdon said. He gripped the back of a kitchen chair and stared down at his knuckles as he unburdened himself. "I was approached by someone from the government, who was concerned about ... a business matter at Harper and Bow, and naturally being the true patriotic Englishman that I am, I agreed to help them."

"Good, so far..."

"Well, as to that," he said, coughing slightly, "I was misled. To my everlasting and undying shame, the person from the government was not who they said they were. I passed on my company's information to them, and now they have information which privileges them, and puts me in a most awkward position."

"You must speak to the authorities!" she said in shock. How could he have been so stupid?

But he was an honest man – usually – and expected everyone else to be exactly who they said they were, too. He would never have done such a thing, so it was hard for him to imagine someone else might do it.

"I cannot," he said. "Every day in the papers we read of one more scandal. If even the Earl of Euston can be named in the paper, then I do not think that I can be overlooked."

"I hardly think your ... case ... is similar to the affairs of Cleveland Street. Is it?" she added forcefully.

"No, no! Good heavens no. Nothing of the sort. This is just a little light ... aha ... blackmail."

"Oh no."

"I am afraid so. But they assure me that as soon as I have furnished them with the required amount, they will say no more

50

of the matter."

"Rubbish," she said. "Blackmailers never stop. They will return again and again and bleed you dry. Your only recourse is the police."

"Think of the shame that would be brought on my poor, dear Phoebe. Anyway, I have the money and I will pay them. Except I do not yet have the money. Much of it was tied up in the bank in China, and it has collapsed, and I am in something of an awkward position."

"And you want my help? No, sir, you want the police." *Just as I told Mr Bartholomew just a few scant hours previously.*

"No police! I thought, actually, you might advance me a loan."

She nearly laughed. "I? I am hardly a lady of means." *I travel in the second class coach,* she thought, *and steal old bread from the kitchen. My gloves have been darned so many times they are grown very tight and I can only remove them by biting at the fingertips.*

"You are a woman of independent business, and your father has enjoyed much fame in his time. I do not ask for a gift. Only a temporary arrangement. I have taken a loan from a bank in the City but I have to be careful who I approach. If I went to a large, well-known place, everyone would speak of it, and I cannot have people think that I am in trouble."

"Honestly, you men are worse than women for all the emphasis on appearances," she said. "I cannot allow people to think that my hair might be artificially coloured, but you cannot allow anyone to think you have a problem with the flow of credit. My father has no money at all. Science was not the career to make a great fortune."

51

"Please," he said in a begging tone, "anything that you might be able to do would help us enormously. Now that I have brought you into my confidence, I feel sure that you will be able to assist. Why not take on a new job? You set your own rates, do you not?"

The only potential investigation at the moment was the one suggested by Mr Bartholomew. Mrs Silver was currently telling everyone in London to avoid Marianne. Mr Bartholomew's ridiculous begging loomed into her mind with a wearying inevitability. "Very well," she said. "I will see what I can do."

He left the room swiftly and she waited until he had definitely gone before trudging her way back to the garden wing.

***

She took the purloined food into her study rather than fill her bed with crumbs, and sat at a desk. This room was attached to the other side of her father's laboratory, though it was mostly herself that used the long bright room these days. His recent experiment had fizzled out, and had produced nothing more than an acidic smell which had persisted for days. She picked out the largest and most easily handled lumps of egg and cheese and bread, and ate with her left hand while she flicked through her diary with her right.

It was as she suspected. Now that Mrs Silver's heir had withdrawn his retention of her services, she was uncomfortably free. The gossip about her would soon die down, and she did not fear that it would affect future commissions too severely. But for the moment, the diary was bare.

She wondered how much money Price needed. He was

utterly foolish to begin paying the blackmailer. It would all have to come out, sooner or later. Her heart ached for Phoebe. Marianne vowed that she would be there to protect her, as much as she could.

She smoothed out the scrap of paper which displayed Mr Bartholomew's address. It was not too hard to get to his house. She tapped it with her fingers as if she were thinking about the job.

But she had already made up her mind.

She'd accept.

A crash came from the laboratory and she jumped to her feet. Seven different unpleasant scenarios crowded her mind, but when she wrenched the connecting door open, she was met by the eighth possibility – her father, in a state of delirious distress, trying to prise the lid off a bottle of something green.

"How did you even get hold of absinthe?" she said sternly as she strode across the room and snatched it from his grasp. "If I tell Mrs Crouch, she will cane you like a child. Come along. To bed. Now!"

Six

Marianne found Phoebe in her morning room the next day, languidly avoiding answering letters. She had a stack of them on her writing bureau, sent by people who wanted her support in their philanthropic endeavours; they came from people who sought her patronage; from people who just wanted to introduce themselves in the hope that they might be admitted to her social circle. Instead of attending to them, she was gazing out of the window at the morning sun lighting the wide lawns yellow and green. It was to be a pleasant and warm day.

"I think we need more roses," Phoebe said. "I fancy them all in shades of pink, with marvellous scents. I told Fletcher but he said something about soil and stamped off to the pineapple house."

"He would know. Gardeners know everything."

She smiled as they both had the same remembrance. When they were young girls, sharing long holidays together, they had often played outside when they could sneak away from the adults. But Phoebe was a year older than Marianne, and had been much stronger. One day, the gardener at the old house had seen Marianne well and truly beaten, and decided to show Marianne how to best her cousin in a fight. She had done so, and they had not fought since. "Phoebe, listen. I am going to see Mr Bartholomew."

"Oh no! You mustn't! Yet how thrilling. Tell me why." Phoebe's ennui disappeared in an instant.

"I have no other work," Marianne said. "I am wholly without business at the moment."

"Well, you do not *need* to work. You have everything you require in life."

"I do need to work. It is not just for the money. A successful case brings in more work, and it is my name, my reputation. I need to win something to offset my recent failure, after all." Marianne walked over to the window and gazed out at the lawns.

Out of *Phoebe's* window, at *Phoebe's* lawns. One day, Marianne vowed that she would have enough money to run her own household. But such ambition was not spoken of, and though she thought that Phoebe would not blame her for such longings, she didn't want to insult the generosity of her cousin.

"When are you going?" Phoebe asked. "I should tell you not to. But you will go, won't you? How I wish I were as free as you. I wonder if..." She tailed off, but her eyes were bright.

"I shall call on him this afternoon. He has given me his address."

"I know where he lives anyway – well, Price does; he invited him, after all."

That sparked something. "How long have they known one another?"

"I do not know. Price does not speak of business, and I do not listen if he does, which he doesn't, so I have no need to ignore him. I am an excellent wife," she added with a grin.

"Whose idea was it to invite him?"

"Price, of course. He said that Mr Bartholomew was only lately returned to England and due to his long absence, he knew nobody."

"This is more and more suspicious. Mr Bartholomew hinted at something that had happened abroad."

"I shall come with you, then," Phoebe declared impulsively. "I do not care that I should not. You can go alone, of course, but it would be better, would it not, if you were accompanied? I will not tell Emilia or Fry. They will only fret."

"Please do come, if you think that you can. It is not a visit I should care to make alone, in truth."

* * *

And yet now she was alone, after all.

Just before lunch, one of the children had fallen ill, and Phoebe was unwillingly dragged into an altercation between the governess and a nurse. There were accusations, tears, and a great deal of fuss about carbolic acid. Marianne waited for Phoebe to extricate herself but Phoebe told her that now the governess was threatening to leave her situation, and a whole new mess of secrets amongst the servants was unravelling: "The children's nurse has been carrying on with the stable boy – can you imagine! – and both must be threatened with dismissal. I shan't, of course, but the threat must be real and immediate. We can call on Mr Bartholomew tomorrow."

Marianne decided she had to leave the house rather than be drawn into the tedious drama. She'd known about the stable boy

57

and the maid for a long time, anyway. And the stable boy was a far better choice than the nurse's previous liaison, which was one of the carpenters engaged to do some work in the stables. Marianne had stepped in, and the carpenter had been dismissed for another trivial matter; Phoebe had known nothing of the goings-on but it was she who garnered the praise for her astute management.

Such was the usual way of things.

Marianne decided this was not her fight, today, and she prepared to slip away, intending to walk briskly to the railway station.

As she went silently down the stairs, she came across Mr Barrington standing at the front door, looking out over the gravel path. He had his hands on his hips, making him look like a squat teapot from behind.

"Is everything in order, Mr Barrington?" she asked as she approached.

He jumped and turned, and scratched his head. "I do apologise, miss. I hope I have done right." He had a card in his hands and he looked down at it with puzzlement and a little embarrassment. "I am afraid I panicked. What with the burglary and everything, miss, it does set one on edge."

"I am sure you have done right. You always do. Did someone call?"

"Someone most unfavourable-looking, to my mind, miss. It is not the hours for one to call, so he is not quite of your class, I should say."

"My class? Someone called for me? Was it Mr Bartholomew?"

"No, miss, a Mr Monahan, and he was insistent that he left his card for you."

She held her hand out and he passed it over with reluctance. It had the man's name and an address.

"You did very right," she reassured Mr Barrington. "He should not call here at all. If you see him again, feel free to dismiss him just as you have done today. Thank you."

He was crumpled in relief. "Thank you, miss. I should not like to have bothered Mrs Claverdon."

"Of course not."

He closed the door after her and she slipped the card into her bag as she walked down the drive towards the railway station. She tried to think about Edgar Bartholomew, and the business with Price Claverdon and the blackmail, but her mind kept returning to the unpleasant persistence of Jack Monahan.

Why had he suddenly started to harass her? What else was happening? She began to form an unwelcome connection between Monahan and her cousin-in-law.

It was not beyond the realms of possibility that Jack Monahan was the blackmailer. She nodded to herself. That made a kind of sense. Though why Monahan now pursued her was a mystery.

She vowed to unravel it. She stamped into the ticket office and turned her mind, instead, to the journey.

She did not need to travel all the way into London. With the aid of one of the huge railway manuals, she managed to plot a route that took her part-way into London and then out again on another branch line, just one stop, so she was still technically in the capital city. She adored the creeping network of lines across the country. Sometimes she fancied she would spend a year of her life just travelling the railways.

Except that she had to look after her father.

But he would not always be around.

She stopped that selfish and unworthy thought before it went too far, and turned her attention to her surroundings as she descended from the carriage and made her way towards the Bartholomews' address.

The Bartholomews lived in a large fine house on the very edge of London, yet it was handily close to all amenities by dint of the railway. It was built of impressive white stone and hedged all around with severe black railings. It was reached by a long driveway past a lodge, and was surrounded by trees. She stood on the main road, which was relatively busy, and populated by small shops, houses and a church.

She could call in now. It was a socially acceptable time to do so, and the butler or housekeeper would politely inform her if the day was wrong or her visit inconvenient. She would be received in a ground floor public room and she could easily request to keep the door open. Mr Bartholomew himself had asked for her to visit him. She considered herself one of the new breed of women – indeed, a New Woman – and though she had never actually worn rational dress in public (in spite of the newspaper illustration's suggestion) she refused to be stuck in the restrictive mores of yesterday's society. She had a degree. She had a business. She had a life of her very own.

She also had a burning curiosity.

Her mind was made up. She'd call at the house.

Before she could talk herself out of it, she ran lightly up the steps to ring the bell of the house. It was modern all over, on the outside, but when the front door was swung open, she was greeted by a very cold and unwelcome bare hallway.

And it was Mr Bartholomew the son himself who opened the door.

His eyes widened at first but he smiled in grateful welcome. "Ah! Miss Starr. I am so pleased. Do come in. Are you alone?"

She entered with one glance behind. "I think so."

"I mean, did your cousin not come with you?"

"No, she was detained with domestic duties."

"What did you think I meant? You seem startled. Did you encounter trouble on your journey?"

"It is nothing. A passing fancy. Does your father not engage many staff?"

"Many? He has none! Not a single one resides here. A woman comes in to do for him, daily, but otherwise he is quite the hermit."

"And is he at home today?"

"He is neither at home – to visitors – nor at home at all. He is away for the day and I do not know what he does or where he is. I have not seen him since last night's dinner, and he grew abusive and threw a glass of brandy at me. A full glass," he added.

"What a waste."

"Indeed. Please, let us step into the drawing room."

She hesitated. The bare hall echoed with her voice. There were no tables, no pictures, no portraits, no clocks, nothing at all – the house was as if it were up for auction, stripped of all comforts. She thought of the clutter of Woodfurlong with something almost like affection. "There are no servants *at all* here? I am quite alone with you?" She had intended on keeping the door open but what was the point of that, if there were no staff within earshot?

He sighed. "We could step down to the lodge where there is a man and a boy. I rather think you are safer here. Wait one moment – I have an idea." He spun around and ran lightly up the stairs.

She wanted to open doors and peek into rooms while he was gone, but her footsteps would have revealed her snooping, echoing around the empty hall. So she waited, close to the front door. When he returned he had smoothed down his hair and thrown a cravat around his neck, though it did not match his jacket at all. In his hand he held a small revolver, and she reacted instantly – she plunged her hand into her bag and pulled out her own weapon, a ladies' pistol, and levelled it calmly at his face. Her hand barely shook at all. She counted her breaths to keep herself out of panic.

This was not one of the gardener's tricks from her childhood. Her own father had given it to her when she left for college. "I know what the men at Cambridge are like," he had said darkly. "I was one. And I ought to have been shot."

Mr Bartholomew gasped at the sight of the pistol in Marianne's hands and then laughed with incredulity. The revolver in his own hand was hanging loosely by his side. He had made no move to raise it. He let it now dangle from one finger. "Miss Starr, I can assure you that I brought this to give to you so that you might feel more protected against me. But I see that you are already so provisioned."

"Of course. I would not have come here at all, alone,

without some care for my safety."

"Then why are you so concerned about being alone with me at all? You could blast my head off at any moment."

"Oh, it is not my physical safety that worries me; not armed as I am, with this. But you must know that every moment a woman moves, in the street or indeed in her own home, she is threatened by the potential of harm from strangers and friends and family alike. No, I did not wish to be caught here utterly alone, for the sake of my *reputation*. Bodily injuries heal but once a woman is fallen, she is never going to rise again."

He spluttered. "I would argue that your reputation is already somewhat grey."

She lowered her pistol. That was true. "Yet you still want my help. Enough of all this. I am here, and that is that. Put your gun to one side. I shall keep mine close by. Is the drawing room more comfortably furnished?"

He stepped back and put his revolver on a lower step of the stairs. "Not particularly, but there are, at least, some chairs."

He led her into the large room. The windows were huge and bare and lacked any curtains or drapes. There were a few scattered and mismatched armchairs, and one chaise longue. A folding table stood by the dead fire. It was the dreariest room she had ever stood in.

She settled on the least-dusty chair. "You must tell me everything," she said. "And I shall need part payment upfront."

Mr Bartholomew dragged a chair closer to her and sat down. He spoke in a hasty rush. "My father is called Edgar Bartholomew and he inherited a great deal of money as a young man. He has always been wealthy and has invested wisely. My mother and he … did not make a great marriage. She fled from him when I was small, though he did not pursue her. I think he was content to be rid of her. He paid for my education and I spent long lonely terms at school. In the holidays, at first I went to my mother but she lived in a succession of small rented rooms, and eventually I simply stayed at school with a handful of other sorry boys whose families were in India or Africa."

"That sounds like a hard upbringing. And your father did not call for you at all?"

"He did not. Were he not paying for the fees, I should have imagined that he had washed his hands of me completely. I had no letters and no communications. In the strange gap between school and university, I came here to see him, many years ago. I felt that I was a man, then – looking back, I was not! – and that I ought to confront him as a man does."

"And?"

"And he was not here. The house was shuttered up. The man in the lodge said that my father was never here. He could not remember the last time he came."

"Where was he?"

"London, I was told. But I did not find him. It turns out that my father is a very secretive and closed-off man. He shunned society although society did not shun him – I mean to say, he did not seem to be alone except through his own choice. He was mentioned often in the company of one friend, a man called Wade Walker. And that was all."

"An American? Wade?"

"I don't think so but yes, it is a strange name. When I asked what they did together – business, friendship – I was given all manner of answers, but mostly people shrugged and said that they 'talked rot and imagined fancies' or words to that effect."

"I must ask a most delicate question. Did any hint of … *scandal* attach to these two men?"

"Absolutely not!" he cried in anger, but quickly mastered himself. He said more gently, "I understand. It is a question that I asked myself. No, they were simply close friends, and no salon door was closed to them in London – they did not socialise much, but they were welcome wherever they might have chosen to go. As I said, he shunned society but it was open to him should he have wished to move among it."

"I see. Where is Wade Walker now? Have you ever met him?"

"I have not. I went to university and then abroad, so this friendship was over a decade ago. I can get no word of him in the city. And now we come to the present day. I came home just above a fortnight ago, and sought out my mother, of course. I have not found her. I was informed that she was dead, found soaked in gin in some rookery, and thrown into a pauper's grave."

"You must find her! Oh, I am so sorry for your loss. Surely she ought to have a decent burial?"

"I shall. I have been combing the city for her resting place, though now I am into some low dives, and progress is slow. Now you know why I have a gun. It is not just for protection against lady-scientists."

"Indeed so; very wise."

"When I could not find word of her immediately, I decided to look up my father. I asked around and found his club, and they informed me that he had recently moved back here, to this house."

"How recently?"

"A week before I arrived back."

"Three weeks ago, then," she said. "Did he know that you were returning? His move back to this house might not be a coincidence."

"He didn't know — or at least, I had not told him I was coming, but it was not a secret."

"Why did you return?"

"I was tired of being abroad." His effusive manner had changed and his answer was now strangely terse.

"Really?" she asked, watching him closely. "You have been living abroad almost as long as you have been in Britain. And you mentioned something to me at the dinner party. What happened?"

"Yet I am still an Englishman," he said stoutly, ignoring her main question. *That was suspicious*, she thought. "This is not about me. When I came here, my father received me with some surprise — I do not think that he expected me at all. He was ill the first night and could not receive me and the next morning, when we met at last, he was cold and distant. Indeed, it took some persuasion on my part to get him to allow me to stay here. He thought I would lodge elsewhere."

"He doesn't lack for space here, but perhaps he only meant that because of the lack of servants. Does he mean to stay here? He must engage help, and soon."

"I have no idea. The daily woman cooks us a rough meal every night, and outside of that, we fend for ourselves. I eat breakfast standing up in the kitchen, chewing on bread like a labourer. I do not know what my father does. He spends all day in remote rooms of the house. I hear strange noises at night, but when I go to investigate, I find nothing. Mediums come and go. This is what makes me suspect…"

"Go on…"

"I wonder if my mother really is dead?" he said in a rush. "And how did she die, if she is? Did he have something to do with it? If so, perhaps he is trying to contact her."

"Perhaps. But that would suggest that he truly *is* your father," she said. "Many fathers are cold and distant. And perhaps he feels remorse at your mother's death and seeks only to apologise to her. There does not have to be foul play. And grief would account for his strange behaviour."

"She died last year, by all accounts that I have heard. He will not still be sunk in grief when they had been estranged almost all their married lives. Oh, I do not know what to think! Perhaps it is just that I do not want my mother to be dead, and I am clutching at straws. But you must believe me. He is *not* my father, Miss Starr! He did not correct me when I mis-explained the rules of cricket." He grew animated, and jumped to his feet, pacing around as he beat his fist into the palm of his other hand. "I know you ask me for evidence, hard facts, real reasons, but this is a matter of what the *heart* knows. Still, my father had a deep and abiding love of cricket. I have few memories of him, but one is of playing the game with him. My father, I am sure, was not quite as tall, and I know that you will say this is but a child's remembrance, but it is *true*. This man won't speak to me, won't acknowledge me, and only allows me to stay because he has no reason to throw me out."

He stopped dead. Marianne followed his sudden panicked gaze. They both stared at the door that led to the hall.

Footsteps echoed. It was a slow pace, dragging, almost shuffling. Marianne looked back at Mr Bartholomew and mouthed, "Is that him?"

He nodded.

The footsteps stopped. Then they came towards the drawing room door. It was flung open with a vigour quite the opposite to the heavy steps. Marianne remained seated.

The man in the doorway clutched Mr Bartholomew's discarded revolver in his hand. He was a tall man, spare of build, and his age made him look underfed rather than lean and lithe. He had hair as dark as George's, though it was coarse and stood out stiffly like it had been dried out in a desert sun, and he wore no hat. He must have left it by the front door with his outdoor things. He had rather pale brown eyes that were small and shadowed by thick coarse grey eyebrows, and his cheeks were sunken. The lightness of his eyes seemed strange against his darker hair, but she wondered if he suffered from cataracts. He stared at Marianne in shock, and a great deal of displeasure.

Yet he spoke in a measured and polite tone. "Good day, madam. I am the proprietor of this house. I do not know your business, and I hope you will forgive this bluntness, but you must leave. I was not expecting visitors, and we are not arranged for such calls." Then he glared at his son. "You trespass mightily upon my goodwill, and you shall answer for this."

She got to her feet and tried to answer him with dignity but she kept her attention on the gun in his hand. "I beg pardon for my intrusion, sir. I am Miss Marianne Starr, and I–"

"I do not care who you are," he replied. "You must go now. George, take her to the door. And come back here immediately, to explain yourself. Or leave, with her, and do not ever come back."

He sounded like every inch the father, and now a new suspicion entered Marianne's head. If one of them was a fake, it might not be the man now standing to one side of the door, in his own house, very much the confident landowner. Had the son not spoken of a great deal of wealth that the older Mr Bartholomew had inherited?

Mr George Bartholomew went to Marianne's side and led her out of the room. She half-turned at the door to bid the older man farewell, but he walked away from her, towards the empty fireplace, and remained with his back to her. She revised her first opinion of him. He was not measured and polite. He was measured and rude. Very rude.

George Bartholomew took her to the main door, and begged her to wait. Once more she found herself uneasily alone in the vast hallway, and she was relieved when the younger Bartholomew returned quickly. He had an envelope of paper money to be drawn at the Bank of England, and a small bag of gold coins. "This will get you started in the investigation," he said.

She took it and examined the five-pound notes. The whole sum was far more than she was going to ask for. But she was sensible, and said nothing to that effect as she slipped it all into her bag to live among the handkerchiefs, combs, books and gun already in there. It was not just payment. It was future freedom. "Thank you."

"And one more thing." He pressed a wavy-edged card into her hand. "Take this. It is the name of my solicitor in the city. He knows my business and he has more money there, should you need it, in the event that you are unable to contact me. I will be trying to find my mother's final resting place and I do not know where my search will take me."

"Sir, you could contact the police, or a runner to act on your behalf to find her."

"I have spoken with an investigator and a detective. They have not achieved much. It is of little importance in the grander scheme of things. I am also seeking out Wade Walker, and that search too is equally fruitless. But I know he is out there! He must be."

"Just as you know that man is not your father?" she asked.

He missed her flippancy. "Yes," he replied earnestly. "Exactly so."

Seven

Marianne got home without incident, and took to her rooms for the remainder of the day. She wrote everything down, so that she would remember it clearly in the future. She also began a list of things she had to do and people she had to find.

Jack Monahan was a problem. Not only had he thrust himself upon her at the séance, but he had also come to the house. She would have to find out about him, and discover if he was a man to be pitied, or a potential danger. She started a new page in her notebook for him.

Then she began to read the latest journals and periodicals, and a stack of newspapers that had been read already by Price and Phoebe. She missed the constant debate and meetings of university and tried to keep up to date through magazines and newspapers. A story about the events in East Prussia caught her eye, simply because George Bartholomew had been there, but it was all about the Junkers – the aristocracy in the region – and their refusal to give up their ancient rights to keep serfs under their thrall. *For serfs,* she thought, *you may as well say slaves.* But the legal language in the article bored her and her eyes flitted on, caught suddenly by the word *Maskelyne.*

But the story was not about the celebrated stage magician from the Egyptian Hall. She was eager to discover what he was doing, as all the rumours were that he was closeted up and writing a book that would shatter the public's illusions about magic. Instead, it mentioned a "true heir and perhaps rival" to Maskelyne called Harry Vane, lately arrived in London and already stirring up the salons with his shows and talks.

She had been hearing more and more of him, and she made a new note to seek him out. She would be interested to hear what he had to say, and saw him as another potential ally in her mission to lead the British public away from superstition and firmly into the future – a future of science. She travelled to public lectures as often as she could, and it was heartening to see more and more women attending these events.

She was a member of the University Club for Women, a rather new venture that linked up the recent graduates of all the colleges that now accepted women. They met at Bond Street, and she thought it would be worth her while popping in soon, and asking if anyone there knew anything. She looked at her list of questions again. She wanted to find out about Edgar Bartholomew and Wade Walker. She wanted to know exactly why George Bartholomew had returned to England. She wondered about Price Claverdon's ill-advised situation of blackmail. She flipped the page of the notebook and studied the barest, blankest page: who was this Jack Monahan?

She was interrupted in her thoughts by a knock at her door. Her father was in a lucid period, and requested that she spend the evening reading to him, and she agreed though she could not persuade him that there were more interesting things to read than a journal of chemical science. The evening dragged, but he was happy, and she had to remind herself that she should be a dutiful daughter. She owed him a lot, and it was her turn to repay that debt.

She stifled her frustration and smiled like a pleasant young lady and counted out the minutes until she could finally abandon the discussion of Graham's effusion and diffusion of gases, and head to bed.

The next morning, she was startled quite early by a quick rapping on her bedroom door. She was not yet dressed, and pulled her loose robe around her as she called out, "Who is it?"

Phoebe, as immaculate as if she had been up for three hours, danced into the room. Of course, she had staff who would dress her. Emilia, her personal maid, was a particularly patient genius. "Who do you think it is? Have you a stream of gentleman callers? What happened yesterday? Oh! You have changed your curtains. I like the red. When you came home, I was being held hostage by Mrs Digby and her half-dozen daughters, and they simply wouldn't leave. I hoped you might manufacture a disaster to save me."

"Oh, I didn't realise. What is that?"

"This," said Phoebe, waving the newspapers at Marianne, "is a revelation. You must see it. They have just been delivered. I wrestled it from Price's grasp before he took it to breakfast and covered it in egg and fish. He will be annoyed with me. I don't care."

"You do care."

"Yes, I do. I shall be awfully contrite later though. Now, look!" She opened one of the wide papers up and flung it onto

Marianne's bed. "Look. Just look!"

"An electric corset with health giving properties?" Marianne said, peering at the half-page advertisement. "No, Phoebe, we've spoken of this. It is nonsense. It will kill you more likely than do anything useful. Just like that headband of zinc and copper discs that you bought for your migraines. Useless."

"The discs do work but I cannot stand the smell of vinegar. But surely, Marianne, the corset will fill me with vibrancy?"

With a sigh, Marianne sat on the bed and pulled the large paper closer. "There will be ink on my sheets and the maids will be angry," she remarked as she scanned down the narrow columns of tiny print. "Anyway, you have quite enough vibrancy, I feel."

"There are quotes there from some eminent people."

"Anyone could print anything. No, Phoebe, I really would not recommend this. But I do not think this is really why you've come to see me so early."

Phoebe slid onto the bed alongside Marianne. "So astute. Go on. Tell me everything. You went without me to the Bartholomew place, and I am unhappy, though it could not be helped."

Marianne told her cousin everything that had happened at the house. Phoebe nodded seriously when she was finished.

Phoebe began to fold the newspapers back into manageable sizes again, ready to take into the breakfast room for Price. "Are you definitely taking the case, then?"

"Yes."

"Thrilling! You must find out all you can about Edgar Bartholomew. Marianne, do you not ever worry about making enemies?"

"Mrs Silver is hardly a terrifying nemesis."

"Perhaps not, but there are others. What about that dreadful little man you exposed last month?"

"Oh, the Incredible Duke Illanni? Wasn't he vile! He swore to disembowel me in Downing Street, which I thought was a curious threat. For safety's sake I have avoided calling on the prime minister, of course."

"Of course," laughed Phoebe. "But seriously, are you not sometimes afraid? He was very upset that you made such a fool out of him. And not just you, too. Didn't that man, the one you admire, Harold what's-his-face, do the same?"

"Harry Vane," said Marianne with a sigh. "Oh, I simply must meet him. I keep reading about him since he came to London and I do so want to talk with him."

"I am sure your paths will soon cross. But once this Vane had hold him of, coming after your exposure, well, that fake Illanni was quite done for. He has been run out of town."

"And with good reason. He really was a menace. Simeon was annoyed, of course. He admired the man's tricks and wanted to learn more."

"Well, your Simeon is a menace all of his own."

"Hush now. He is a good friend."

"Marry him and be done."

"Oh goodness, no, I should as rather marry a fish. We are too much friends, and that is all. I know him too well to ever want to marry him." Marianne got up and began to choose her clothing for the day, laying it out on the bed and checking for stains.

"I'll send my Emilia to you," Phoebe said. "You have repairs and darning to be done there."

"Thank you."

Phoebe stood up and shook out her skirts, then scooped up the papers. "Come along. You shall miss breakfast at this rate."

"I intend to. I have other things to do."

***

She was not going to sit around and wait for the next thing to happen to her. Marianne had never sat around and watched life go by. She simply wasn't built that way. Instead, she sallied forth into the fresh open air and took the next train into town.

She marched briskly, buffeted by crowds and street hawkers and tourists and workers and children and dogs and noise. She headed for Simeon's workshop, wanting to tell him what had been going on, and perhaps to ask for his advice in how to find out more about Edgar Bartholomew and the irritating Jack Monahan. She found her old friend hard at work on a cabinet of mirrors, set at cunning angles to disguise their true purpose, and instead the mirrors merely showed the contents of a hidden compartment.

"You are very clever," she remarked as he demonstrated it.

"Yes," he said. "And everyone knows it, which is why they target me so much."

Ah. She had thought he might have moved on to a new paranoia by now, but obviously not. "They seek to emulate you," she said soothingly. "They are copying you out of flattery."

"Then why do they do so much better than me?" he wailed

suddenly, and flung himself dramatically into a shabby armchair, his legs sticking out at angles like an abandoned puppet. "There is a conspiracy against me, I can tell. There are whispers."

"Why would there be?"

"I am different. I have no background, no history. It marks me."

"Oh, tush. What rot. You are what you make yourself. The world is changed, Simeon. Even the meanest man can rise, now. You are not what your father makes you."

"And as I have no father, that is all to the good. Do you want some cake?"

"Yes, please."

He jumped up. He had to be in motion. When he stopped moving, thoughts and worries would overwhelm him. So he bustled around the end of the large room set aside as the kitchen, and came back with a slab of something sticky and gingery on a clean plate. His own, she noticed, was marked with pickle and the remnants of a pie. But at least he knew how to treat his guests well.

She blamed his slovenly habits on his erratic upbringing. The son of a prostitute, he had been in a Foundling Orphanage until he was adopted by an impoverished but well-meaning clergy couple, who doted on the young boy but brought him up with equal measures of discipline, praise and the fear of Our Lord. They had encouraged him to pursue his interests and apprenticed him to a carpenter who specialised in the theatre. The clergy couple then promptly expired, leaving him very little in the way of inheritance, but no lasting troubles, at least.

Marianne had met him when she was still in her first year

at college. She had come back to London and was attending a public lecture about the possible use of electricity in telepathic transference. She had listened to the start of the lecture with deep scepticism and finished it utterly unconvinced, and a little sad that she did not believe it. They had sat next to one another and very politely ignored one another as they were perfect strangers, and that would have remained the case. Except when the lecture ended, Simeon had risen to his feet, seen that she was unaccompanied, and said, "Oh, I suppose I ought to offer to escort you to a cab or the station? Only I need to go quite quickly because there is a show on I need to see. There will be an elephant."

And that was it. She, too, needed to see the elephant, and they became friends with a shared interest in the workings of magicians, mediums and mystery.

She told him about the visit to Mr Bartholomew, and he listened with interest. "And you have taken the case, then?"

"Yes."

"So what is your next move?"

"I shall find out all I can about the older Mr Bartholomew. And I must hunt out Mr Wade Walker." *And look up this Jack Monahan*, she thought, but decided not to tell Simeon that. He was concerned enough for himself; she didn't want to add worries about her to his burdens.

"How will you find out about these men?"

"By using my innate charm when speaking to people."

His face flickered for a moment and she was offended. "I can, you know," she said. "I can be charming."

"Good luck," he remarked. "Would you like some eel pie?"

***

She had eaten far too much, and wasted rather too much time at Simeon's workshop. It was after midday when she continued on her journey. She decided that she would walk back to the station, and get home, and begin to write letters of enquiry. She walked slowly, as it was hard to breathe and digest at the same time in her narrow clothes. She didn't tight-lace her corset – only a few, madly fashionable women ever did – but she had dressed herself when she had been empty of food, and now her belly was rebelling. Acid burned the back of her throat.

She paused by a bench, and debated whether to sit for a moment. As she did so, a man stopped alongside her.

The cologne in her nostrils told her who it was.

"You, again," she said.

"Of course," replied Jack Monahan with a grin. He swept off his hat and bowed low. "Didn't I tell you that we should be friends? I shall watch you and I shall follow you until I convince you."

"Sir, you cannot do such things!"

"It seems that I can."

"There ought to be a law against it."

"Perhaps there is. Shall we go to a police station and ask?"

She frowned at him. "I am going nowhere with you." She felt powerless under his onslaught.

"Then let us sit here, and discuss ... *business*."

"No." But curiosity finally burst out of her, "Well, sir, what business?"

"Aha! At last. Excellent. I always get my way, in the end."

He grinned and she felt a little ill. He would not take no for an answer, and she began to wonder about men like that. How dangerous would he become if she kept refusing him? Had she become a point of pride and principle – someone that he had to break?

He put his hand up as if to stroke her cheek, and she stepped back with a hiss. He let his hand drop but he continued speaking as cockily as his gesture had suggested that he was. "I knew that you were a woman of sense. And that is exactly why we will go into a kind of partnership together. I speak only of business, Miss Starr. I know better, now, than to appeal to your womanly nature. This business arrangement will be a temporary one, but it will serve us both well."

"Doing what?" she asked, in spite of herself, and slightly miffed at the insinuation that she had no womanly nature worth appealing to. She remained standing though he had taken a seat on the bench now, and lounged, with one arm resting along the back of it. She could not sit down without it looking as if he had his arm around her shoulder. She kept her chin held high.

"The exact details can be worked out as soon as you agree to it," he said. "But suffice it to say that I think your talents for spotting the tricks of mediums and frauds could be very useful to my current line of work. You are a talented investigator. Very well-known, very clever. So let us harness our cleverness together. Yes, that's it exactly."

"I will not agree to anything that has only the barest of details. I am not that stupid," she said scornfully. He had made his excuse up on the spot and she didn't believe a word of it. He was riddled with lies, and he was simply saying what he thought would appeal to her. "You are making things up as you go. What exactly is your current line of work? For I am beginning to imagine that you are a fake and a fraud yourself, sir."

"Are we not all composed of layers and not all are revealed truly even to ourselves?"

"No," she said.

"There are many perceptions of truth," he went on, like he was giving a philosophy lecture. "For example, while I believe you to be an able and indeed talented woman of science, others think you to be a shrill harpy."

"How dare you!"

He opened his hands wide. "Not my words, dear Miss Starr. The words of others. There are those in this town who don't appreciate your talents as I do."

"Who?"

"Rivals in your very own business."

"I have none! We all work towards the same aims."

He shook his head sadly. "Would that this were true. Some resent a woman's influence in the masculine arts. But I do not! All I want, Miss Starr, if I may speak plainly, is a little time in your company. I should dearly love to see your laboratory! May I not call?"

"You have tried and you were rebuffed. I am sorry, sir, but you may not call."

His face darkened and his fists seemed to briefly clench. "What must I do to be able to be accepted at your house?"

"It is not my house," she said through gritted teeth. "Sir, if you have any decency in your heart, you will leave me alone. I am very busy."

"With what? I can help."

"You can help by allowing me space. Good day, sir."

She strode away and counted to thirty before she looked back. When she did so, he had gone.

Eight

"So you have discovered nothing?" Phoebe said to Marianne, later that evening. Price was dining at his club in the city, and there were no visitors expected to Woodfurlong. Marianne was already dressed for dinner, and she was in Phoebe's own rooms, watching Phoebe's maid Emilia attend to her cousin's hair.

"No, nothing so far. I admit I am feeling unsettled by the whole thing. A natural reaction, you must agree, to that dreadful man Monahan. He was most bullying. And you have found out nothing about him from your gossips and contacts?"

"Well, there are a few whispers," said Phoebe. She stayed perfectly still as the talented fingers of Emilia worked through her hair, pinning and curling and twisting. "There is actually a link between him and Lord Hazelstone – you know, the member of the House of Lords – I've never met him."

"I know the name. He is involved in trade and so on. Does your husband not know him?"

"Lord Hazelstone? Perhaps. I shall ask him. But as for this Monahan, well, he might have been in his employment once, but no longer."

"So whom does he work for now?"

"He seems to be quite placeless. He is a low sort with high airs that are not quite finished. Some of the ladies tittered at his name. They like to be charmed by him but would not dream of letting him anywhere near their daughters. He sounds the perfect cad. Emilia, does the name mean anything to you?"

Emilia de Souza was the bright daughter of an impoverished gentle family who were sunk too low to even be able to afford commissions in the army for the sons. One was working as a humble clerk and the other had taken to the church and ended up in a living so remote that Emilia sent him food parcels when she could. She was a good-natured soul who lacked any bitterness as to her reduced situation. She sprayed a little perfume over Phoebe's hair, shading her mistress's face with her free hand. "Jack Monahan ... no, my lady, I don't recollect having heard it. I can ask around. Are you expecting him to be known among the staff?"

"I don't know – Marianne, what do you think?"

"He is placeless, as you said. I recognise that in him. Perhaps he was once an officer. He carries himself with the confidence of a gentleman and he had, of course, gained admittance to Mrs Silver's salon. I should go and ask her how she knew him but I fear she'd slam the door in my face."

"Ah, then here is a job for me." Phoebe sat forward and Emilia tutted. "Hush, girl, listen. I will go and talk to Mrs Silver. She can hardly close the door to me. Do you know when she receives calls?"

"I have her card. But you have no introduction."

"I will obtain one. I know enough ladies in London to be

84

able to tease out a thread of connection to this woman. And, while I am at it, I shall put out more feelers for this other mystery of ours – Edgar Bartholomew."

"He seems to be a recluse."

"Luckily, I am not. And I need another project if I am not to have a rose garden. Let me mobilise my forces."

"You sound as if you are on campaign."

"Indeed I am!" Phoebe said. "I shall hunt this man down through the drawing rooms of London."

"I suspect he does not frequent many. We are more likely to find him in clubs and private dining rooms, surely?" Marianne said in frustration. "We need a man. I would ask Simeon but he would be next to useless, and cannot get to the high places anyway. I need someone who can move in all circles and… dash it all, I am describing Jack Monahan."

"Try Simeon. You never know. He has a good reputation, for what it is worth. As for this Monahan, could we use him, do you think? Use him, as he is intending to use you?"

"I do not know what he really wants from me, but it cannot be good. I think he lies out of fun, half the time. I have the dreadful feeling that none of this would have happened if I had not refused him at the start. Now I am a project to him. He only really seems to want to get me alone. He wants to come here."

Phoebe nodded. "We need to know more about him before we allow that. What am I saying? We can never allow that!"

Marianne sat up straight as something occurred to her. "No man is without a past. Not Monahan, and not Bartholomew. He must have attended school, and a good one, I think. Perhaps there is still some old master who remembers him."

"How old is this man?"

"He must be in his mid-fifties, perhaps less. His son is around thirty."

"It is unlikely that you will find a master who taught him. But I suppose that it is worth a look. Well, then. Tonight shall be the last night I dine soberly at home, Marianne: tomorrow I, too, begin the hunt!"

***

It was a hunt from which Marianne was largely excluded, partly from her own nature – she knew she would be useless at polite conversation in elegant dining rooms and more of a liability to her cousin than a help. Though they had shared something of the same upbringing, they had known from early childhood that their futures would be very different. Phoebe had been schooled into society and loved it; Marianne had chafed under any instruction that tried to make her into an acceptable lady. But as she had no fortune to inherit, and a sad inclination to speak her mind, Marianne had abandoned any attempts at fitting into polite society and had embraced the more radical and shocking groups that accepted her into their circles. Bluestockings, liberals, and suffragists.

She left the comfortable drawing rooms to Phoebe without a murmur, and concentrated on exploring other avenues. While Phoebe flitted from fine house to fine house, charming everyone she met into gossip and revelations, Marianne moved among the middle circles of society, and those on the edges – often, well-bred folk with dangerous ideas. She spoke to old graduates that she still knew at the University Club for Ladies, and tradesfolk she had dealt with at Woodfurlong, and governesses and merchants' wives and schoolteachers and, in a few cases, old colleagues of her father who still remembered him fondly and would indulge his wayward daughter. She had a list of the very best public schools, and sent letters to them all, enquiring as to former pupils and naming Edgar Bartholomew.

Marianne did not see Phoebe for three days, so intent was she on her task. While Marianne moved around town, she kept her eyes very open to any sign of Monahan, but if he was watching her as he had threatened, he was subtle about it. Nor did she hear from Mr George Bartholomew.

Yet all the while she had the prickling of unease at the back of her neck. Jack Monahan had promised to come after her, and soon he would, she was sure of it.

She even went into the police stationhouse on Bow Street, when she was passing, and spoke to a dismissive sergeant behind the desk. "There is no crime in walking about and looking at people," he told her. "I do it all the time. Indeed, it is my job."

Unless she had been physically harmed, then they might act – though her father would be more likely to be heard than she herself. If he brought a complaint that his daughter had been harassed, all of the Metropolitan police force would spring into action. She reminded the police that their own house had been broken into, as it was common knowledge that the penalties for house-breaking were harsher than for leg-breaking, but still he was unmoved.

She had suspected that the police would be of no help to her.

But on the evening of the third day, she had a stroke of luck. She received a reply to one of her letters, and it merely confirmed that there had once been a pupil called Edgar Bartholomew at the Westminster School. She was on the first train to London the very next day. She bought a newspaper to read in the ladies' waiting room and for the journey itself.

A civil war still raged in Chile, she read. That did not interest her as much as an article about the now-ancient Reverend William Stainton Moses who was still proclaiming his skills at automatic writing as a revelation from God. She felt sorry for the old man, now, though his books still influenced the young and foolish and impressionable, and that made her angry. His ridiculous Ghost Club was an embarrassment.

She sought any mention of Harry Vane but he was absent this time. She had not yet found where he might be lecturing publicly and decided she needed to call at the Egyptian Hall to find out; also, Simeon might know. Or he might instead tell her all about how he intended to levitate a piano down Pall Mall.

She skimmed the trade section, out of a kind of respect to Price and how he made his money. He had lived in Prussia in his youth, for many years, and still used his experience to guide policy. The recent shift in power had unsettled things but as she read the article, her eyes unfocussed and she drifted, instead, to thinking of other things, especially how she was to persuade Phoebe that an electric corset was a terrible idea.

The train arrived. She left the paper on the seat for the next passenger to find and enjoy.

She walked along the side of the Thames and approached along Great College Street, passing the famed college garden on her right. It was said that it was the oldest cultivated garden in England. It was a shame that she couldn't see any of it, with the tall grey wall keeping everyone out. She ignored the various doors along the wall, and headed for an archway at the far end. It was a school of high, but problematic reputation and the dispute over the future of the ownership of one building, Ashburnham House, was dragging on in the courts – it had been going on for twenty-two years now. She persuaded a porter to allow her into the main yard by using her very best upper-class accent as borrowed from Phoebe, and she was led up some steps and into a chilly, cavernous corridor. There the porter dithered, not sure if he could leave her alone while he went to fetch someone with more authority to tell her to leave.

Luckily a black-robed master came flapping along like a bat, and he took charge, drawing Marianne into a cluttered side room that smelled of dust. "My dear, are you looking for a particular boy?"

She was initially confused and wondered what kind of underhand and shady market they were running until she realised he had taken her to be the mother of a student. "No – my apologies!" She quickly explained about the positive reply to her letter, and asked if they had any master old enough who would possibly remember a pupil from almost thirty years previously.

"Oh my goodness, there is a tall order. It is true we tend to wear ourselves out here and simply die as we teach, and they do say that one Latin master expired during a lesson and his unfortunate state was not realised for three days. The boys simply filed in and out as usual, and assumed he was sleeping – such was the status quo. However, thirty years is a very long time. We would surely notice a cadaver in that length of time." The master mused, his hands behind his back, staring at a blank bit of wall. "So, hmm, old masters, still present and hopefully still breathing.

Luckshaw? Maybe. He smells particularly dusty. Collins? Oh, no, no, he came from Eton, didn't he, though he probably started there in the last century. Oh! I have it. Wait here."

She had no intention of going anywhere until she had her answers. She smiled and perched against a pile of boxes, and the master swished away.

He was gone for some time.

It was a strange and lonely place to be, in a windowless store room, while all the noise and clatter of a boys' school went on outside.

Finally, the man returned, and he wasn't accompanied by another gown-wearing teacher. Instead, the man by his side was tiny, ancient, and dressed as a gardener. She remembered her old childhood mentor, and felt a rush of warmth for the man. She was already disposed to like him just through simple association. He coughed with a creak like a rusty door.

He was probably as old as the college garden itself.

"Bert has been here since Waterloo, haven't you, eh, Bert?" The master clapped him on the back and disappeared.

Bert scowled at the door, which was left half-open, and then flashed Marianne a toothy and genuine smile. He touched one finger to his forehead, and said, "What may I do for you, madam? An old boy, was it?"

"Edgar Bartholomew." She furnished him with as many dates and details as she could. She doubted that the man could possibly remember any pupil at all, even from so long ago, and she was right. He was not a teacher, after all.

He shook his head. "I have a remarkable memory," he told her, in a voice as strong as a twenty-year-old man's. "I can tell you everything I know from decades ago. I cannot tell you what I had for breakfast, alas."

"It is often the way, in …"

"Us ancient decrepit folk, yes. Oh, don't worry. If I cannot admit I am old, what can I say? No, there is no Edgar Bartholomew coming to my mind. Was there anyone else?"

"Perhaps you might remember a certain Wade Walker?"

And his face lit up, to her delight. "A singular name for a singular boy. Ah yes! The pair of them – I see them now, one so dark and one so pale – yes! Both good lads, good students, and inseparable. Quiet, and respectful in manner."

"Do you know what they went on to do in life?"

He shook his head. "No, no. I only know them as they passed through my gardens. I know all the good boys, who walk the paths and appreciate the flowers, and I know the bad ones, who scuff the gravel and pull up the plants. But that is all I know, I'm afraid."

"Thank you." She got up to leave, and brushed the dust from her skirts. "One last thing. Which one was blond, and which was the brunette?"

"Walker was as a pale as a ghost, with hair like sun, that a maiden would kill to have. Bartholomew was like a pirate who had spent his whole life at sea. Dark eyes that the ladies would soon swoon for, swarthy as anything you ever did see."

She trudged out into the suddenly-bright streets, and felt despondent. For the Edgar Bartholomew she was investigating was also dark of hair.

***

When she got back, Marianne found Phoebe waiting for her in the hallway. "I am glad to see you are dressed for a trip to town," she was told. "Let us take lunch somewhere secluded."

"It is a little late now for lunch."

"A mid-afternoon tea then. I have a fancy for cakes. Price said I looked peaky this morning, and that I should treat myself. I must obey my husband! It is written in the scriptures, after all. Come along!"

By half past two they were back in London, in a pretty little teashop down a cobbled side-street. It was a favourite haunt of ladies who wished to have a break from a day of shopping. They could hardly stray into the raucous coffee houses which were full of men and politics, but tea rooms like this were springing up all over the place. They ordered a few light sandwiches and pastry delights, and a large pot of tea.

"Now, I have news," Phoebe said. "Do you? Shall we toss a coin for who speaks first?"

"You may as well, for I have little," Marianne said morosely. "I have been paid for nothing, you know. We are chasing shadows."

"Not so. Listen! I did not discover much more about Jack Monahan. I cannot discover why he was dismissed from his employment with Lord Hazelstone – yes! He was dismissed. He did not leave of his own accord. So that is even more reason to avoid the man. Now, there was also Mrs Silver, and I managed to meet with her at another friend's afternoon salon. Alas, Mrs Silver was unhelpful. She had no good words to say about you, by the way. I pretended that we were not linked in any significant way. She told me that Monahan had insisted that he attend a séance with her, and did so by claiming some affinity with me! Because he dropped *my* name, she allowed him to be present."

Marianne scowled. "The snake."

"I know! And as neither he nor Mrs Silver herself had ever met me, I feel most doubly used. How many others use my name as a way to open doors?"

"I wouldn't think it is widespread. Such deception always gets found out."

"True," Phoebe said. "Anyway, he is said to be a charming man when in company, according to all accounts, just as I said before. I also discovered that he is definitely a bachelor and his family is unknown. He has no name. Beyond that, no one could say much at all about him. Some women turned to laughing and blushing, so he must be an attractive man. Is he?"

"I could hardly say."

Phoebe twitched her nose. "Indeed. I am sure we can trust you not to have your head turned by such frivolity. A little of it would do you good – but not now, not with this man. Now, as to Edgar Bartholomew, there is more to say. He is known as a quiet and sober man of business, generally. His wife's departure all those years ago, and her tragic death last year, has made him an object of pity and sympathy. He has not taken advantage of his marital freedom, and in fact has been praised as a man of narrow morals and good standing."

"So far, so good."

"He does not dine out. He does not hold dinners and he does not receive callers. He does not attend invitations. He has been a recluse for these past ten years or more."

"Where?"

"He has mostly been living in a small suite of rooms in London, close to his very small and exclusive club, and it is a place I do not think even my own dear Price could simply walk into. Most of the people I spoke to say they were surprised to see him suddenly emerge into the streets again."

"When did he suddenly emerge?" Marianne asked. "No – I can guess. Three weeks ago?"

"Yes. But he still refuses dinners and parties. He has moved back to his country house on the edge of town, they say, and given up his rooms, but he comes into London almost every day."

"And does what?"

Phoebe grinned in triumph. "Here is where it does involve you, and I can understand why his son thinks that you are the best person to help. He is closeted up with all the different mediums and magicians in London."

"His son said as much. But I wonder why?"

"No one could say. So, what do we do now?"

"Eat all the cake here, and then go out and find him, and follow him."

"How thrilling."

***

It turned out to be rather hard to find an individual in London. They had a wasted and pointless day, as they trailed from one place to another. Sometimes it felt as if the whole world lived in London. They hung around the houses of the better-known mediums, and spoke with neighbours and servants and got nowhere. Sometimes they were told, tantalisingly, of Mr

94

Edgar Bartholomew being spotted – "he came yesterday, madam, miss, you've missed him" – but they did not see him. Even fewer words could be got about Wade Walker. People simply said, "Ask Edgar Bartholomew. They are always together, or so it is said."

They had one tiny piece of luck as they trudged on their way back towards the nearest railway station. Phoebe had wanted to ride in a cab, but Marianne knew of a "spiritualist" woman who had lately arrived in London, purporting to hail from India though Marianne had spotted her at a gathering and felt that her skin tone was more of a dark Celt, and her accent likewise tinged with the Welsh valleys. They passed by the tall narrow house where the woman had set up her rooms, and Marianne spied a maid throwing water out of the door.

One small coin and a hurried conversation later, and they knew that Bartholomew had been visiting "Madame Dipali" regularly and was booked to attend a small, private sitting the very next day.

"Say nothing to anyone," Marianne said to the maid, whose eyes remained hard until Phoebe revealed another coin for her.

"Well, wasn't that a stroke of luck!" Phoebe said as they turned away and linked arms. The streets were busy and they did not want to get separated. They had their bags on their inner arms, sandwiched between their bodies and well out of the reach of most pickpockets. People buffeted them from all sides.

"I am pleased," Marianne replied. "I wonder if there is any way of getting into this séance, or perhaps sneaking into a room adjacent to it, and hearing what Mr Bartholomew has to say." She kept her voice low, but something caught the ears of a man who was walking a little way ahead of them, and he half-turned his head in surprise.

Marianne faltered. It was too late to hide. There he was – the man that they had been seeking – heading towards the same railway terminus. As he had been known to visit the medium, it was not too strange to see him on the same street. But for him, it was an uncommon surprise. He spun around and blinked. "I know you," he said. "Oh! I saw you at my house. You were talking about me? I heard my name."

It was a bizarre and terse stream of short sentences. He looked ill at ease, and stepped forward with a looming air over them that Marianne could not help but interpret as threatening.

"Oh, no, sir," Phoebe said, "I doubt that we were talking about you... Bartholomew? It is not such an unusual name."

"Indeed it is not, but coming from this woman, I am suspicious. Why have I seen you now, twice, in two days? What has my son been saying?"

"About what?"

Edgar Bartholomew pressed his lips together as if he were trying to stop himself shouting in exasperation. He nodded to the side of the pavement. "Step this way. There is something that you must know about my son."

They moved out of the way of the busy pedestrians and into a little alcove formed by the jutting edge of a building and some stone steps. Peeling notices and advertisements hung in strands from the flaking walls. It smelled unclean, as street corners tended to do. Edgar Bartholomew glowered at them. "My son has been abroad," he said. "He has been away from home for many years, and as you can imagine, this has unsettled him. Even, if I can go so far as to suggest such a thing, it has unhinged his mind slightly.

The air in foreign climes can make a strong man ill, given enough time. We are not suited to it. I have read Mr Darwin and I find his arguments compelling, and so it is with my son; he was born to live here, not there, and it has made him ... well, it has made him mad."

That is not how it works at all, Marianne thought. Yet she could also believe the man's final argument, even if she didn't agree with his logic to get there – the son's ideas about his father, that he was an impersonator, could easily be seen as delusional.

Phoebe was attempting to turn on her society-lady charm. She smiled sweetly and said, "We quite understand, sir, and if my cousin has done or said anything that might be offensive to you, please know that it has only been done from a place of concern."

"Concern? What about? What exactly has he said to you? How did you meet, and why *were* you at my house?"

Marianne was feeling like she was drowning. She should have had a nice, pat cover story ready to trot out. She felt her face flush. She gabbled, "Ah, nothing. Oh! Yes, we met at a dinner. He works with my cousin-in-law, Mr Claverdon, and he came to dine. Isn't that right, Phoebe?" Her truthful words came out in a rush and sounded fake to her own ears because of her panicked breathlessness.

And he clearly didn't believe what she was saying, either. "Oh really? I think you might look into his employment a little more. Works! And why did you come to my house? I do not receive callers."

"He invited me. He wished only to talk," she added hastily.

Phoebe began to squeeze Marianne's arm. "We should go," she murmured, saying then to Mr Bartholomew, "Once again, I apologise for our intrusion. We have to catch a train."

"The train can go without you. They run frequently enough, and I mean to have this out," he said. "Come now. What is your name? I asked it before but did not care to remember the answer. Now, I find I must look to my business. So who are you?"

In spite of all the reports of him in town as being of a quiet and sober-minded man, he presented a rough and bullying manner. It seemed to surprise Phoebe, but Marianne remember his bluntness from before. She said, "I am Miss Marianne Starr, and this is Mrs Phoebe Claverdon."

Phoebe tugged Marianne's arm. But he was blocking their way now, standing between them and the street. "And what did my son want to talk about?"

"It is a personal matter," Phoebe said, as Marianne struggled for words. "Come along." She pushed past Mr Bartholomew, unashamedly knocking him with her elbow, and dragged Marianne into the flow of people heading towards the station. "Good day, sir."

"If I see either of you again, I shall alert the authorities!" he bellowed after them.

Everyone turned to stare at the pair of them. Marianne could see that Phoebe's face was now aflame, and they heard muttered speculation as to their occupations – people were assuming that they were well-dressed whores.

Neither spoke until they were safely in a first class carriage, and quite alone, and then Phoebe began to giggle as the shock wore off, and Marianne frowned and stared out of the window.

She wondered if Simeon had a way to get her into the private séance that was to be held the following day.

Nine

They knew that the private sitting between Edgar Bartholomew and Madam Dipali was due to be held in the afternoon. Unfortunately in the morning, Phoebe woke up unable to see. She suffered attacks of hemicranias or migraine opthalmique, and would be confined to a darkened room for many hours. Various doctors had prescribed an array of remedies, from a few grains of aconitine in alcohol to triphenin in water, but nothing worked so well as a day and a night of silence and darkness. Marianne went to check on her, and whispered that no amount of electricity – administered by headband or by corset – could possibly help. Phoebe had moaned and burrowed into the pillow.

So Marianne checked on the governess, the cook, the housekeeper, her own father, her father's nurse, the children, and Emilia, and set everything to rights before leaving the house just before midday in a fearful rush, hoping to get to see Simeon and conjure up a plan of action before the scheduled séance.

Simeon laughed at her. "Of course I can do what you ask," he said. "But not within a week. Ideally, longer. I need to know the layout of the room. Where are the entrances and exits? What materials have been used in the walls? It is a ground floor room? Who else will be there? What tricks are planned?"

"All I want to do is to spy on him!" Marianne wailed in frustration. "Is that so hard? You can make invisible tigers appear, and handkerchiefs dance in the air. You can surely do this, simply with the objects that you have lying around in here!"

Simeon ran his fingers through his hair. "You are clever – how would you do it?"

"I am no magician."

"What do you hope to achieve?"

"I want to know why he is visiting mediums. I simply want to overhear what is happening."

"Why does anyone visit a medium?" Simeon said. He threw himself into a chair and pulled one ankle to rest on his opposite knee. "You tell me."

"To ..."

"To be duped?"

"No," she said. "They want to make contact with people they've lost, to find reassurance, to ... well, to be entertained, too, but as this is a private meeting, that means really he is trying to ... talk to someone who has died. He must truly believe in the possibility."

Simeon said, "Well done! You are thinking at last."

"Stop that. If I could listen in to what is happening, I could find out who he is trying to contact. Maybe it's his wife!"

"Is she definitely dead?"

"Yes, she is definitely dead. But the main problem with that hypothesis is," Marianne went on, "they were estranged, and for an awfully long time, so why would he want to speak to her now?"

"Maybe she had the last word and he resents it."

Marianne picked up a small stuffed mouse and threw it at Simeon's head but he caught it with his lightning reflexes. "Careful. This one bites."

"It's dead."

"It was never alive, and that still doesn't mean it can't harm you." He tucked it into his breast pocket, letting the head peep out. "I can understand what you want to do. He's a regular at this medium's house, is that right? So I can plan something if you really want me to, but you need to be able to get next door, and report back to me."

"I shall do so."

"How?"

"I have no idea." Already the initial rush of enthusiasm for the idea was waning. She was in danger of becoming like Phoebe, hurtling from one idea to another without planning and thought. She was a woman of science, she reminded herself. Method, analysis, reason and rationality.

Simeon pulled the mouse free from his pocket and threw it back at her.

***

Marianne walked. Walking cleared her head. Phoebe, when she came to town alone, was not really alone; if her maid Emilia did not accompany her, then Price's valet Mr Fry would. She could ride in a carriage and have men carry her boxes. She did not see the city as Marianne did.

Marianne gloried in the freedoms afforded to her middling status. She ambled through the more respectable streets of shops and businesses, though as everywhere in London, the lower classes pressed in from all sides, in a jumble of noise and vision. People called out – begging, selling, preaching, warning.

Huge advertising hoardings screamed out their wares, and posters were pasted upon posters. Beggars wheeled or crawled, some with their life story chalked on the ground or scribbled on board that was propped at their feet, if they had feet. Street sellers offered her everything from ribbons to pies. Dogs barked, boys fought, and cabs trundled through the roads doing battle with delivery carts and horse-drawn omnibuses.

She walked and she thought – *if* Edgar Bartholomew was someone else, pretending to be him, then how would he do it? He would have to know the original man well enough to know he could fake it. He would have to be similar. And if he was not similar, he would have to change his appearance.

How did one change one's appearance? You couldn't grow taller, and while you could get fatter or thinner, it was not so easy. You could change your hair, but not your eyes.

Edgar Bartholomew's eyes had been pale, though his hair had been dark.

Something skirted around the edge of her memory. Someone had said something. Was it about hair, or eyes?

If anyone was going to impersonate Bartholomew, would it not be his closest friend, Wade Walker – of whom no one could speak? She only knew he existed based on the testimony of a few scant people.

It was the most tenuous of suspicions. But it was all she had.

She could not even imagine *why* he might be doing such a

thing.

She knew that she would need help for her next move. With Phoebe out of action, she decided to head back to the Bartholomews' country house, and ask for George Bartholomew's assistance.

When she reached the lane at the bottom of the driveway to the Bartholomew place, she stopped. If the older Bartholomew was at home, she was going to walk right into a world of trouble. She couldn't risk that.

Instead she knocked on the door of the lodge and it was answered by a pleasant man with deeply lined cheeks and a ready smile. "Can I help you, miss?"

"I hope so. I was hoping to call upon Mr George Bartholomew but I am aware that his father is not always amenable to visitors. I have no wish to cause trouble. I was wondering if you might be able to convey a message to the gentleman, the son, asking him to meet me down here?"

"As to that, I should love to help you, miss, but it is not possible."

"Has Mr Edgar Bartholomew banned all visitors then?" she asked in dismay. "Even to his own son?"

"Oh no, it is not that – though you are correct in that he does discourage them. No. Mr George is no longer here."

"When did he leave?" she asked. She was amazed at this news.

"I wouldn't call it leaving. I am sorry to say that he was ejected."

"By his father?"

"Exactly so. There was some manner of argument, I believe,

and then he was gone. He walked to the station, I understand, with not much more than a bag and the clothes on his back."

"And where did he go from there?"

The gatekeeper flicked his eyes over her shoulder, and said, "London, I should imagine. He does not know any soul there, though. Perhaps he will obtain a place to live through his company."

"Perhaps," she said. "Thank you." She gave him a coin, which he tried to refuse, but she insisted. As she turned to go, she thought of something else.

"Why did Mr Bartholomew come back to this house? When was it, three weeks ago?"

"Aye, nearer four now. I have no idea. I have not seen him above ten years or more. Back then I was not gatekeeper – I worked in the village. I only took this position on four years ago, when the old man here previous to me died, sudden-like. Mr Bartholomew took me on."

"So you saw him four years ago?"

"No, miss, it was all done by correspondence. I can read tolerably well," he added proudly. "My lad has been up the school for a few winters and he taught me."

"And you have no idea why Mr Edgar Bartholomew came back alone?" she asked again. This man did not know Edgar, so could not vouch for the son's accusations.

"No idea at all, but he did not return alone, miss."

"His son arrived a week later, yes."

"Yes, he did," the gatekeeper said. "But when Mr Bartholomew came back that month ago, he came in a carriage here with another man."

"Who?" she asked as her heart beat faster. "Was it Wade Walker?"

"I do not know. He stayed for three days and then he was gone, but I did not see him leave."

She turned around to look up the driveway, all unkempt and mossy, and hedged around with uncut conifers and yew trees. "He could still be there."

"There could be a troupe of circus performers there, miss, and none of us would know."

Her spine tingled.

***

She caught the very next train back to London. The man in the ticket office, recognising her as having alighted from the previous train, gave her a curious look but she held her head high and ignored it. It was now early evening and if she were being sensible, she would head home to Woodfurlong.

But the chase was on. She felt that they had wasted time hunting around London to try and follow the older Bartholomew man. She went directly to the main offices of Harker and Bow, and hoped that she was not going to bump into Price Claverdon. Since he had confessed the blackmail to her, she had done absolutely nothing on his behalf, as she had been so caught up in the other matter. Not that he had requested her help, of course – he just wanted money as a loan. She wondered if she would ever see that money again, and was sad. What of her plans? One day she had to secure her future.

Price had seemed tense and quiet at mealtimes, and was spending more and more time in London and away from the house. She assumed that he was at his offices.

Sometimes she caught him looking at her intently. But they could never speak of the issue in the presence of Phoebe. So she would quickly look away, and hope that the sudden movement did not raise any unfortunate suspicions in Phoebe's mind.

She had passed on the money she had obtained from George Bartholomew, and Price had been awkwardly grateful. She promised him more, if she were able, and he stuttered and thanked her. He wanted to refuse – but he could not.

It was a situation with no good ending, she could see that. Not for him, nor even for herself. Was she only delaying the inevitable? She wanted to hide Phoebe from this pain for as long as she possibly could.

Her uncomfortable ponderings had to be put to one side as she reached the magnificent portico that surrounded the main entrance of the offices of the import and trade company, Harker and Bow. Clerks hurried in and out. They would work late, she knew, even until ten o'clock or later, though the more senior staff had greater freedom. It seemed as busy now as it did at any point during the day. A young man dashed past her from behind, and he was clouded by the aroma of hot pies. She took a step to the side – directly into his path, deliberately so – and he stumbled. He lost his grip on his paper-wrapped parcels and they tumbled to the ground.

She gasped, in a convincingly coquettish manner she hoped, and helped him to gather up his precious cargo as she offered a stream of apologies. She let her gloved hand brush his as they reached for the same packet, and he reddened and coughed. He was as innocent as he was young then – that was good, and had been by no means a given.

She could make use of his blushing manner. As they stood up, she reached out and brushed some invisible specks from his lapels. "I am *so* sorry!" she said, trying to lighten her voice. "I am *so* clumsy! I do hope that nothing is damaged. How awful of me!"

"My pies are fine, miss, thank you. Ah. Yes. Oh."

"I did not mean your pies," she said, looking at him from under her lashes, and thinking, *what would Phoebe do in this situation.* "I mean, I hope that you are not damaged!"

"Yes, no, I mean, no, thank you." He tried to get away but she closed her hand over his wrist and he froze in absolute terror at her bold touch. She was being positively shocking. He couldn't pull away. What, that he should appear to push a lady? He simply couldn't do it.

"Please, perhaps you can help me. I am supposed to go inside and ask but ... well, it is a large and scary place for a mere woman, as I am sure you understand. I fear that I have not the courage for such a thing."

He gulped.

She pressed on. "I am trying to discover where a certain George Bartholomew is staying. He is an employee of this company. He has had to leave his father's house quite suddenly."

"I am sorry – I am only an office clerk. I do not know him."

"But perhaps you might go inside and enquire on my behalf? And if he is at work today, here, would you ask him to step outside?"

He seized the chance to escape from her, nodded furiously, and ran up the steps.

She moved to one side and fiddled with her bag, trying to

look like she was there by chance, until he returned. He had a slip of yellow paper in his hand and an address was scrawled across it. "This is where they sent him, miss," he said, thrusting it at her without making eye contact. "He is not at work at present. He is on some sort of leave and could not say when he might return. They made faces at me and I did not know what they meant. He might be in trouble but they would not tell me. I am of no consequence," he added helplessly.

She thanked him – well, she thanked his rigid back as he shot away from her. It didn't matter. She had what she needed. She had no idea where the street was, but she hailed a cab and spent twenty minutes sitting in almost stationary traffic to reach a place that she could have walked to in less than five minutes.

The building was a respectable-looking one down a narrow street. They were on the edge of the trading district and these rows of houses were all residential. From the mish-mash of curtains and coloured paint, she could tell that the houses were all sub-divided into flats and apartments or single rented rooms. But the front steps were scrubbed and the windows mostly glass rather than board, and there was an air of industry about the place.

She knocked on a blue door and it was answered promptly by a small and ancient woman in layers of black. She peered at Marianne, thrusting her face forward so that she was only a few inches from Marianne's chest. Her eyes were milky and almost opaque. "Hello?"

"Good day, madam. Is this a lodging house for employees of Harker and Bow?"

"Indeed it is. We take many of the clerks here. Are you from the offices? Come in, come in, dear, out of the cold."

It was not remotely cold, in spite of the evening sun now dipping behind the roofs, but Marianne accepted and stepped into the long dark hallway. "I'm looking for Mr George Bartholomew," she said. "I was told he arrived here yesterday."

"Oh yes! Poor man. I'm afraid the only spare room was up in the eaves, hardly fit for any soul, but he took it readily enough. I've not seen him stir since."

"Oh – is he here now?"

"He is, I think, unless he sneaked past me, but I don't miss a thing, no I don't. I have the ears of a snake."

Marianne had no idea how good a snake's hearing was. She smiled, even though the woman probably couldn't see it – no doubt she could hear Marianne's smile in her voice. "Might I go up and see him?" she asked.

The woman frowned. "And you are from the company, are you? Who exactly are you?"

"No. I am a family member of one of his colleagues, Mr Claverdon."

The woman lost her frown and began to beam. "I know all the big managers," she said. "I know him! Mr Price Claverdon! Oh, he has been a company man for years. Well, well, off you go. Up as many stairs as you can, and then it's the door on the left."

Marianne ran up the stairs, and paused for a minute to get her breath back before she rapped on the door.

But he did not answer when she knocked.

She tried again, and then stood still and silent on the uncarpeted landing and pondered the situation. He could easily

109

be out. He wasn't at the offices, if the young clerk could be believed, but he could have slipped past the blind housekeeper and gone out into London in spite of her claim to reptilian hearing.

Then she heard a cough from within the room.

She knocked once more, and called through the wood, "Mr Bartholomew? It is Marianne Starr." She tried the knob and it opened, but she only let it go a few inches, enough for her to talk through the gap. She hardly wanted to burst in on the poor man.

"Miss Starr? Come in – oh. Please excuse me. I find that I am somewhat unfortunately indisposed."

She had opened the door as he said *come in*, and stopped as he got to the end of his sentence. She didn't know where to look. Mr Bartholomew was lying in a narrow bed, low to the floor, at the far end of the room, where the sloping ceiling came down almost to the wooden floorboards. There was a window above him that was letting in light but no air. Luckily ventilation was provided by a slim gap where some of the plaster had fallen away from the lath on the walls, revealing the greying sky beyond. She sniffed. There was the distinctive odour of garlic in the room, and sickness.

There was a wooden chest on the floor, standing closed and draped with clothes, and a bag to the side of it. She examined everything in the room in depth, because she didn't want to look at the man in the bed.

He appeared to be fully clothed, right down to his suit jacket, and she assumed – hoped – that he wore trousers underneath the blankets. But even so, the fact remained that he was in bed. The only other man she'd seen in such a personal place was her father, and he resented it every time that his illness brought his dignity so low.

"Forgive me," he said weakly. "This is hardly the attitude that you expect." He struggled to sit upright.

Her compassion finally overruled her morals. "You're ill. Have you called a doctor?"

"No, no. But please, can you bring me the water? I knocked over my glass…"

She went into her efficient and capable self, and set about the task. The glass was rolling under the bed in a pool of water, and there was a half-full brown earthenware jug not far away on the floor. Also under the bed was a bowl and a chamber pot, and neither seemed fit for her to examine. She left them well alone. She passed him the refilled glass, and stood awkwardly. He invited her to sit on the bed, but that was a move too far. She could manhandle a clerk's wrist but she would not sit on this man's bed. She remained standing, but she looked at his face at last, and was very concerned with what she could see.

"You need to see a doctor. What has happened? Why are you here? I apologise for the questions but…"

He waved away her concerns. "I understand. It is your job. Why, I am paying you to ask questions!"

"And it will help my job if you can answer them."

He nodded, and then grimaced and clutched at his stomach. "Ah – ah! It comes in waves, the pain. I must have eaten something that was past its best. I took oysters from a street seller last night."

"Were you ill at your father's house?"

"No. This came on in the middle of night, quite suddenly, and has been worsening all morning. But I have been ill before and I am strong. It is a hazard of the traveller and we learn to bear up. These things never last above a day. I am not concerned."

"You must keep drinking water. So, why are you here, in this room, and not at your father's house?"

"I think you could tell me that."

"What?"

He smiled weakly. "My father has thrown me out, and he mentioned your name. He came home yesterday in a fearful temper, and found me exploring the unused and empty rooms of the place. He dragged me out of them – literally dragged me, as if I were a dog! – and demanded to know why I had been talking to you."

"And what did you say?"

"I said that you were my colleague's cousin-in-law and that I had met you at a dinner party. He believed me, but he was still furious. And when I challenged him on his movements and his secrecy, he ejected me from the house, quite forcibly. He had kept hold of the revolver that I had placed on the stairs – do you remember? Well, he had that, and he waved it at me. I did not think that he would use it, but..."

"Oh my. What did he do? Is this the cause of your illness? Are you shot?"

He laughed while clutching his stomach. "And you a woman of science! A bullet would not cause nausea like this. No, he fired to one side of me, and ruined the wall. I do not know if he meant to miss me, but thank heavens that he did."

"How awful."

"And so I am here, and I am impressed that you have found me."

"Speaking of finding, have you any word of your mother's grave?"

"I have heard nothing."

"Do you think your father has killed her and now uses these mediums to find her, and speak to her beyond the grave?"

"It is possible. Yes, I have often thought that. Perhaps all my idea that he is not my father was just a way of preventing myself seeing the truth – that he is a murderer! Don't we all lie to ourselves about something? We try to force the world to be as we would wish it to be, rather than seeing it as it is."

"Like a vast version of the willing-game."

"And maybe the world is more full of tricks and deceit than we can ever know."

As the conversation took its gloomy turn, he sagged back against the wall, and drew the blanket higher. He knocked his head back and closed his eyes, and his cheeks stiffened. She recognised all the signs of a man trying to hide his pain. "Might I go and fetch some food for you?"

He shuddered. "No, thank you. I fear I am about to be most unpleasantly indisposed again. I am so sorry, Miss Starr. I tend to … erupt. Please could I ask you to leave me?"

"I am worried."

"Call upon me tomorrow. Perhaps some bread. Oh. Miss Starr. Do go. I think. Before I humiliate myself and shock you. Oh." He spoke in bursts through gritted teeth, and his fingers gripped the edge of the blanket tightly.

She retreated to the door, unwilling to leave him in such a poor state.

He opened his eyes. They were red now. "No doctor, no

point. Remember my solicitor. And do not let that man win. You know. You know who. Please go."

She closed the door quietly behind her and heard him explode instantly into paroxysms of unpleasantness. Feeling nauseous herself, she went down the stairs and left her contact details with the old woman.

"If he gets worse, send word immediately. And here is payment in advance," she said.

The old woman tasted the coin, and smiled. Marianne caught a glimpse of her tongue and was disappointed to see that it was not forked.

Ten

The next morning, Phoebe was feeling much recovered from her debilitating headache, though she could not stomach strong-smelling foods. She told Marianne that all the colours of the furnishings were bright and new in her eyes, and all her senses were improved. In return, Marianne told her about the sorry state of George Bartholomew, and together they raided the kitchens to put together a basket of nice food and drink that would appeal to an invalid. Mrs Cogwell, the cook, was delighted to unleash her caring side, and the cousins ended up having to carry the parcel between them, it was so heavily filled with tempting treats.

It was only just before mid-morning when they reached the building with the blue door. The blind housekeeper greeted Marianne with no apparent recollection of the day before, at first.

"I came to see Mr Bartholomew yesterday, do you not remember? I gave you my address?"

"Oh, yes, so you did. I have it still." She patted her skirts.

"I take it he is well?"

"I have not seen him yet. He is such a quiet man."

That alarmed Marianne. They didn't hesitate. They dragged the basket awkwardly up the stairs and dumped it on the floor outside his bedroom door. Marianne rapped and partly opened the door to speak through the gap.

But there was no reply to her calling out this time.

She peeped in, holding her breath. The smell of garlic was stronger now, and mixed in with all the vile odours of a sickroom, staleness and unwashed clothes being the very least of it.

He lay on his back, rigid, and his eyes were open, staring at the ceiling.

Phoebe came to her shoulder, peering over, and gasped. "He is dead."

"Step away. Don't go in – go back into the corridor. You will soil your nice clothes. Let me check." Marianne went forward. The floor around the bed was a mess of fluids, and the bed itself was worse. He had died hard. She pulled off her glove and pressed it to her mouth with her left hand, as if that might block the smell. With her right hand she felt for a pulse in his throat, and found nothing. He was cold and the skin felt rubbery, as if it would mould to her touch and remain in place if she pressed it.

"He is most definitely dead," she called back to Phoebe. "Now what? Who do we tell? A doctor is no use."

"Do we not inform the police?"

"In case it is a suspicious death?"

"It does not seem suspicious. He has been ill, not stabbed in the heart or shot in the head. But the police will know what to do. Come away, Marianne. You can do nothing for him."

"Oysters, he said," Marianne mused. "He had eaten bad oysters. But I can smell garlic."

"I can smell many things, and none of them are pleasant."

Marianne could not help herself. She peered down at him. His face was not his own, not any more. His flesh sagged towards the floor and new folds had appeared in his cheeks. It was not as if she was looking at the man she had known. He was a lump, an object. The blanket was tangled around his feet. His trousers were stained and his shirt rumpled. His jacket had been discarded and lay on the floor. The skin around his face was yellow, and his belly seemed distended.

Oysters, she thought – *really?*

But she was no pathologist. With reluctance, she followed Phoebe out of the room and downstairs, where they raised the alarm with the housekeeper and a boy was sent to the nearest police stationhouse and they were plunged into a world of questions that had very few answers.

***

"Now what?" Phoebe said as they were released from the stationhouse. One conscientious young policeman had insisted on furnishing them with smelling salts, small glasses of sherry and a pork pie each, while they had been inside the stationhouse. Neither of them had eaten the pies, though Marianne had pocketed both for later. It was a little after lunch time but Marianne didn't think she'd want to eat for a while. She could still smell the room.

"I would like to go and tell his father," Marianne said to Phoebe.

"There is no need. Someone will be sent to him from the police, soon enough."

"Yes, and I would like to beat them to it. I want to see what

117

this man's reaction will be."

"Ah, I understand you! Yes. But are you sure you want to see him? I must get back to Woodfurlong as my dressmaker is coming – in fact, she will already be there, and wondering where I am."

"You go on home. You have duties. I will visit Mr Bartholomew alone."

"No, you will not. He has spoken roughly to you, don't you remember? He has a gun, and he tried to shoot his son."

"I also have a gun, and unlike him, I will not miss."

"Marianne!"

"I promise."

"What, to not miss?"

"Exactly. Go on with you – I shall be home for dinner."

"If Price ever knew what we were about, he should divorce me completely."

"He would indeed," Marianne said, but she thought, *perhaps he would not. If you knew what he was about, you would divorce him if you could.* She forced a smile onto her face. "I expect that I will arrive there at the same time as the police. Let me compromise with you. I shall wait in the gatehouse with the man there, until the police arrive, and then I will go with them, and let them break the news, and simply watch for his reaction."

Phoebe relaxed. "That is a much safer plan."

It did not, unfortunately, turn out quite so neatly.

***

When Marianne reached the lodge at the end of the driveway, she fully intended to call on the gatekeeper and follow

118

the plan she had laid out to Phoebe. She did not go straight to the door of the lodge, however. She walked up the driveway for a short distance, looking for any sign of the police having arrived before her.

And there was someone standing on the front steps of the house.

It was no policeman.

It was, in fact, a woman. She was very tall, and held herself like a queen, with dignity and confidence in every line of her. Marianne didn't follow the latest fashions but Phoebe and Emilia ensured that she did not disgrace herself in company and she had a rough idea of what was current. She could recognise that the woman was wearing the very latest in elegant tastes. Her dark jacket was slim and fitted, with plump peplum sleeves and scarlet trim. It skimmed over her hips and her skirts were a dark grey, ideal for moving about the city, with artful folds to convey restrained fullness, narrow at the sides but bunching up over a bustle at the back. She held a furled umbrella, in the exact shade of red to match her jacket's trim, her shoes and her hat.

Marianne's first thought was that this could be George's mother, at last, and Mr Edgar Bartholomew's estranged wife. Yes, perhaps she had never been dead at all. Her heart gave a tight pang. If so, did the mother know what had happened to her son? Marianne stopped walking. She would definitely wait for the arrival of the police. She could not possibly intrude on this private tragedy.

But the woman was talking to Edgar Bartholomew, and he was standing on a few steps up above her, and getting increasingly angry. He waved his arms around, and Marianne could hear his voice faintly, though not the words. The woman did not make any move to respond. She did not seem remotely intimidated; she didn't bend, or quiver, or hunch her shoulders, or put up her hands in supplication. Instead she stepped back, moving down the steps to the gravel without turning her back to the man.

On an impulse, Marianne began to walk towards them.

She heard Edgar Bartholomew shout, "– ever again!" and he slammed the door of the house. Now she was alone, the woman turned, and suddenly saw Marianne approaching her.

They both slowed down but they continued to walk towards one another.

The woman was not old enough to be George's mother, and Marianne felt relief. She was pretty, with high cheekbones and wide eyes that lacked any obvious upper lid, giving her a fey look. Her skin was very fair, and her hair was the sort of blonde only generally seen on young girls. When they got to within ten feet of one another, they stopped.

The woman was scrutinising Marianne as hard as Marianne had been observing the woman.

Marianne smiled politely. "Good day. I am Miss Marianne Starr."

The look on the woman's face said, very clearly, *why do I want to know that?* But she smiled in return. "Delighted, I am sure. Please do excuse me. He is not in the best of moods."

"He rarely is. Was it the older Mr Bartholomew that you wished to see? Or perhaps his son?"

"Oh!" The other woman's demeanour changed instantly and she closed the distance between them. "Do you know George? Yes, it was his son I actually hoped to meet. Oh, do forgive me. I am Anna Jones."

They shook hands as if they were in a drawing room, not someone else's driveway.

"Are you quite all right?" Marianne asked. "You seem pale. Would you like to walk into the town? I know a pleasant tea room."

"Ah – thank you, yes. I should like that. Do you really know George? Mr Bartholomew said some terrible things about his son. I hardly know what to believe. I hope that he spoke from a place of spite and not from truth."

"Oh dear. I am so dreadfully sorry to have to tell you this," Marianne said, as they fell into step alongside one another. It was somehow easier to break bad news when one was not facing the other person directly. "I do have some awful news about George Bartholomew –"

"Then his father was telling the truth?" Anna cried out. "Is he really dead?"

"Is that what he said to you?"

"It is! And is that what you meant?"

"It is." Marianne kept walking but now her mind was whirling. How did Edgar Bartholomew already know? She could see, up ahead, a black cab approaching along the road. It pulled up at the lodge as they passed, and a policeman got out to speak to the gatekeeper.

"I can hardly believe it," Anna said with a catch in her voice. No one took any notice of them as they went past the cab and headed towards the town. Women were of little importance. "What did he die from?"

"As to that, I am not sure," Marianne said. "Did his father

give no hint?"

"He did not. He didn't seem upset, just angry, but grief is a strange thing. When did he die?"

Marianne felt uncomfortable talking about the subject in the open air. It was a bright, fresh day, and the topic was more suited to rain and twilight. "I hope I do not shock you, but I found the body myself, this morning. I had visited him yesterday, so he must have died overnight. I am so very sorry." She cleared her throat before asking, delicately, "Were you close?"

"I suppose that you mean, were we lovers? And no, I am not shocked, by anything you might say. I am a woman of the world – perhaps even a worldly woman. Ha! So *they* might say. But tell me, how is it that you found him? Was he not here at this house? Why was he not here? Indeed I could ask about you and George … were *you* two lovers …?"

Anna had sidestepped the question about their closeness, Marianne noticed. "He was not here," Marianne said. "And no, we were not lovers. His father had asked him to leave this place, apparently, and he had taken rooms that had been found for him through his company."

"Bow? Really, they would still do that for him, after…?" She bit her lip and looked away.

"Yes, Bow, the very same, and why not?" *She knows a lot about him,* Marianne noted. *That he works for Harker and Bow, for a start. Interesting.* "I knew that he was ill when I visited him yesterday, and when I went back today, that was when I made the unpleasant discovery."

"How tragic."

They stopped outside a tea room. The windows were small

and covered in lace, preventing anyone from seeing in, but Marianne assured Anna that it was a fine and genteel place. "But I do understand if you find you have no appetite," she added.

"I do not. But I think I could take a little tea." Anna flashed her a small smile. "One must remain strong, don't you agree?"

Eleven

They made awkward small talk at first, as they were shown to a table, and they gave their orders to the plump serving maid. Suddenly facing one another added a layer of stiff formality to their interaction. Anna was a dignified woman, and well-bred, but the manner of their meeting threw a pall over the proceedings.

"What a sorry state of affairs," Marianne murmured. "It does make things disagreeable. We can hardly now chatter about fashion or gossip about well-known people in the newspapers, can we?"

Anna's perfect eyebrows quirked a little and she looked up at Marianne under her wide lids. "And those things are your everyday and preferred topics of conversation, Miss Starr?"

"Why would you think otherwise?" Marianne felt immediately defensive. Was this woman about to reveal that she, like Jack Monahan, already knew all about her?

Anna said, "You are not a slavish follower of fashion, for one."

"A polite way of saying I am dressed in a rather out of date way."

"I would say classic, and restrained; not showy. Your hands – forgive me, but you did ask – have curious stains. Ink on your finger, so you like to write – maybe letters, maybe other things. But there is a slight roughness, too, and a hint of sun. You might enjoy gardens and you do not have an attentive maid, but you speak as if you are of the class to have a maid, so you are a poor relation. A governess?"

Marianne sat back in her chair and smiled. "I ought to be upset but I thoroughly enjoyed following your chain of thought! You are like the mediums but do not pretend that your insight comes from spirits. And you are correct in many particulars, except I am neither a gardener nor a governess; I am a woman of science."

"Ah!" said Anna. "And here is the best place in all the world to be such a thing. London is so... forgive me. I run on, like a child."

"There is nothing to forgive. Are you a visitor here?"

"I have recently moved here."

"From?"

Anna turned her head to the approaching maid and their conversation had to be dropped in the flurry caused by setting out the tea things. Marianne decided, as Anna had said earlier that she was "not shocked", to be blunt in her speech and approach. The tea arrived in an ornate pot. Marianne fiddled with the cups, and said, "So, how did you know Mr Bartholomew? You did not answer me, previously."

"No, for it was a personal question."

Marianne made steady eye contact with Anna but she didn't blush or look away. Then Anna raised her left hand, and showed

Marianne the silver ring set with pearls.

Marianne understood. "You are married – what, to...?"

Anna laughed. "No, not to George. Poor George! No, my husband remains ... abroad. There, I hope he stays. I shall never see him again. But this tells you all you need to know."

It did not. It could have been hinting that Anna and George had been engaged in a scandalous affair, or it could simply be saying that their friendship was platonic. "I still do not follow," Marianne said stubbornly. "I am not a clever woman."

Anna sighed. "I rather think that you are, because of – or in spite – your education. I am a clever woman, too, and I know one when I meet one. Well, I met George in Prussia," she said with reluctance, "a few years ago. Our paths often crossed at parties and banquets. He was lively and made me laugh. This was a rare thing. So we often spoke together."

"Does your husband also work for Harker and Bow?"

Anna twitched her nostrils. It was a fleeting movement, but she blinked heavily at the same time. "He does not," she said. "My husband and I are estranged, as I said. Naturally you understand that this is a sensitive topic and one that I am not prepared to discuss any further with a stranger."

Yet you blithely analyse me as if I were a specimen, and speculate as to my background, quite openly. You are an arrogant woman, and I am too polite to say this. "Naturally. If I have offended you, please accept my apologies..." Marianne made a number of other pleasantries until Anna waved at her.

"Enough, now. Why do we English carry on so?"

We don't, though, do we? Marianne thought. There was a hint of an accent in Anna's speech. She had said she was not a

127

Londoner. "Are you …English?"

"Yes, of course. I attended school in Cheltenham. Though I have travelled widely since I was married."

You are not at all who you seem to be, Marianne thought. Before she could say anything else, she was now on the receiving end of Anna's questions.

"And how did you know George?"

"Through my own business," Marianne said. It would profit her nothing to lie about this. "I said that I am a woman of science, but do not think that I spend my time on beaches, scrabbling for fossils, or drawing plants. I am a scientific investigator. I am particularly concerned with exposing fake mediums."

"Oh!" Now Anna sounded genuinely fascinated and she leaned forward. "You do not believe in a world beyond the veil at all, then?"

"I will believe it as soon as I have evidence and facts."

"Do not the testimonies of a thousand people convince you? Human experience, in a sense, is all that we have, is it not?"

"No – I will not believe it, not until these phenomena are tested in a laboratory."

Anna cocked her head. "The very fact of being in a sterile place makes the manifestations far less likely, or at least, that is the argument that I have heard. As for me, I would like very much for there to be more to life than … than … well, all of this. Have you not read the phenomenologists? I urge you to look at Husserl."

"He is not familiar to me," Marianne said. "Are you a philosopher? You know about me but I know nothing of you."

"No, I am no philosopher, but I have studied widely, across

Europe, in every institution that has been open to me." Anna sniffed. "Which are few. But tell me, why had George come to you? He is a ... he was a straightforward and honest man."

Marianne sipped at her tea while she considered the question. But there was no reason not to tell Anna about this, so she said, "He believed that his father was an imposter and had asked me to investigate."

"But that is nothing to do with mediums and all that you are engaged in."

"I know," Marianne said. "And so I initially refused him. However his father was acting suspiciously and in the end, I agreed to help. Now, though..." Now there was only George's final exhortation to her – *Do not let that man win.*

"Well, that is your task over with. I am sorry," Anna said. "In fact, it is a sorry business, all done, is it not?"

"It is. Although I am not sure that it is all over. Well, thank you for the company although it would have been nicer to have met under better circumstances." She meant it, too. She could have had long and intense conversations with this woman.

They both stood up and began rearranging their outdoor clothing while the waitress hovered. Marianne insisted on paying and Anna only made the briefest of protests.

Once outside, they had another awkward moment as they faced one another for the parting. Impulsively, Marianne asked for Anna's address in London. "As you were friends with George, I will pass on details of his funeral to you."

Anna flinched, and frowned. Marianne wasn't sure if it were just the mention of the funeral, or something else, but when Anna said, "I have rooms at number forty, Bird Street," Marianne didn't believe her. She had never heard of Bird Street, and found the name unlikely; but she did not know London as intimately as a cab driver, so she nodded and decided to check it.

"And your address?" Anna said, intently.

"I live in a house called Woodlands," she said slowly, trying to sound confident, and worrying that the lie would be obvious. "Woodlands, just off the High Street in Upper Holloway."

Anna accepted that, and gave no sign of suspicion. They shook hands again, and parted. Marianne walked slowly along the road and spent a long time looking in shop windows, and Anna seemed to do the same along the other side of the street. It became a test of nerves as they both watched each other while pretending not to.

Eventually Anna called a cab and rode away.

Marianne caught the train into town, and then asked a cab driver to take her to Bird Street.

"Ain't no such place, miss," she was informed chirpily.

She had suspected as much.

It was just her luck to have met another woman with broad interests and a high intellect, and have her to be an imposter full of lies.

Twelve

Anna was a mystery, Marianne thought, but not the biggest or most interesting one at the moment, and she tried to convince herself to put the woman out of her mind. She had other things she had to attend to. Anna had likely been having an affair with George – really, she had admitted as much. She had seemed plausibly shocked and upset about the news of his death.

And Marianne felt a pang of genuine sympathy. For how could Anna openly mourn the loss of her lover? They should not have been together and society would not tolerate her shedding a public tear for him. Anna's lies – at least, some of them – were understandable misdirection.

Marianne walked slowly, keeping to the edge of the road, out of the way of hurrying pedestrians. Her main focus now, she felt, was to get to the bottom of the blackmailing of Price. He himself seemed content – well, that was not the right word: resigned, maybe? – to continue paying the money to his unknown blackmailer, but it made Marianne's blood boil. It had to be stopped. Though how she was to do that, when Price would not tell her who was blackmailing him, was a problem. He seemed convinced, naively so, that once he had paid "enough", they would stop. Of course they would do no such thing.

She felt an uncomfortable obligation to the dead George Bartholomew, to "not let that man win" but she had known, from the start, it was a pointless chase and she had taken the case simply for the money. She felt none of her usual fire to expose Edgar Bartholomew; he was not making a fool of anyone but himself. She exposed mediums, because she objected, on moral grounds, to their deception. They preyed on the weak, the vulnerable, the lonely and the bereaved, and it made her blood boil. Plus, it was a way for her to earn money. Money meant independence, of a sort.

Money didn't cut you loose from family responsibilities, though.

However, the only real paying job she had at the moment was the Bartholomew case, and it was something that she had to do.

But her final problem was Jack Monahan. She had some tantalising snippets of information about him – who he had once worked for, what manner of man he was – but nothing real and concrete.

Except that she did have his address, printed on his card that was shoved to the bottom of her bag. She fished it out from underneath her revolver, notebook and handkerchiefs. She recognised the street name, and knew it to be close by the river. She set off at a brisk pace rather than call for a cab or take a crowded omnibus. She hoped that he lived in a respectable house with servants that she might pump for information. She organised her possible tactics in her head, as she refused to be caught out again. She would ask sweetly and charmingly at first.

If that did not work, she could try a little bribery. Her last resort was, of course, threats and intimidation.

The house appeared respectable but on closer inspection, it was yet another property that had been divided up. On the ground floor lived a thin-looking woman who said she was married to a middling clerk in the post office. She opened the door but left Marianne standing outside while Marianne asked if she was in the right place. She told Marianne that the two upper floors were taken by Mr Monahan, but that he retained only a daily girl and a man servant who was "as dirty as he was rude, and as silent as he was ugly. And unlikely to be home, while there was drinking to be done."

"Can you tell me what Mr Monahan does for a living?"

"I thought that you knew him," the woman said with narrowed eyes. "You said as you were calling on him friendly-like."

Marianne leaned forward and dropped her voice. "Our paths have crossed a little, lately, and he left me his card and invited me to call." She showed the woman the proof. "But there is much I do not know and I think it is wise for me to find out *before* I let the acquaintance progress … if you read my meaning?"

The woman nearly rolled her eyes but she stepped back into the corridor and said, "Come in out of the wind. You're wise to feel him out first, as is. I wouldn't like to say as he's a good match for a likely young woman, at the end of the day. Oh! Miss, step this way sharpish." The woman grabbed Marianne's arm and hauled her through the front door and into her own front room, partly closing the door to the corridor, shielding her from the two men that entered the house and went on up the stairs.

"That was him," Marianne said in a whisper.

"Yes, with his grubby man along with him."

"So what does he do for a job?"

"He does nothing, as far as I can see. He used to do the dirty work for Lord whats-his-face, but they had a set-to and the Lord gave him the boot, and none too soon, if you ask me. Heaven knows what he got up to, sneaking in and out day and night. Now he roams around trying to get his old job back. He's always in some scheme or another."

"He does not sound at all like the sort of man I wish to associate with." Marianne was making up her mind. She'd continue on her way, and look no more into Monahan.

He probably only thought that she was more wealthy than she actually was.

The woman was nodding. "You do right, miss. I'll see you out."

But as Marianne turned to go, there was more knocking on the street door. The thin woman sighed. "Now who?"

"I'll get it, Mrs Hathaway!" called the familiar smooth voice of Monahan from upstairs. "I'm expecting someone."

Marianne and Mrs Hathaway remained behind the slightly-open door as Monahan's footsteps bounded down the stairs and he greeted the new person with warmth and laughter. "Dunston, you're late!"

"I'm never late, eh! Here or there?"

"Bill's upstairs. Let's go out. Drinks?"

"That'll do nicely. Got into that girl's good books yet?"

"Not a sniff of it. She won't be got through flattery."

"Precious little to flatter her about, eh? Too much reading does terrible things to a woman's face."

134

"Oh, I just need to use the right sort of flattery. Science is her thing so I realise I need to praise her brain, that's all —"

The voices faded and the street door slammed closed.

Mrs Hathaway had a look on her face that was halfway between sympathy and told-you-so, and Marianne could only nod with a wry smile. "That confirms him as a cad, a cheat and a liar," she said.

"I am sorry, miss."

"Oh, don't be. I knew from the start. My main question is — why me? Have you any idea? I am a woman of no importance at all. I have no money and no means."

"That do seem strange, but all I can say miss — if you forgive me — is that perhaps he mistakes you for someone else."

"I cannot think who."

***

She left the house and intended to continue on her way. Unfortunately her way back to the railway station lay the same way as Monahan and his friend Dunston. She lagged behind and tried not to look as if she was following them, but she was also eaten up by curiosity and could not help but keep them in her view.

Monahan must be a man with a fear of the law, she thought, *for he looks about himself constantly*. She tried to stay behind other people, but it was less easy for a well-dressed woman to blend in than a man in a hat and a dark coat could. She jumped behind a clergyman too late. Jack Monahan saw her, said something to his companion, and strode back along the pavement to apprehend her. She slid her hand into her bag as he approached, and let her fingers brush her gun.

"Good day, Miss Starr! Well met. You have been watching my house, then, and following me. What larks!"

"I have done no such thing," she said. "Yes, I admit I have been to your house – for I, sir, am no liar. I went, and then I left. Now I am simply returning home. You, however, have been following me, plaguing me and threatening me. You cannot deny it."

"I have done no such thing! The threats, I mean. I have never threatened you. I do admit the rest. I have followed you from time to time! Such fun. It does me good to stay in practice."

"But one cannot *do* such things," she said in exasperation. It was like trying to chastise fog. He seemed pleased with himself, rather than repentant. "Practice for what? Who are you, and why do you think that you *can* do these things?"

"I am Jack Monahan, and that is my real name. I am sure you have looked into it. It is known, around town. I am a gentleman, but one who must work, and I have travelled widely, which might account for my manners if any seem rough or brutish – for which I do apologise."

"Oh. I did wonder about your manners," she said. "We thought you might be one of those fallen gentlemen who fight abroad and come home thinking they can carry on as if they are in Kabul or wherever still."

"I was never in Kabul," he said. "But yes, I suppose you have me right. Well done!"

"And what is this to me? Why do you plague me so? Your insistence is troubling and I suspect you mistake who I am."

"No, not at all! I believe that we have the same aims. We

both want to expose people. Come, there is a private dining room that I know, not far from here. Let us go there, and I shall buy you lunch, and we will talk. It is past time that we do. As you wilfully refuse to come to me, I shall insist that we dine out together."

"It is late for lunch," she said, trying to turn away.

"I am hungry. Let us not be bound by the rules of when one may eat and when one may not."

Much as she longed to run away, this was her chance to get to the bottom of things with the infuriating man. Of all the various people who had plagued her over the years, he was by far the most persistent. Even the random letter writer of Hastings had given up after a few rebuffs from her. But Jack Monahan, it seemed, really had something to gain from her, or he thought that he did. And she did want to know why he was so determined.

"Is it a respectable place? I will not enter a low dive with you."

"Thoroughly respectable, and we shall send word home to your cousin to tell her where we are, and who you are with, almost as if you are a decent sort of woman."

She did not rise to his insult. "What of your companion?"

"Don't worry. I have told him I must attend to this. He will go on elsewhere."

Grudgingly, she agreed to his plan, and he reacted as if she had said yes to a marriage proposal. With a grin, he marched her around a corner and up some steps into a pleasant hallway where they were met by a smartly-dressed man. A boy was despatched with a note to Phoebe. The smart servant took them to a small but warmly furnished room, and promised them that a light meal would appear within moments.

"This is excellent," he said, beaming at her. "Thank you for trusting me. I can be honest with you and tell you that there are certain people, in particular, that I need to get close to. Never mind why. Now, you happen to have the way in to get close to those people. I have been trying other tactics to gain entry to certain places but these have been fruitless. Alas, my past does precede me. I have been away too much, and I lack certain essential contacts. And I have tried to pay a woman to be on my arm and give me some respectability but that did not go well."

"I should imagine not, if you had to pay her."

He grinned ruefully and she studied him. For all his casual confidence, he seemed to desperately need – *something*.

He did need her.

But she was not sure that she cared to be needed in this way. He was yet still too secretive.

"Well," she said. "*Who* is it that you want to gain access to? Is there any connection with mediums and séances? Otherwise I must tell you that I am useless to you. I do not really move in society."

As she said that, she realised that she might not be the end target. She did not move in society much but Phoebe did. Was she simply being used as a stepping stone? His next sentence confirmed that suspicion.

"We should get to know one another properly first," he said. "I have told you this all along, have I not? I have a plan! Why don't you have me invited to dinner? That way, when I begin to accompany you to …ahh, these séances, we will not arouse questions or comment."

"And you cannot get invited to other gatherings to meet these same people?"

He blinked. "No, I cannot. They would not be at those gatherings."

Marianne sat back. *What rot*, she thought. *He says one thing but he means another.* The food arrived and picked at the selection of sandwiches delicately and with little enthusiasm. He tucked in, and watched her, waiting for an answer. He was smiling, as if it was a foregone conclusion.

Does he think I am stupid, she thought. *Does he really imagine I do not already see through him? Clearly he has had no dealings with women – well, women of any class – at all. We are not so easy to hoodwink as a streetwalker.*

"I need something from you, too," she said at last.

"Of course. We will be a partnership. If you need me in the future, just send word."

"I need you now, before I will aid you. I need to gain access to a particular room, and spend some time there, without being noticed."

He stopped, mid-chew, and frowned. "Excuse me?"

She felt a little rush of triumph. It was rather marvellous to have surprised the man. "A man has died under strange circumstances and I wish to know exactly what happened. The body will have been removed by now, but I want to get back into the room, and look for any evidence as to how he might have died." She took a deep breath. "I suspect poisoning."

"You said you want to get back into the room. You've already been there?"

"Oh yes," she said, airily, and enjoying every minute of his shock. "I found the body, after all."

***

She had expected Monahan to make complicated plans to be undertaken at night, but when she described the situation and layout of the room, he rolled his eyes and said, "Oh well – come on, then." They went out into the streets and it did not take them too long to get to the right road. They marched up to the lodging house and stood on the opposite side of the street, looking at it.

"You say the housekeeper is blind?" he asked.

"As a bat."

"Then it is simple. I shall talk to her and you can creep upstairs. There is no need here for complicated subterfuge, exciting though that would be. Oh, there is one issue," he said and sighed. "This plan won't work if the door is locked."

"Don't worry about that," Marianne retorted. "I have methods."

He looked at her sideways but she was already striding across the road. It never did for a man to know too much about a woman, after all. One must have one's secrets. Especially if those secrets were marginally criminal.

She waited for him to catch her up at the entrance to the building. She stood to one side as he rapped sharply on the door. "Have you a cover story?" she hissed as they waited.

"I am always prepared with at least seven," he said. "For any eventuality."

That was something to aspire to, she thought.

The door was opened and the plan sprang into action. He began to charm the old housekeeper with long tales that kept

140

suggesting they had a point but seemed to go nowhere, while Marianne slipped past them both and crept as silently as she could up the stairs to the attic.

Once at the door, she found that it was locked, and she was almost pleased as it gave her a chance to practice the tricks that Simeon had taught her. There was no lock that he could not break – even while blindfolded and upside-down. She had a small kit in her handbag, nestling next to her gun. As the door was an internal one, with no need for real security, it was a simple matter of using one of her skeleton keys in the warded lock. Within moments she was in the room.

She pressed a handkerchief to her mouth hastily. The body had been removed, but the smell remained. There were more signs of disarray. The bed clothes had been flung to the floor, and the chest now stood open. The police had not done any investigation as, to them, there was no suggestion of foul play.

But Marianne had a deep suspicion about George Bartholomew's father.

She prowled around the room. The housekeeper had not even begun to clean up yet. Perhaps she was going to pay someone to do it for her. The place was still foul with sickness but she fought past her revulsion and tried to identify what she was smelling. Vomit, diarrhoea, and garlic. There was also sweat, and unwashed clothes, and general staleness.

She steeled herself to peer under the bed. It was dark, and she blinked, not sure what she was actually seeing.

The chamber-pot appeared to be faintly glowing.

She pulled it towards her very carefully. Inside was mostly bloody solid matter, and very little liquid. In the pale light of the bedroom, there was nothing that was obviously emitting a glow now.

She pushed it away, thoughtfully.

She had thought that she might take samples back to her laboratory but now the idea filled her with revulsion. She could not carry a full chamber pot through the streets of London. She did pick up one of the bedsheets and rolled it carefully so that the stains were inside, and did not show. She glanced once more around the horrible room but there was nothing that leaped out at her.

She ran down the steps, tapped Monahan on the shoulder as she passed him, and shot right out into the street. She was hailing a cab as Monahan extricated himself from the housekeeper and came to join her.

"Was it a success?" he asked, and recoiled as she pushed the bundled sheet at him. "By God – that stinks!"

"Yes. Are you riding in the cab with me?"

He glared at her. "With that? You know that I will not. Now remember our bargain. I have aided you, and you must now help me. You have my address. Let us attend a dinner party together, soon, at Woodfurlong, and then we will proceed."

"We are basically to show the world that we are courting lovers?"

He shrugged. "I think it's for the best. If I do not hear from you within a week, I shall call on you most publically. You will not like the scene that I create. We are partners, remember?"

She leaped into a cab and did not bother to reply. As they drove away, she realised, with a slight pang of guilt, that she hadn't actually thanked him for his help.

142

Thirteen

"Father?"

Russell Starr was reclining in a darkened room. Dusk was coming early to his quarters. The curtains were drawn almost fully, letting in only a half-foot of bright light that made a searing vertical line in the otherwise gloomy room. He muttered something which she decided was probably "Come in, dear daughter" but could just as easily been a raving about sparrows and their evil ways.

"Are you well today, father?" she asked in a low voice.

"I am not dead, which is as good as it gets, these days."

"Does the light still hurt your eyes?"

"Like knives, Marianne. Like the sharp bitterness of my erstwhile colleagues. Like the professional jealousy of a man of letters."

"You seem quite lucid."

"I am always lucid. I always speak sense, but sometimes the world is not ready to hear sense. But I am always most perfectly lucid."

She took a seat on a padded chair near to his chaise longue. "You're not," she said. "Two days ago you were trying to look at the moon through a microscope."

"What of it? Maybe I saw it, too. Not *the* moon. Perhaps *a* moon. Like the ghost of a flea."

"Don't read Blake, father. You know he will give you nightmares."

"Are you come here to lecture me?"

"No. Actually, I would like your help."

He sighed. It became a long and protracted exhale. It went on for so long that she half expected him to deflate and become nothing but a pile of clothes. Eventually he dragged in a fresh breath and said, "Go on."

"There is an awful lot of explanation that I ought to give you, to explain how I have got to this point…"

"Do I need to hear it to answer your immediate questions?"

"No."

"Then leave it. Life is short. I should not wish to die before you get to the important points."

"A man has died, and I would like to know how it happened."

"It was the will of God. Next question."

"Father! No, listen. You are an avowed disbeliever anyway. He was poisoned, I am sure of it. I went to see him – oh, it's complicated, I shan't say how – and he had stomach ache, and nausea. He was racked by pain, in truth. There was a strong smell in the air –"

"Almonds?" he asked. "You would know what that means."

"No, it was garlic."

"Hmm. Curious. *Interesting*. Go on."

"And the next day, he was dead."

"More details. Come on, girl. Were you trained for nothing?"

She had been trained mostly in electricity and its wondrous properties, not chemistry, but she didn't argue. "His stomach was distended and his skin yellowish. His eyes were yellow-brown where they should have been white. I took a sheet from his room, which I have left outside in the corridor, as it smells most vile."

"Anything else?" he said. He began to stand up, unsteadily, and she went to his side. "Come, fetch that sheet and let us take it to the laboratory. Is there blood on it?"

"Blood at the very least, yes."

"Excellent."

The laboratory was in a perpetual state of readiness. Half a dozen experiments were in progress, or forgotten and abandoned, making the place rather dangerous to the unwary. They spread the stained sheet across one of the polished benches. Marianne could not help grimacing at the smell. Russell merely sniffed once and said, "Yes, garlic."

They looked at the sheet. There was a crusting of various things, and the blood had run for some way. "Was he bleeding heavily?" he asked.

"No," she said.

"Look at these patterns," he said. "Either he had been injured, maybe stabbed, or the blood that did flow from him carried on flowing."

"What does that mean?"

"I am trying to say that the blood was not clotting as it ought to have done." Russell leaned on the bench and tapped his fingers on the surface. "Garlic. Blood flowing, not coagulating. Distended stomach – liver? Yellow skin. Yes. Liver. Stomach cramps. Did you look at his stools?"

It felt like a horrible thing to admit to. "Yes. It was strange, but I had a fancy that they ..."

"They glowed," Russell said, and he smiled, for the first time in many weeks.

"Yes! How on earth did you know?"

"It is the garlic. He was definitely poisoned, this poor friend of yours. White or yellow phosphorus, I should say. If I could have access to his body, I should be able to confirm it."

"No, that's impossible. We have enough evidence here, though."

"Not for a conviction."

"Maybe not yet." Marianne pulled up a stool and sat down. "Who uses phosphorus?"

"Match manufacturers," Russell said. "Those poor girls – their jaws fall off."

"Not so much these days, father. But there is another group of people who use phosphorus," Marianne said. "And they are the bane of my life ... and my livelihood."

***

Marianne could not get Phoebe alone that evening. They had a few of Price's friends over for dinner, and they monopolised the drawing room afterwards, leaving Marianne no chance to get to her cousin. The next morning, she hastily grabbed Phoebe as they went into the breakfast room. Price was waiting, impatiently. Marianne pressed Phoebe against the wall. "We must have a dinner party soon where I can invite Jack Monahan," she said.

"Oh my goodness! Why? Oh, do not say that you have fallen

for him. We spoke about this, Marianne!"

"Fear not. But listen, I know how George Bartholomew died – he was poisoned by phosphorus. And in getting this knowledge, I made a promise."

"Ladies, please," Price called from the dining room. "I wish to eat."

"Marianne! Tell me all."

"I will find you later." They scurried into the room and Phoebe soothed the grumbling Price.

But halfway through breakfast, Phoebe was called to a crisis in the nursery, and Marianne ate quickly to escape the disapproving and silent glare of Price. Rather than hunt for Phoebe, Marianne left the house and made her way quickly into town, and to see her friend Simeon. She told him everything that had happened recently, and asked for his advice.

"I need to find out more about Edgar Bartholomew," she said. "He is my main suspect and my main concern. You said you would help; I think the idea of breaking into rooms next to his séances will not work. I have considered it, but there is too much risk. You were right. But I had another idea. There must be clubs where he would be known, don't you think? If he is not at home, he must be somewhere. Sometimes he is at the houses of mediums but at other times, he is a man of society – he must go somewhere, surely?"

"Perhaps."

"Would you be able to gain access to them? These clubs? Dining rooms? Coffee shops, even?"

"Not the exclusive ones, no. Yes, I can get into coffee shops, but that is all. You know that I cannot move in the right

147

circles."

"But could you ask around?" she begged. "I would not ask if I had other options." She was scraping the barrel. She had known all along that Simeon would not get into the higher clubs, but surely someone would know someone who knew someone. That was how it worked, was it not? Among men? Even she had her own club now.

"Marianne, you have evidence now – so you must take this to the police."

"I intend to, this very day. I am asking you to help me because I think it is linked to what George asked me to look into. Please, Simeon."

"I am so busy," he said. Then with a sigh, "Yes, I will try. But you must promise to go to the authorities." He sank into silence for a moment, before suddenly declaring, "You know, I am delighted that my instruction in lock-picking had paid off at last. I shall make a magician's assistant of you yet."

"What has happened to your last one?"

"She objected to my manner. I don't know what she meant. What is wrong with my manner?"

"We've spoken about this. You don't meet people's expectations of a flamboyant showman."

"No, because the magic should speak for itself."

"People want to be entertained, not educated."

"Well, they are wrong," Simeon snapped. "People simply don't know what is best for them."

"You look tired," she said, and went to make a cup of tea.

"You mean, I am grumpy," he said. "Of course I am tired. I have been on the trail of the men who have stolen from me, all night in fact."

"Oh, Simeon. Not this again."

"It simply won't do, Marianne. I cannot continue like this. I am a good magician, am I not?" he added imploringly.

"Of course you are! Dear Simeon. You are marvellous." She brought him the hot drink and sat down, leaning forward to gather his hands in her own. "But I cannot fill your head with empty platitudes just to make you feel better…"

"Why not?"

"Don't pout, it is unbecoming. No, if I lie to you, it will do you no good. Your act is brilliant magic, Simeon, but poor showmanship. People want spectacle and drama. Even, dare I say it, moments of laughter."

"Laughter? I will not have them laugh at me."

"Not at you. With you. At your wit and splendour."

"I do try. I wear greasepaint though it makes me itch. Marianne, will you help me?"

"I will do anything."

"Will you be my assistant and devise a new routine with me?"

She nearly broke his hand in shock and horror. "I cannot! Oh – but I am honoured that you ask me. But you know that I am busy, with my business and my father too. And even if I were not, I have no show experience at all."

"Yet you advise me as if you have."

"No, I am speaking as a member of the audience. You need an experienced assistant who has worked with others. Like Nellie."

"Nellie who has left me because of my manner?" He snorted with derision and got up. "Look at all this! All this! For what?

149

For others to steal from me, and for my closest friends to tell me that I *need* to be laughed at."

He stamped around, picking things up and discarding them, occasionally running his hand through his hair, and growling at everything. He was like a demented spider, skittering from corner to edge to table to chair, full of pent-up frustration.

"You need sleep," she said. She got up to leave. "I'll come by again, soon, when you're rested, and I will help."

He turned to her as if he were going to beg her to stay, but she didn't have time, and when he saw her face, he knew it, and kept silent.

***

She kept her word, and she went to the same police station that had dealt with George Bartholomew's death. She boldly went into the wood-panelled room to speak to someone, hoping that she might see the same policeman that she had met before. The desk officer was an elderly man with a bald head and grey whiskers, and he got up from his stool with difficulty. His eyes were kind and he spoke softly.

"I would like to report some suspicions around the death of George Bartholomew – do you know if Sergeant Giles is available?"

"He is not, miss, but if you will give me all the details, I shall be sure to pass them on." He spoke in a friendly way and it put her at her ease.

"Very well. I am Miss Marianne Starr and I discovered the body. My father is Russell Starr." She paused but the policeman gave no hint that he recognised the name, and unless his hobby

150

was chemistry, there was no reason why he should. "Due to the circumstances around the man's death, we believed that he had not died accidentally. Upon closer inspection, we have determined that he is likely to have died of the ingestion of white phosphorus – and not by his own hand."

The policeman wrote it all down and then tapped his pen nib on the paper. "Upon closer inspection," he said. "Can you expand on that? When, and what did you do?"

"It was simply that when I found the body," she said, "there was a strong odour of garlic in the room. When I had seen him previously, he had complained of stomach pains and sickness. His belly was distended and his … his … his stools glowed in the dark."

The policeman snorted and then swallowed his laugh hastily. He laid the pen on the desk. "Thank you, miss. I shall be sure to pass these on to the relevant authorities."

"Please do. There needs to be a proper autopsy and now they know what to look for."

"Indeed. Thank you, and good day."

"Do you want my address? You can contact me or my father for further information."

"Thank you. We have everything we need. Good day."

"And you'll investigate this further?"

"Of course. Good day."

"Someone killed him!"

"Indeed, indeed. *Good day* miss." He started to inch his way around the counter as if he intended on propelling her out of the door.

She turned and huffed out of there.

It was very clear that the paper he had written on would be nothing more than kindling for a fire before the day was out.

***

Marianne walked aimlessly for a while through the ever-crowded streets, wanting to kick at things. She wove her way into the fashionable West End, where theatres and opera-houses and galleries all vied with more and more eating places. Women were enjoying a freedom that was unknown to their grandmothers, and they were making the very most of it. The exploding class of merchants and middle classes led to wealthier wives, and they had to fill their days with something: culture, art, shopping, gossiping, visiting, eating, and walking around so that other people could see them. As Marianne found herself shoved against a shop window by the passing of a family of daughters, towed along by a stout matriarchal figure, she felt a pang of loneliness. She missed Newnham College. The atmosphere there had been lively, yes, but studiously so.

It was true that many of the women who attended the university were simply rich daughters who were filling their time before marriage. Not everyone took their studies as seriously as Marianne had done. But the overriding impression was one of eagerness to seize the new opportunities and make the most of every moment.

The family had passed by now, but Marianne remained where she was. Simeon was too busy to help her. Phoebe was likewise pulled this way and that by her domestic duties, with the added restrictions of her position in society. She was expected to be at home at certain times, and to repay the visits at other times. She had to show her face at charitable events, and become a patron of worthy causes. She didn't attend church or help out there, not half as much as she ought to have done. And now the police had shown themselves to be stupendously unconcerned.

So Marianne was on her own.

I can do this, she told herself sternly. She drew herself upright and turned around. She would not linger any longer in the showy part of town. She had investigations to make.

Fourteen

George Bartholomew had told her that he had a man in the city that acted for him – a man that Marianne could trust. She had his name and address on the wavy-edged card, and found him easily in a busy part of town. Mr Harcourt occupied a rich set of offices in a building shared by other solicitors, lawyers and agents. She was shown into a pleasant waiting room of polished wood and brass, and brought tea until Mr Harcourt was available to talk to her.

But he could not tell her much that she did not already know.

He expressed all the usual sympathies about his client's death, and assured her that he was aware of her role, and that there was a significant sum of money set aside for her, should she be successful.

"And what do you think of Mr Bartholomew's claim?" she asked the yellow-toned man.

"I am afraid that I cannot comment on that matter."

"Professionally? Or because you simply don't know?"

He opened his hands and ducked his head to one side. It was a complete non-answer. She said, doggedly, "Had you met

Mr Bartholomew often?"

"Twice only. We were not of a long acquaintance. But he seemed trustworthy enough."

The solicitor's manner was far cooler than she had expected. She had thought to find an old family retainer of many generations' standing. "Do you think his death was suspicious?"

"It was deeply unfortunate."

Again, a non-answer. He was either guiltily tied up in things, or he was simply an infuriating boor who liked to control situations just for the sake of exercising power.

"What do you know of his situation at his company?"

"Bow Imports, as you know, is a global trading concern and he was one of their overseas agents. That is all."

She blinked. "What?"

He repeated himself slowly but she had heard him perfectly well; she simply hadn't understood what he meant. *Bow Imports.* "Where is their office?" she asked.

He wrote out an address on a slip of letter-headed paper. "Here," he said, and handed it over. "Please wait; there is one more thing."

He went over to a safe in the corner of the room and brought back an envelope with her name on it. "He asked me to furnish you with all the funds you needed for this investigation," he said. "As you are here, you may as well have this now. The rest, of course, will be supplied upon completion." He handed her the fat packet.

She didn't even want to peek inside. She stashed it into her bag, thanked him hastily, and dashed away.

***

Bow Imports was only three streets and yet a world away from the offices of Mr Harcourt. The narrow road was just as busy, but the atmosphere was of graft and dirty hands, not leisurely lunches as money piled up in secret piles, unobtrusive and silent. Here was where the work was done. London was a patchwork of tiny areas, all dedicated to different things, and harbouring different classes of people, yet they all abutted up against one another with barely a mark between them.

There were only low and working women along this street. Marianne walked briskly, aware that her status – though not high – marked her out, here. She held up her head and made directly for the offices of Bow Imports, and everyone got out of her way, recognising the air of intent about her.

Everyone but one man.

"You!" she said. "Following me again, Mr Monahan?"

"No, not today," he said in equal surprise. "Are you not following me?"

"I most certainly am not."

"I can assure you I am here on different business. As we are now partners, I felt it unnecessary to stalk you at the moment, although I am still awaiting the promised invitation to a dinner party."

"Oh, it is in hand. Believe me; I have already broached the subject with Mrs Claverdon. What are you doing here, may I ask?"

"I am here due to your cousin-in-law, of course. And you?"

Marianne gaped. "My cousin-in-law? You *know* Mr Claverdon?"

157

"I ... do, yes. He is well-known." He thinned his lips as if he had said too much. She remembered her very early suspicion that he could be the blackmailer, and she glared at him.

"If you know him, you could have come to dine with us at any time, then," she said.

"No. That would be impossible without your intervention," he said, almost stiffly.

Damn him, she thought. "Will you be welcome in the house? I shall not have you, if you will make a scene."

"There will be no scene. I know him. But he does not know *me.*"

"Hmm." She would have to go back to Price and press him further, before she made any accusation against Monahan.

Marianne gazed up at the elaborate sign that hung over the double doors. They were constantly opening and closing, with clerks and office workers running in and out, clutching papers and telegrams and letters and parcels. Marianne and Jack Monahan stood to one side, out of the way. She said, "Is Bow Imports part of Harker and Bow, then?"

"Of course it is. Goodness, you are slow, for a clever woman."

"I hardly specialise in trade matters. And who did George Bartholomew really work for? This place, or the other?"

"Bow Imports, until he was sacked. But this is but a subsidiary of Harker and Bow."

"Sacked? But he was given a place to stay in London, through Harker and Bow. And it is Harker and Bow that my brother in law works for."

"Oh, they are all linked, in ways that make the most money

158

with the least hassle and tax and duties and so on."

"Is there some foul play going on here?"

Monahan laughed. "Yes – and no! It is business, that is all."

"What was he sacked for? And when?"

"Bartholomew? I don't know. I don't really care. I am here on *other* business."

"Please – there is something strange about why he had returned to England. He came from Prussia. There is someone else here, now, also asking about him."

"Who?"

"A woman."

Monahan's eyebrows shot up. "Oh really? Who is she? And where is she from?"

Marianne quickly described Anna, and he laughed as if Bartholomew had performed a magic trick right there in front of them. She did not like the edge of triumph in his voice, as if one man could celebrate the low actions of all men. He seemed to think that Bartholomew and Anna were certainly carrying on together. He told her to wait on the step, and he disappeared into the offices.

He returned after an interminably long time, and he was still grinning. "It is as I suspected, and no doubt – in spite of your prickly sensibilities – so did you. He was dismissed for having an affair with a married woman."

"With Anna Jones?"

"Indeed so, when they were in Prussia. Was it not obvious?"

"It was a strong possibility. And what of her husband?"

"I have no idea," Monahan said. "Maybe he is on his way at this very moment, hot in pursuit of them both, armed to the teeth like a Teutonic knight in a *pickelhaube*."

"This is a tangled mess," she said.

"I would give it up as a bad job," he told her. "The affair was conducted in Prussia – he was recalled to Britain under investigation – and they dismissed him the very night that he died. So there you go. He most likely ate those bad oysters deliberately, to avoid public shame." And before she could speak, he tipped his hat to her, and disappeared back up the steps into the offices.

She turned away, and headed for home, and wondered if he were right.

No wonder his father had thrown him out that night.

***

She was still thinking about the affair all the way back to Woodfurlong, The train's rocking and clattering was hypnotic and she almost dozed off. She was still feeling a little woozy as she made her way through the town towards home.

She was glad to find Price Claverdon in his study. She had thought she might have to wait until nightfall but he had taken that day to perform his duties from home. She avoided Phoebe, and got admitted to his study unseen by her cousin or any servants.

He looked pale and haggard, and she rushed towards him, but he turned away and sat down behind his desk, effectively screening himself from her. She stopped, and pulled the envelope from her bag.

"Mr Claverdon – sir – how is … it? The … situation we have spoken of?"

"It is as bad as ever," he said wearily. "They ask me for

160

money, more money, and I have to provide it. If I do not, we shall be ruined."

"You must stop! They will ruin you anyway, financially." She thought that to his old-fashioned and stubborn mind, financial ruin was still better than social ruin.

"I will bring this to an end. If I can find a way." His eyes fell on the envelope in her hand, and he brightened. "Ah, is that...?"

"Yes. It is for you. But I do not want to encourage this malefactor." She kept hold of the envelope as he stretched out his hand for it. "You said that they had an amount in mind, and when you reached it, they would cease with their demands. But as I warned you, they have not."

"It buys me a little more time," Claverdon said. "Please ... Marianne."

She shivered as he said her first name, and reluctantly let him have the money.

"And do not lecture me," he added, his voice hardening. "This is a difficult situation."

"It is an impossible one, and must end. Tell me the name of the person doing this."

"I cannot."

"Is it Jack Monahan?"

Claverdon registered not a hint of recognition. "Who?"

Now she was confused. "He claims to know you."

"I do not know him. No, you must leave me to deal with this."

"I am involved now. The police must be told," she said.

"Leave it to me, I tell you!" He dropped his voice. "If you

say anything to anyone, you and your father will have to find alternate accommodation."

It was as clear a threat as she had ever heard. She gazed at him in wonder. He was a man on the edge, and unpredictable.

He met her gaze and she saw no warmth in his eyes at all. "I will do as I say," he warned her. "I will find a way to end this. But for the moment, you must mention nothing."

She nodded. She left quickly, and went a little way down the corridor before slowing down. Her heart was pounding, and she felt unsettled. She had often felt trapped by the largesse and generosity of Claverdon and his agreement to let Marianne and her father have the garden wing. But this was the first time she had felt uneasy or insecure.

If Phoebe knew, she would be horrified.

One day, Marianne would move out. She longed for it. She would have to take her father, and she tried hard to rejoice in the chance to be seen as a dutiful daughter. However, with most of her money currently passing through Price Claverdon and into the hands of some blackmailers, the chances of her being able to run her own household were currently looking very slim.

Marianne heard a click from a door behind her, and she slid silently behind a tall mahogany cabinet that housed atlases and maps of many countries around the world. She felt sure that the sound had come from the door to Claverdon's study. She heard footsteps, very light, just scuffing the carpet, and they were going away from her. She peeked out from around the cabinet and saw Claverdon was heading towards the head of the back staircase, not the main one. He was dressed in an outdoor coat and hat, and he was tucking the envelope into an inside pocket.

She decided to follow him at a stealthy distance.

He paused at the door at the top of the servants' staircase, and pressed his ear to the green baize, before pulling it open and darting into the uncarpeted gloom. She followed swiftly. She was in a better position than he was – no one looked twice at Marianne walking the back passages of the house, but for the master of the place to do so was very odd indeed. They met no servants, however, and soon he was sneaking through one of the smaller doors that went past the kitchen and out into the yard. He could not go through the busy kitchen itself, but he made it out, unseen, via the narrow passageway between the scullery and a store room.

She continued to follow him, her heart hammering. She felt uncomfortably hot and sticky. He had threatened her with the loss of her home – what would he do if he discovered that she was following him now?

So she lagged behind at as great a distance as possible. He walked into the small town, and she kept herself hidden behind pedestrians. He didn't look over his shoulder – *but then*, she thought, *why would he?* He walked very quickly, with a purpose etched into every swing of his legs. He was not carrying his cane, and it was obvious he had left in a hurry.

She had a suspicion that he was going to meet his blackmailer, and she picked up the pace, trying to rush around people to catch him up without getting too close.

He headed for a hotel. It was a classy place, catering to wealthy travellers who wanted to pause before entering London, and it also served as a little get-away for those who were tired of the city but who did not want to stray too far away. He was greeted at the door by a uniformed man, who waved him in with familiarity and respect.

She hesitated only a moment before following him inside. The hotel servant bobbed his head, recognising her as Claverdon's cousin-in-law. She pointed at his disappearing back, as if she were with him and simply failing to keep up. She was allowed in with barely a word.

Claverdon was heading up the main sweeping staircase. Her cover was sparser here, and she had to wait until he had turned to the right at the top of the stairs before she took the plunge and followed him.

At the top, she looked to the right and saw him go up another flight of stairs, narrower ones this time, and she went up after him. He turned along a corridor, and rapped a quick code on a door – three long, with a space to count to five, then three more raps.

The door opened. Marianne risked her cover and peered around the corner. She could only see Claverdon's back, and he doffed his hat to the person who opened the door. She could not see the person within, but she saw a very pale hand extend from the entrance. It wore a sleeve trimmed with lace, and the voice was feminine.

The voice belonged to Anna Jones.

And she drew Claverdon into the room, and the door closed, and Marianne sagged back against the wall.

Anna was the blackmailer? It was not Jack Monahan at all?

Or was it all a terrible lie – a horrible deceit being performed on Marianne, and worse – Phoebe?

For it looked, for all the world, as if Price Claverdon was

having an affair with Anna Jones. After all, it wouldn't be the first time for her. She had shown herself to be a woman of that ilk.

And no wonder he wanted money, if he were keeping a mistress of such unusual beauty.

Marianne went home wearily. She could not think how she might tell Phoebe, or even if she ought to, but this was a heavy burden to bear alone.

Fifteen

It was almost fully dark by the time that Marianne reached home once more. She was starving. She'd missed the main evening meal, so she crept silently past the drawing-room door and into the kitchens, where she was swallowed into the warm embrace of Mrs Cogwell's domain. Ann and Nettie, two very giggly maids, were sitting by the fire, darning socks and discussing men. They subsided when Marianne first entered, but relaxed and quickly forgot her presence. Anyway, Marianne was just a few steps up from being one of them, if rather large steps, and everyone knew it; she never even tried to put on airs and graces.

Emilia de Souza came in from the servants' hall with a stack of dishes, and Nettie who was one level below Ann – Nettie being the laundry-cum-scullery maid and Ann being the slightly more elevated kitchen-cum-housemaid – jumped up to take them to the scullery. Emilia caught Marianne's eye as she passed the table, and held her gaze.

"Is everything all right, Emilia?" Marianne asked.

Emilia nodded, but she kept on looking, and Marianne took the hint. She thanked Mrs Cogwell for the food, and shouted a farewell to Nettie and Ann, and left by the back ways to get to the garden wing, and she was not surprised to be followed by Emilia.

"Does something ail you – or your mistress?" Marianne asked as soon as they were alone in the cold corridor and screened by the green baize door.

"I am perfectly well, as always," Emilia said. "But I am bothered by some change in my mistress's demeanour."

"How so?"

"She seems – don't laugh – thoughtful."

Marianne did nearly laugh. Yes, a turn for the intellectual would be a startling and concerning change indeed. "Emilia," she said gently, "she is helping me with that most fiendish investigation. I rather think you already know about that."

"I do know about that, yes, but there is something else on her mind. Oh, perhaps it is the investigation that weighs heavy upon her. But she is secretive, and has taken to peering around corners, and craning her head to see what her husband's correspondence is. I suspect that *she* suspects that her husband is…"

Marianne's laughter had gone quite cold by this point. "Emilia," she said sternly, "what exactly do *you* suspect?"

"I cannot believe it. I shall not utter it. Mr Claverdon adores my mistress. It shines from him. It always has. And he is an honest and upright man. I do not know where she got this idea from, but it is eating her up."

"Has she said anything at all to you?"

"No, not a word. I think she seeks evidence first. Please talk to her. For don't we all know that if you look for something hard enough, in another person, you will see it, eventually? Whether it is there or not?" And Emilia turned away to blink rapidly, and Marianne saw the history of a failed love affair there, and put out her hand to comfort the young woman.

Emilia smiled slightly, and composed herself. "Forgive me," she said. "And I do hope that I am speaking out of turn and that this is all my imagination."

"So do I," said Marianne, and she knew that it was not. "I will speak with her. Go on, now. Do not worry."

***

Marianne avoided breakfast the next morning, and she went straight back to the hotel in the town where she had seen Claverdon visit Anna. She strode past the man on the door, and up the stairs, walking with a confidence that made people step out of the way.

She used the same pattern of knocks that Claverdon had used. It was a while before the door opened. Anna was in a state of undress, wrapped in a long silk gown, with her hair tumbling around her shoulders, and no paint or powder on her face. Her left cheek was creased slightly, and she blinked her pink eyes sleepily. "How – what? Miss Starr?" She started to close the door but her reactions were slow and befuddled, and Marianne pushed her way rudely into the hotel room.

"Tell me what Price Claverdon is to you. Are you aware that the man is married?" Marianne said. She stood herself squarely in the centre of the room, with her hands on her hips, taking the attitude she had seen in the governess when scolding the children.

The room was comfortable but small, and served as a sleeping area as well as a space for day to day living. It was only intended as a stop-over for a relatively wealthy traveller, not as somewhere to stay for any length of time. It was crowded with fine clothing and books and papers. Anna stayed by the door, her hand on the knob, the other hand clutching her robe firmly closed. "How dare you enter my private chamber! I will call for help," she hissed, keeping her voice noticeably low and in very little danger of calling for anything.

"Tell me what Price Claverdon is to you!" Marianne repeated. "Oh, please do call for help – I shall have your evil practice exposed and you will be ejected onto the street. This hotel would not care to be revealed as a place for *certain women* to ply their trade, would it?"

Anna's eyes were shining, but Marianne thought that she was not near tears – this was an angry woman, not a distressed one. She flared her finely chiselled nostrils and stared at Marianne. Then, as she woke up properly and thought about the situation, her expression turned to one of confusion.

"One moment, Miss Starr. You ask me about Price Claverdon – but what is this man to *you?*"

"He is my cousin-in-law, and the head of the household."

"You … live with him? Your household?"

"Yes. He was kind enough to take my father in when he became ill. And as I am unmarried, I live there as well … it is not so unusual," she added. "Why do you look so? Does this make any difference to your immoral actions?"

"It … does," Anna said slowly. She was pale of skin anyway, but to Marianne's eyes, she seemed even more strained. She let her hand drop from the door handle. "Miss Starr, I have to tell you that you are here under quite false information. There is not a hint of an affair between Mr Claverdon and myself. There, I said it. The word itself. There is no criminal conversation happening. As far as I know, he is a loyal man to his wife. Your sister?"

"My cousin. But he came here…"

"I respect you and your education, Miss Starr. I am telling you the truth. It was a business matter only."

"What business have you with him?"

"An arrangement, only. Oh, this does not make sense to you, does it? I find myself alone here, in London, Miss Starr, and in need of all the friends that I can get. I cannot tell you why, but I am an outcast, and I must find a way to survive. If you knew, you would understand and perhaps even forgive me. But Mr Claverdon is nothing but a businessman to me."

Marianne opened her mouth to say, *Then you are the blackmailer,* but the door was flung open, inwards, with such force that it struck Anna and sent her tumbling to the carpet, her robe fluttering, exposing her long white nightdress. Marianne rushed to help her up, out of sheer instinct, and both women were standing together when the intruder strode into the middle of the room.

He was a tall and broad man with a large bushy beard, unkempt and sorely in need of a trim, though his clothes were very fine and well-cut. There was a military air to his jacket but the insignia on his epaulettes were unfamiliar to Marianne.

As was his language.

He barked something out to Anna, very roughly, and she shrank back against Marianne. She shouted back at him, in the same language, a guttural one with rolling r's.

171

Marianne's hand slipped into her handbag which hung from her arm. Her fingers touched the hilt of her pistol and it gave her strength, tinged with the fear that she might have to finally use it, and she did not know how she would manage that. She could not kill a man. She would aim for his legs, she decided.

The man was shouting again, and he gesticulated to the clothes on the bed. Anna was shouting back, their words tumbling over each other, and pointing to the door. She clearly wanted him to leave.

Marianne stepped to one side and pulled her gun out. She held it straight, with her other arm bent to make a kind of rest. She pointed it at his chest, and slowly cocked it.

The man opened and closed his mouth, but this time no sound was coming out.

Anna squeaked.

"Get out," Marianne said, pitching her voice low to avoid any hint of a wobble. "You won't be the first man that I have shot," she added.

The look of fear in his eyes was gratifying. He snarled one more thing at Anna, and fled from the room.

Anna collapsed to her knees. "Lock it! Lock the door!"

Marianne looked down at her. "I do not know what trouble you are mixed up in, but I am warning you, that you are to have nothing more to do with Price Claverdon." She went to the door, and pulled it open dramatically, jumping out into the corridor with her gun still raised, in case the man was still in the corridor. He was not, but a maid squealed and ran away.

"Lock the door yourself," Marianne said, and shoved the gun back into her bag as she walked away.

***

The language had been unfamiliar to Marianne, who was schooled in Italian and French, and quite a bit of schoolboy Latin, due to her studies. She had never made any grand tour, nor even visited anywhere further afield than the Isle of Wight. Still she had heard every language of the world spoken at some time or another in the streets of London – the whole globe passed through the greatest trading city on earth, after all. She rolled the accent around in her memory. It had seemed very close to what she knew of German. It was a dialect of that language, or Russian, perhaps, or something similar from that part of the world.

And Anna had spoken it too, without hesitation. Marianne had wondered before if she had the trace of an accent, and now she knew: Anna was definitely not an Englishwoman born, though she might have spent much of her life here. The comment about her education at Cheltenham might have been true.

So what was going on? Marianne made her way back to Woodfurlong quickly. She had promised to help Claverdon, but how could she do that if he would not tell her the whole truth? But then, the help that he wanted from her amounted to nothing more than money.

If he was having an affair, rather than being blackmailed, she could understand now why he didn't want to tell her any more.

It was not impossible, Marianne thought, for him to be doing both – having an affair *and* being blackmailed. The question then became, was Anna the other party in both of those situations? Or should Marianne be looking for yet another player

173

in this sorry game?

At any rate, Claverdon was lying, and he was risking Phoebe's good reputation. Marianne would not have him make a fool out of her cousin.

He was also risking losing everything. And that included Woodfurlong, and then where would Marianne and her father live?

***

She asked Mr Barrington, the butler, if Mr Claverdon was still at home, and he said yes, but he was in the morning room with his wife. Marianne sighed with frustration. She went upstairs and changed her clothes, which took up a good half an hour, and then prowled around the public rooms downstairs, awaiting the emergence of her cousin and her husband.

She could hear no raised voices so they were not arguing. Marianne hoped that Emilia had not said anything to Phoebe. She stalked up and down the hallway, and her ceaseless aimless movements unsettled Ann who was polishing the wooden bannisters.

Marianne eventually went outside, intending on taking a turn around the gardens, as it was a dry day with a light breeze and not too hot. She took a newspaper with her. She scoured the foreign pages for anything to do with Prussia.

It was the link, she was sure of it. Anna was either from that region or had lived there; she had met George Bartholomew there. Something had happened – an affair, most likely – and he had been dismissed. So he had come home, and she had ... what, followed him?

174

Then there were missing pieces. Marianne tried to fit together Jack Monahan's pursuit of her, Price Claverdon's affair with Anna, and the strange antics of Edgar Bartholomew and his ultimate death.

There was nothing in the newspaper. She folded it up and tucked it under her arm. She had just completed a circuit of the house and was heading across the wide front lawns when she noticed a man striding up towards the house, with a dark blue top hat, and a cane swinging jauntily at his side.

She knew that manner of confident walking.

She ran down the steps to intercept him before he reached the house.

"You should not be calling here!" she told him angrily. "Were you not warned off before? Come away. Come down to the road. If anyone should look out of the windows…"

Jack Monahan grinned at her. She could have slapped that toothy smile right off his face. "I am only calling to ask when the dinner party is to be held. There is a matter of some urgency. Now we are friends, you may tell the butler that I am welcome here, surely?"

"I am waiting for my cousin to set the date. She is awfully busy, you know."

"I hardly think so."

"Why are you so frantic? Why here? Why me?" she demanded. "I really haven't believed a word you've said." The experience of the previous few days had left Marianne feeling frazzled. She almost didn't care that she was coming across as a strident harpy. She had no need to impress this man, anyway. He had shown himself to be a liar.

"I helped you," he reminded her.

That was true.

"Come away from the view of the house."

Monahan allowed himself to be led. She walked quickly but he kept pace with her easily. "I need to get to know Price Claverdon," he said at last. "I know *of* him. But I need to get much, much closer to him."

Claverdon, again. Just what was her cousin-in-law doing?

"But why?"

"I cannot say. I would not want to prejudice the investigation that I am involved in. You understand that, don't you?"

She stopped walking. He spun around to face her. She was at the very end of her patience. She said, with tones of doom in her voice, "Mr Monahan, I have had enough. I have made a promise to a dead man to discover the truth about his father. I have a business that I am neglecting, which bodes ill for my future. I have a father who needs me, and a good friend in difficult circumstances who likewise demands my time. Your ridiculous and childish attempts at seeming to be intriguingly mysterious are simply tiresome. You are wasting my time. Speak plainly, or go away. I know you worked for Lord Hazelstone and I know you were dismissed. I know you are up to something. Now, will you tell me who you are and why you are doing this? For I have a busy day ahead of me."

Monahan sighed. He had lost his cocky attitude. He leaned his hands on his cane in front of him, and mulled her words over.

"As you wish. But I must warn you, that this knowledge comes with a price."

She raised an eyebrow at him. She really could not care any less.

"If you know who I really work for, it puts you in danger," he went on. "Are you sure?"

"Danger?" she said, almost laughing at him. "You have no idea of my past few days. Go on."

"I work for the government," he said.

"And...?" *It's another lie,* she thought. *How utterly tedious. And I've promised to get this man invited here to a dinner party!*

"That's it," he said.

"Well, I am not terribly impressed. I have met government men," she said. "All it seems to mean is that you like long dinners and even longer words."

"I am employed in a clandestine capacity," he said. "I undertake necessary but unpleasant tasks that would not do to be revealed in public."

She shrugged. "You are some sort of spy, then."

"In a sense, yes. A domestic one. Amongst other things."

"Jolly good," she commented blandly. "I do not know what Claverdon is to do with this."

But she did know. It was now becoming more obvious even to her.

He had given away his company's secrets, he had said. And now he was being blackmailed.

If Monahan was telling her the truth, then the authorities already knew what he had done.

And he was going to be dealt with – secretly.

She shivered. That could mean anything, but certainly nothing good. She had to cancel the dinner party invite. Surely

Monahan was going to cause a scene: she could not allow that.

She trudged back up to the house, and was apprehended by Phoebe in the hallway.

"We have set the date for the dinner and the invitations are all sent out," she said. "Including to your Mr Monahan. Isn't that good news?"

Sixteen

Marianne wanted to get out of Phoebe's company as quickly as possible. She claimed there was a crisis with her father, and that it was time for his next bout of medication, and fled away to the garden wing. When she got to their own rooms, she found that her father was dressed – for the first time in a few weeks – and tidying up the laboratory. He held up a round-bottomed flask as she came in.

"What were you boiling in this?" he asked.

"I cannot remember. Was it not one of your experiments? What does it smell like?"

"Death and beetles."

"Lovely. It is definitely not mine. Are you going out? Are you sure that you are quite well?"

"I have never been better," he said. "Apart from my eyes. And the headaches. And the strange feelings that I am swimming in a choppy sea. And my sore neck. Oh, and the itching. I shan't describe that. But yes, I am perfectly well. You, however, are not. You look as if you have found lice where there ought not to be lice."

"Father, that's awful."

"Yes, lice in one's bedclothes are horrible."

"Oh. Yes, they are." She trailed up and down the long benches and stared despondently at the random articles – a stack of galvanic plates, an earthenware jar that once housed leeches, a tangle of copper wire – and sighed heavily.

"Tell me what bothers you. I am your father, and I command it. Speak!"

"I think we are a little beyond such paternal demands," Marianne said, but she slid onto a rickety stool and rested her elbows on the bench.

"It must be to do with Phoebe," he said, and he took a seat opposite her, and knitted his knobbly fingers together. "Otherwise you would have spoken to her about it, and you would not be here looking like a well-slapped fish."

"Thank you, father, for your astute comment and helpful, supportive advice."

"I haven't started on the advice yet. Tell me what is wrong, and I will tell you how to solve it. It is simple."

His current period of lucidity was lasting longer than usual. His illness came in peaks and troughs. She was reminded of the brilliant scientist that he had once been, and felt a pang of loss for the man that had gone. But that man was back, at least for a little while, and she had to enjoy the relationship while she could. So she began to confide in him.

She told him about Jack Monahan. It was easier than trying to explain what was happening with Phoebe, Price and Anna, and she didn't want to cause him concern about the possible loss of his home. She outlined everything about the strange man – what he claimed to be, what she knew he actually was, and what he wanted from her.

Her father was immediately suspicious.

"This man sounds like a chancer, a cad and a thoroughly untrustworthy sort. And Phoebe has really invited him to dinner?"

"She has. I felt obliged to him, as he helped me get back into the room to find evidence about how poor George Bartholomew died. But that evidence has done little good; I feel I am stuck, now. I must find a way of linking it to Edgar Bartholomew. Meanwhile I am plagued by this Monahan and I agreed to help him to make him stop following me. What else could I have done?"

"Shot him."

"That was a consideration." Marianne rubbed her temples. "Anyway, I changed my mind but it was too late. The invitations have gone out. So, he will be coming to dinner. That, then, should be an end of it. That was all he wanted."

"To come to dinner here? Marianne, that is madness. What does he want to do?"

"He wants to speak to Mr Claverdon."

"Why? He can speak to the fellow anywhere."

"I don't know." She could not tell him her other suspicions. She did not want to drag Price Claverdon into this, for various reasons. She was not sure what he was up to, for one thing. And she was afraid that the threat of losing their home would unhinge her father's mind once more. So she stayed quiet, and hoped that he would not notice.

Russell was too wrapped up in contemplation to spot her reticence. "We need to find out about this Monahan fellow."

"I have tried, father. Phoebe has been making enquiries all

181

over town. I've even asked Simeon."

Russell snorted with pure derision, and slid off the stool to stand squarely on the floor. He was as straight as a rake, and he said, firmly, "No one can do what I can do. I am still *known* in this damned town. You will see."

He turned and walked out of the room, stiff-backed and proud, and she would have laughed, if she had not been so concerned about what he was about to do.

***

The problem of Edgar Bartholomew was weighing on her mind. Now that her father was unleashed onto the Jack Monahan issue, and she had warned Anna off from Price, she felt she only had one thing left to do.

She had to uncover the truth, one way or the other. She had to get proof that Edgar was the father of George – or proof that he was not. If he was not, then that opened up the problem of George's death, and that was something she could then take to the police.

As to why he might be, or not be, the father was a different matter and not one that she was concerned with.

She only had to prove identity, produce it for Mr Harcourt, collect the rest of the money, and rest easy that she had done the right thing for a dead man. Evidence could go to the police for them to deal with as they saw fit.

It would be simple.

Then she could publicise her success, and drum up a little more business, though she had to admit it had been getting harder of late. There were fewer mediums on the circuit around

London, and more stage magicians. The world was growing cynical, which warmed her logical scientific heart but did nothing for her bank balance.

She headed to see Simeon. His madness always made her feel like her own wild schemes were actually quite sane.

He opened the door cautiously but when he saw it was her, he flung it wide and hauled her inside. "Aha! I knew you would be back!"

It was at that point she remember that she had promised to call on him again, and help him with his own issue. She tried not to groan. She did not have time to run around after fantasy thieves. "Good day, Simeon, I wonder if ..."

"Let's get a pot of tea going while we work out our plan," he said happily, bouncing around the workshop. "Oh! I have made a new device that can hide a live bird in my sleeve. Do you want to see it?"

She threw herself into an easy chair. He had a little arrangement of comfortable furniture around the range at one end, where he was making the tea, and she settled into the soft cushions. "Let's have tea first," she said. "Simeon, what do you hope to achieve? Are you wanting to simply prove to yourself that someone has stolen your design, or do you want to make them stop, and if so, how will you do that?"

He had his back to her. He clattered the kettle against the china pot, and she saw his shoulders rise and fall, as if he had sighed heavily. "I just want to know," he said.

"Don't you know it already? Isn't that the point?"

"I just want to know for sure. Yes, yes; look at me." He turned around. He was the picture of dejection, and the opposite man completely to the one who had opened the door to her ten minutes before. "Of course I cannot confront them. The least they will do is laugh at me. I cannot threaten them or promise violence nor do I have any recourse to the law. I just want to know for sure."

"And then what?" she pressed.

"I don't know. I have not thought beyond that. It's just that my thoughts run so fast and jump around my head, and I think it's because I feel so persecuted, and if only I can know this one thing, for sure, it will help, won't it?"

"Simeon, before this current obsession, you were convinced that the family in the upper rooms of the house next door were following some strange religion that involved chanting, and the overthrow of parliament."

"I admit that I was mistaken, and my actions were not helpful."

"No. I think that we can all agree that your night-time raid upon the poor family was ill-advised, and that the police were very generous to let you out of the cell the next day."

"Well, they have moved away, anyway, and this situation is not the same."

But it was, and she knew it. She wondered if he knew it too, somewhere, deep inside.

"Oh, Simeon."

He sagged.

"Simeon, make the tea."

He moved mechanically, and brought her a hot cup, and took the seat opposite to her. He stared at his drink. "So why did you come around, if not to help me?"

She felt like a cruel and selfish woman then, because she had to say, "Because I would like your help. If possible. Please."

"Is this the Bartholomew matter? Or the Monahan one? Or a new problem entirely? And you say that I have obsessions! You are collecting them."

"Does it look that way from the outside?"

"Yes."

She sighed. "I can trust you, can't I?"

"You do not even need to ask. I am insulted that you do."

So she told him everything, absolutely everything, and all of her suspicions, and it was a huge weight being taken from her shoulders. And in turn, the light and the fire returned to his eyes. He had a new project, and finally decided to embrace it. She hoped that it would replace the fixation on thieves.

"I like how you are thinking about Edgar Bartholomew," he said. "He could easily be Wade Walker in disguise, as both were close friends, and both were something of recluses. Especially as now, no word can be got of Wade Walker at all. One man is dark, one blond. Well, the easiest thing would be to see if the man you suspect to be fake is dyeing his hair."

"Easy?" she said. "I don't think so. What do you suggest we do – sneak into his house and watch him at his ablutions? He has no servants we can ask or bribe, or I should have done that at once."

"Maybe we do not need to go to such lengths," Simeon said. "That's a pun."

"I'm sorry?"

"Hair. Lengths. Do you get it?"

"No, for it does not work if you have to explain it."

185

"You told me to add humour to my act. As you can see, it is not working. Listen," Simeon said, leaning forward, "we simply need to obtain a length of his hair. Then you can do your science on it, and tell us if it is dyed!"

"Yes, but also no," she replied. "I am not a chemist. Even so, I am sure that I can work out what tests to perform, yes, if we know what people actually use to dye their hair. I have no idea what people use. However, the main problem is: how do we obtain this lock of hair? Shall we set up shop as barbers and entice him in?"

"Oh no, it could be far simpler," Simeon said. "He is a man who is visiting mediums, is he not? And you know the ways of the séance, and I know the ways of magic and artifice. I have some useful devices…"

"We will not need a sleeve-full of hidden birds," she said. And she smiled. She had realised what he meant. "But yes. I think we can do this."

Seventeen

Planning was invigorating. It made Marianne feel as if she were in control of events. They decided that they would perform a small private séance, and all the other participants would be hand-picked stooges that Bartholomew would not recognise. All they needed was darkness, really, and either Marianne or Simeon could clip some of his hair. As he had never seen Phoebe, they decided that she should play the medium, and she readily agreed to this plan. She was delighted to be involved. Marianne would coach her in what to say. Simeon would be one of the fake participants, and Marianne would hide in the spirit cabinet or some cupboard within the room. They also needed some more participants. In the end, she decided to ask a few old college friends that she knew were in London.

As for premises, Simeon said he could speak to his landlord who rented out many properties in the area. There was a chance that they could gain access to a well-furnished drawing room for the evening.

The final piece of the puzzle was to get Edgar Bartholomew invited. But as he was known to be hunting for mediums who might help him, that turned out to be easier than they had thought. They mocked up some cards declaring Phoebe to be "Mrs Algernon Carter", a middle-aged widow of many years due to a tragic accident early in her marriage. Since then, the spirit world had called to her but she had resisted the vocation until very recently. Now she was newly come to London from Edinburgh, where she intended to live quietly but to follow the promptings of the spirit for a "select few people of status and class." They pasted up a few handbills and paid for a small announcement in one of the spiritualist periodicals.

Naturally, Bartholomew was all over that as soon as he had heard. He sent a letter to the address that Simeon had procured, and the amenable landlord kept up the pretence for them. He was in the process of having work done to the building, installing plumbing so that he might let the rooms to better-paying guests, but while the back rooms of the apartments were a mess of pipes, the drawing rooms at the front remained untouched.

Within a week, they had all the people assembled, and Phoebe sent a note back to Bartholomew saying that she had been led, by the spirits, to invite him to a small private séance to be held the following evening.

He arrived very early.

Marianne was hidden in a large sideboard in the corner of the drawing room. They had drafted Emilia in to act as a general servant, though she needed a great deal of persuasion. She was not confident that she could play a successful role in the charade, but she agreed for Phoebe's sake. She led Bartholomew into the drawing room where Simeon was already present, engaged in a stiff and formal fake conversation with the so-called Mrs Carter. They had taken care to disguise Phoebe as much as possible, so that her reputation be protected against any accidental unmasking. Her blonde hair had been scraped back and hidden under a lace cap more suited to a much older lady. Rather than apply paint and powder to accentuate her beauty, Emilia had shown dexterity that made Simeon gasp. Under her brushes and paint, Phoebe had acquired around ten years on her life, with shadows and wrinkles and sags to her cheeks. Even Price would have had to look twice.

Marianne could hear everything. She was on a cushion, kneeling in the cupboard, and staying as still as possible. She was wearing nothing but a long white cotton dress, a simple sort favoured by young maidens and painters like Burne-Jones. She could not risk swishing silk skirts around.

Bartholomew introduced himself and began to eagerly press Mrs Carter for information about her successes and her techniques. He sounded like a thorough believer in all matters spiritual.

"Although," he confessed with a sad air, "I am finding more and more that mere charlatans are invading this most sacred calling, and I should be devastated to discover that you were of their ranks, my good lady."

Marianne bit her lip. It sounded like a very polite threat, and she was glad that Simeon was out there. The magician stepped into the conversation swiftly, and began to ask questions that were designed to reveal information that could later be used by the medium.

They were also designed to make Simeon and the whole proceedings look entirely innocent. "And does your wife also have your sensitivities, sir?" was Simeon's first question.

"Alas, I am widowed, but that is not why I am here, and nor do I care to speak too much, for this, I know, is how the fakes operate. They seek out information, do they not?"

Marianne, kneeling on her cushion, winced. He knew what he was about, all right. But it did not matter. They already knew more about Edgar Bartholomew than he would realise.

They were saved by a fresh interruption from the two other participants. Miss Mary Sewell and Miss Clara Ettington-Vane entered and there was a flurry of introductions and light giggling. Marianne could not see anything, but she could hear that both young women were faking their personas and enjoying every minute of it. In real life, both had been serious and studious bluestockings, albeit with a penchant for the theatre, which gave them both a release from their daylight routines.

And so the séance began, rumbling along in the usual patterns. Their hands were linked as the lights were put out. Emilia moved silently around, placing a candle at the far end of the room on a side table. She removed herself to stand by the sideboard.

Phoebe began to moan and shake, and the chemicals that Marianne had added to the wick of the candle caused it to flare up, glow green from copper particles, and then go out in a shuddering rush.

The room went utterly silent.

Marianne was stiff with tension now. It was all down to Phoebe and whether she could follow their coaching for long enough for Marianne to get out of the cupboard. In their plans, they had asked Emilia to do the deed, clipping a lock of Bartholomew's hair, but the lady's maid had been so horrified that they had to rethink. She could not, she said, go near a man in the pitch darkness carrying scissors. If she slipped, she would be a murderess. And therefore out of a position, she had added, as if that was the worst of it.

Phoebe began to alter her voice. "There is a man here," she said, "who has some words to speak to one of you." Marianne cursed silently. Phoebe had dropped her voice too soon, but she should not have done that until she was actually purporting to speak as that man. She went on, saying, "He is called John – John Masters…"

Mary gasped convincingly. "My grandfather! Oh! Can it be?"

"Mary," Phoebe rasped, her voice now gravelly. She would have to be careful, Marianne thought, or she'd induce a coughing fit. "You are to pull out the middle drawer in the bureau. Pull it out completely. The will is lodged *underneath*."

Now everyone gasped. "Thank you, grandfather! Mother will be so pleased!"

Marianne longed to be able to see what was going on, but even if she weren't in the cupboard, she would not be able to. She hoped that the calculated revelation would have the right effect. Bartholomew, now, should have all his attention focused on Phoebe.

Phoebe let her voice rise up, and now she was playing the part of a small child, and pretending that she was a long-dead daughter speaking to Simeon, who did a very nice impression of a heartbroken father. His sobs covered the sound of Marianne pushing the well-oiled cupboard door open.

Her instinct was to rub her eyes but it had no effect. The

191

room was pitch-black. She knew roughly where Bartholomew would be seated, and they had practiced the next steps a few times.

As Simeon thanked Phoebe, she gave out a low wail. "Oh! The spirits, they are coming, they are … they are here! Did you feel that?"

Mary and Clara tittered nervously, and Simeon choked back his final sobs. Marianne counted her paces and slowly reached out until her fingers brushed the back of a man. It was Simeon, and he called out, "Oh, I feel a hand upon me!" This helped her to orientate herself properly. "Ah, it strokes my cheek – dear Millie, is that you?"

"It is Millie, come to comfort you," Phoebe crooned.

It really was the most excitingly convincing séance that had ever happened.

While Bartholomew's attention was fixed on Phoebe, Marianne took two steady paces, silently, to the right, and reached out carefully. Her fingertips met the warm skin of a neck, and Bartholomew yelped out, and then coughed, and muttered an apology that barely covered his excitement. "Who is that?" he asked.

The problem was, they were not sure who to say it was, without blowing their cover. It was down to Phoebe to muddle her way through this. They'd practised a few options.

Phoebe said, in her normal voice, "There is someone here for you but they are faint. They are struggling to get through. Come, come…"

Bartholomew leaned forward slightly in his eagerness, and Marianne lost touch. But she had her small embroidery scissors in her hand and she employed the pickpocket's tactic of misdirection. She placed her left hand very firmly, and very suddenly, exactly where she judged his left shoulder to be, and at the same time slid the scissors close to his scalp at the back, closing them slowly to avoid an audible snip.

She caught the tuft in her palm and then released his shoulder, and stepped silently back until her hip caught the sideboard and she was able to retreat into her hiding place once more.

Meanwhile Phoebe was claiming that the spirits were fading away.

Everyone murmured their disappointment, and none more so than Edgar Bartholomew.

"So close! I felt his hand upon me!" he said.

His hand, thought Marianne. *He was not expecting his dead wife, then.*

"I am sorry," said Phoebe, affecting exhaustion. "They have all gone, and I am left as nothing more than a husk … please, girl, let us have some light."

Marianne double-checked that the door to her cupboard was firmly closed and she heard Emilia cross the room toward the candle. The main door to the room opened. Chairs scraped and conversation resumed. Marianne tried to focus on what Bartholomew was saying, but he had evidently drawn Phoebe to the far side of the room. It seemed to take an interminable amount of time before everyone had left, and she was finally released from her prison.

"I have it!" Marianne declared, and held the rough scrap of dark hair aloft.

Simeon, Emilia and Phoebe grinned, but Phoebe's smile died first.

"We might have a problem," she said. "He has spent some time trying to persuade me to give him a private sitting. He is now utterly convinced that I am genuine, and that I am the only person who can help him to contact his dead best friend."

Eighteen

Russell Starr was in bed until late the next morning. He had been out and about around town for half the night, and Marianne hoped that he had stayed out of trouble.

She wrapped a long apron around her clothing and set to work in the laboratory. She placed the lock of hair on a clean white tile, and set her notebook down on the bench beside it. She began to make a detailed visual analysis of the sample, and took meticulous notes. Although she far preferred electricity, magnetism and all manner of other mysterious and invisible forces, she still had a basic grounding in the scientific method, and so she could make a start while she waited for her father to wake up. She hoped that he would be fit and well.

"What have you discovered so far?"

Her father's voice startled her and she knocked her cheekbone against the microscope. He looked tired, grey and lined, and was dressed in a violently red and purple dressing robe trimmed with fur. He was pursued into the laboratory by Mrs Crouch, who was urging him to return to his bedroom, or at least to eat some breakfast.

He turned, demanded strong coffee and a lightly poached

egg, and then came to Marianne's side. "Coarse, rough, and a chocolate-brown. How are the ends?"

"Not recently cut. The outer layer of the hair is not smooth, and it appears damaged. What would one use to dye hair?"

"You are the woman. This is your domain. You tell me."

She sighed. "Hardly. I will go and speak to Emilia."

"Bring me an egg when you come back, won't you?"

***

When she returned – minus the egg – she found her father dining at the laboratory bench, with a yellow-stained cloth tucked into his robe. "Coffee?" he asked. "Crouch was complaining but she has sorted out a fine feast here."

"Thank you, yes, I should like some coffee."

"Well, you ought not to."

"It is a dreadful habit I got into at university."

He harrumphed and poured a small cup for her. She accepted it and said, "Emilia says that there are various ways to turn light hair dark but they are not straightforward. You can use herbal rinses, but she was dismissive of their effectiveness. To effect a strong change, one needs chemicals. You can buy things from the chemist that will do it, she said."

"But she did not know the chemicals used?"

"No, of course not. She is a lady's maid."

"Then go and purchase the relevant items, please. Make sure the ingredients are on the packets, or insist that the chemist in the shop tell you how it was made. We need a starting point otherwise this runs the risk of becoming a wild goose chase."

"You mean it isn't already?" Marianne said, but she took

her cup of coffee into her own room to dress for a quick visit into town. Their local shops should be able to furnish the necessaries, she thought.

When she returned, she had a packet of dye and a sheet of paper scrawled across with the local apothecary's hand. He knew and liked Russell, and had taken time to note down everything he knew that might be relevant.

Russell studied the paper. "Charcoal and grease is used in the theatres and by criminals," he read. "Of course, yes, that won't stand up to much scrutiny. Woe betide you if you are caught in the rain. Oh! Salts of bismuth, lead and silver. Yes, that makes a lot of sense. It is much the same in photography, is it not?"

"I think so."

"If it is this, we would need to steep it in nitric acid. What else?" He turned to the box of *Tinctura Pompeiana* and peered at the writing. Most of the text was a hyperbolic stream of claims as to its effectiveness and there was no strictly factual information – nothing useful like a list of exact contents and their proportions – but it did claim to include "litharge, lime and harmless chalk". She noted they didn't claim the overall preparation itself was without risk. The directions were somewhat intimidating. "Apply to wet hair and allow to permeate for four hours, keeping moist the whole time, and then allow to dry. A dilute solution of acetic acid next applied and finally rub the whole head with the yolk of an egg."

"Marvellous," Russell said. "Nitric acid is our friend again here. Let us get to work!"

* * *

They split the sample of hair into four, each batch consisting of around two dozen strands of hair. Then it was over to Russell. Marianne sat at the bench and watched her father work, and it felt like old times, with an added veneer of pain and regret.

Regret was pointless. He could not be cured and would not live out his allotted span of days. He would descend into madness and pain over the coming years as the bacteria continued its assault on his brain. He bent his head over the flask in which he was steeping a lock of hair in nitric acid, and she had one brief and vain flash of thanks that the syphilis had not taken his now-rugged good looks. He had not fallen prey to the gummas, the large spongey growths that would make monsters out of men.

But she knew that his balance was getting worse, and his headaches were increasing and his tolerance to light was poor. His moods, likewise, swung this way and that. Partly it was the disease, and partly from the effects of the medication he experimented with.

They had never spoken of what should happen when he became unmanageable. But they both knew that he would.

"Aha, see!" Russell said, his cheery shout at odds with her gloomy thoughts. She pushed a smile onto her cheeks and went to peer at the flask.

"Do you see those bubbles?" he said.

"I do ... let me think," she replied, knowing that he was going to challenge her. "That is chalk, effervescing?"

"Yes, exactly so. Good girl. And what is the white substance at the bottom of the flask?"

198

"Um. Lead?" she hazarded.

"Possibly. We shall test it. Fetch me the ferrous sulphate and the bottle of sulphuric acid."

With those things assembled, she was directed – as she had the steadier hand – to spoon out a little of the white stuff from the flask. As she dumped it into a fat glass sample tube that was resting in a clamp, her father casually added, "Of course, if it is lead nitrate, it is highly toxic."

She retreated and let him do the experiment. He added liquid to the tube to make the white stuff into a solution and then the lead sulphate. Marianne was ordered to return to perform the final part of the test – adding the acid, slowly, drop by drop.

Russell stared like a hawk.

"Yes!" he exclaimed. "The brown ring!"

"You sound happier than you have done for months."

"Naturally. Look – do you see that brown line between the acid and the solution? This proves the hair was indeed dyed with a substance similar to the dye in the packet."

The acid had slipped below the aqueous solution and in between, there was a distinctive brown line.

"It is one step closer to showing that Edgar Bartholomew is not who he says he is," she said.

"No, you have that the wrong way around. The man claiming to be Edgar Bartholomew is not him. Logic, girl. Be strict and be accurate. Now your question is, who is he?"

"I do not have to prove that. All I need to do is take the results of this experiment to the solicitor, and he will pay me the rest of the money."

"We shall have a merry few months then. Let us buy better

199

coffee."

She opened and closed her mouth. The money was going to be loaned to Price, not frittered away on eggs benedict and new smoking jackets. She began to clear up, and as she bustled around the laboratory, she asked if he had discovered anything about Jack Monahan.

"You said you had ways and means, father. I hope you have not got into trouble with it."

He sighed heavily and grunted as he sat down to watch her tidy the room. He had done the brain work – it was her place to do the domestic side of things. "Ah yes. He is a slippery fish to catch hold of. My usual place seemed to have no word of the fellow at first."

"But...?"

"Well, I was not such a fine upstanding gentleman in my youth, and I knew of a few other places I might try. Lower sorts of clubs. Still gentleman all, I might add, but those who care less for reputation and more for ... entertainment."

"Oh, the Four In Hand Club, those sort of things?"

"They are nothing more than loud young men who eat a lot and drive fast. No. I did get a whiff of the man at Cobden's but they are all free trade nuts and would not admit me. I had most of my information from a butler at a shady drinking dive where rich men go to pretend to be poor. And there, among the reprobates and gamblers, whoremongers and thieves, they spoke of him with admiration."

"What? Well. Well, well."

"The reason that men of good taste and quality would not speak of him, in public, was that he was in employment to Lord

Hazelstone but dismissed in disgrace. But you knew that already. However, this Monahan is apparently desperate to get back into Hazelstone's good books. He was involved in some investigation into fraud, but did something – I do not know what – which if revealed would have brought Hazelstone into disgrace. Now he is, in the words of my informants, something of a loose cannon and unpredictable. They gave me warnings not to cross the man. He is well-placed but in secretive ways."

"Perhaps we ought to speak to Lord Hazelstone."

"I think mentioning Monahan to Hazelstone would provoke the man to rage. I have met him. I would rather lick a toad than meet him again. Marianne, I forbid you to have anything further to do with Monahan."

"This is going to be awkward, father. For he dines with us tomorrow night."

Nineteen

Marianne went straight back to the police station the next morning. She had asked her father to write out his suspicions and the results of the tests. She saw the same balding old desk officer as before, and demanded to see Sergeant Giles. Or, she added, anyone of authority.

He looked at her, and sighed before going slowly to the door at the back of the office and calling out. In a few moments, she was being led into a private room with Sergeant Giles. He was a pleasant-mannered man of middle age, who had a heavily domed forehead covered in lank black strands of hair, and a yellow-toothed smile. He offered her tea, which she refused.

"I hope you are recovered from the awful shock you sustained when you found the body," he said.

"Yes, thank you. I am here on that very matter. May I ask, has an autopsy been performed, and a cause of death established?"

"I believe the coroner has noted it as accidental poisoning. Did you not mention oysters?"

"Only that he had eaten some – but he was not killed by oysters, sir! You must examine the body again. I have already informed your man out there on the front desk. It was white phosphorus! Did he not pass the message on?"

"Oh, Meeps? I am sure that he did. But it was not deemed necessary to follow up. And anyway, the body is buried now. Poisoning is poisoning; it was a tragic accident."

"No one accidentally dies from white phosphorus. It was deliberate."

Giles's face took on a patient form. He wove his fingers together and inclined his head, to give her the impression that he was listening very hard. Delicately, he said, "And do you have anyone in mind who might have done this?"

She knew when she was being patronised. She replied with studied politeness. "The man who claims that he is his father – Edgar Bartholomew – is an imposter and we have evidence."

"Which is?"

"Here." She pushed her father's note across the table. "He dyes his hair."

"Vain and silly, but not a crime."

"George's father was dark haired naturally. Why is this man, who says he is the father, dyeing his hair to be dark?"

"Perhaps he has gone grey, and wishes to disguise it."

She opened her mouth to lay out all the other suspicions, and then closed her mouth again. She had not even considered the fact that he could have gone grey. She felt monumentally silly.

And the look on Sergeant Giles's face was one of pity and sympathy. He stood up and she followed, mechanically. She knew that there was no point in going any further.

***

Phoebe had spent the whole day preparing for the dinner party, which was to be "merely a small, private and intimate affair." There was no need, then, for twelve courses nor for the centrepiece to consist of an arrangement of ferns around a pineapple, but that was only Marianne's opinion and apparently "you are just a woman of science and what do you know of meringues?"

"I know that they taste nice, and that I should like to still have room in my belly to enjoy them. Are pigeons entirely necessary?" Marianne had said, before being chased out of the room.

But paying attention to such details was Phoebe's particular interest. She had invited the Jenkins, as usual, and also Marianne's father.

To everyone's horror, this time Russell accepted the invitation. Phoebe did not know that he had done such an unusual thing until five that afternoon, just an hour before the guests were to arrive.

It sent the whole ritual out of kilter.

Marianne found Phoebe in her room, being dressed by Emilia, and broke the news to her with trepidation. Phoebe was naturally furious.

"He has just decided?"

"He has. He said yesterday that the fumes from the experiments we had undertaken had upset his system, and he had retired to bed. But he sprang up an hour ago and demanded to know where his invitation was. I said that he was welcome, as always, to join us, and he said that he would."

"But he can't! We only invite him because we know he will

say no. It upsets all the balance at the table! Monahan will escort you in, Price will escort me, and the Jenkins make up the six. If your father attends, he will be a spare!"

"I told him that. But you know what he is like."

Phoebe rolled her eyes and blew out her cheeks, and Emilia tutted. "Hold still, my lady. Your curls…"

***

And it only got worse.

Russell, being the most distinguished guest, held out his arm to Phoebe and took her into the dining room. He had dressed very smartly, and was quite the fashionable figure – if it were still 1860, which it was not. Still, he was at least clean and he walked with confidence. Price brought Marianne in, and Mr Jenkins had Mrs Jenkins on his arm. Jack Monahan preceded them but looked quite out of place. They took their seats. His hands flapped, as he had no lady to attend to. Marianne almost felt sorry for him.

And then she remembered that this whole affair was simply done to please him, and she quashed her softer feelings. *Let him be awkward. This was all his fault.*

The sweetbreads and beef olives came around first, and then a clear soup that cleansed the palate. The talk was kept as light and gentle as the soup, and everyone behaved impeccably. Marianne was not sure who she ought to worry about most – her father, who could lapse into brain-fever at any moment, or Jack Monahan, the unknown entity with unclear motives. She laughed lightly at everyone's comments, sometimes without any reason to laugh at all, and tried to watch both men both constantly and surreptitiously. She wasn't sure what she'd do in the event of her father or Monahan behaving badly. Possibly she could faint to cause a diversion.

It was clear, from the questions around the table, that Price really did not know Monahan at all, and he was somewhat confused as to how and why Monahan was even present. Price kept glancing at his wife with a quizzical look on his face. Price and Monahan had clearly never been involved in business together, Marianne thought, as Price pressed Monahan on his daily activities. Monahan, in contrast, asked Price questions about Harker and Bow without needing to be told what Price's role was. Monahan knew a lot. The information was decidedly one-way. She was starting to build her ideas as to why Monahan wanted to be here.

It was nothing to do with her or with séances.

The liar. She had known that all along.

The fish course was mercifully light, just a lemon sole, artfully done with herbs. Mrs Cogwell was a genius in the kitchen, and to get the fish all the way from the kitchen to the dining room, still warm and flaky, was a much underrated and underappreciated success. The servants moved like swift and silent automatons, bringing and removing each course in practised succession.

There was a simple joint of beef for the main course, with a gravy of rich sauce and a boozy hint of sherry, and some chicken croquettes in mustardy breadcrumbs, fried and dressed with parsley. The vegetables were varied and cooked to perfection – clearly not left to one of the maids this time. Even Marianne had to admit that Mrs Cogwell had outdone herself.

On and on the meal ran, with various wines, a steamed

pudding, lighter sorbets and finally a cheeseboard of the most rank-smelling and delightful blue cheese that anyone could remember eating.

Phoebe, Marianne and Mrs Jenkins retired to the drawing room. Marianne stood stiffly by the fire and stared into the flames, replaying Monahan's conversations in her head. She had brought him here. Now he had spoken with Price. Was that it? Was everything over?

Phoebe came up to her side. "Why do you look as if you want to stab things with the poker?"

"So astute. It is because I do want to stab things. What is Monahan up to? Did you hear him talking?"

"I did and he behaved perfectly well. He seems that he simply needed an introduction to Price. I am expecting him to ask for a job."

"I doubt it," Marianne said. "My father says he wants his old job back. Now he is in there, drinking with my father and your husband. I do not like it. And my father knows other things about him; and he does not like what he knows. You can guess, I am sure."

"Yet they all behaved so very well at dinner. They spoke of general things, and I was very impressed. Monahan gave not a hint of suspicious behaviour, and this time, your father did not shriek at the crackers and try to sing that terrible song about lobster."

"No, for Mrs Crouch and I have dosed him very well before he came down to dine, and it is only a matter of time before he passes out," Marianne said.

"Does he know?"

"Of course not. And he never will."

"Splendidly done. I do hope he doesn't fall face first into the brandy. Try not to fret about Monahan. Your obligation to him is discharged."

"It feels unresolved still, as if I am missing something."

"You will never tie it all up to your satisfaction," Phoebe told her. "Life is not like a household receipt book that can be added up and made to balance in perfection. Shall we have more wine? You will care less about the little things then."

Mrs Jenkins came up to them and gazed at the fire. "Mr Monahan is a singular character," she remarked. "Who is he? I fancy he never did say who his family was."

"No," Marianne and Phoebe said in unison.

"He has some mystery but he is decidedly well-bred," Phoebe added. "I believe it to be a mark of his good character that he is not gossiped about in every drawing room in town, and retains a level of privacy that some people would do well to emulate. Not yourself, of course – you are a paragon of reticence."

Marianne had to turn away in case she had gone puce at Phoebe's bare lies.

Mrs Jenkins did not take offence. "And how did you come to know this gentleman?"

"I, er…" Phoebe stuttered and nudged Marianne. "We, I should say, he…"

Marianne shrugged. Phoebe said, in a rush of confidence, "He is a friend of Price's, of course."

"Of course."

Their extended and, to Marianne's overwrought mind, awkward silence was broken by the arrival of the men, who had clearly drunk a lot of alcohol very quickly. They smelled of cigars and pipe-smoke, and bowled into the room laughing as if they had been sharing the best joke.

Price and Monahan might have been strangers at the start of the party but now they behaved like long lost friends. *Well, he had achieved what he came for*, she thought. *Let us hope that his drunkenness does not destroy his aims.*

Marianne looked to her father, who was red in the face, and stumbling towards a wing-backed chair. He collapsed into it, but sighed happily. When she turned back to study Monahan, she realised that he was looking just as intently at her.

His eyes were clear.

He was not actually drunk at all.

Oh, he is a good actor, she thought in admiration, as he winked at her, and then returned to his conversation with Mr Jenkins and Price, talking just a little too loudly, like an inebriated man would.

After a few rounds of cards, with much cheating and laughter, Monahan excused himself. Marianne assumed he was attending to a call of nature. Her father had disappeared and returned three times so far, and was now asleep in the chair by the fire. Everyone was finding the alcohol and food pressing heavily upon them.

But Monahan did not return as quickly as Russell had done.

Marianne had been watering her wine very severely, making it almost a drink fit for children. She glanced at the carriage clock on the ornate mantelpiece above the fire, and after five minutes, decided that she ought to go and find him. He could be lost although Woodfurlong wasn't an extensive house. Perhaps he was more drunk than she'd thought. As she excused herself, her father stirred.

"Help me up," he demanded, and she went to his side.

"Time to retire?"

He muttered something about his age being no barrier, wilfully misunderstanding her, bid everyone farewell with the passion of a man about to embark on an overseas expedition, and let his daughter convey him from the room. She realised that the room had been hot and stuffy as they stepped into the cool hallway, and it revived him somewhat. He lessened his grip on her arm and stood more securely on his own feet.

"Father, I will take you back to the garden wing, but I am concerned that Monahan has got lost."

"How? Barrington or Dry will have shown him the way."

"Perhaps they missed him." They stood in the downstairs hall, and listened. A door clicked at the far end, under the stairs, and the butler, Mr Barrington, emerged.

"Barrington, good fellow, did you see that chap Monahan?" Russell called.

"No, sir, I am afraid I have not. Is he lost in the house?"

"We think so. Take a look downstairs, will you? We'll go up."

"That's not the way to our rooms," Marianne started to say, but Russell had shaken free of her grasp and was heading up the wide, main staircase, keeping to the carpeted centre to muffle his steps. He turned and put his finger to his lips.

"I do not trust that man," he whispered. "He will not be in a bathroom, you may depend upon it. He asked Price too many questions and they were too probing. I know exactly where that snake will be, and so do you, if you stop to think about it. Follow, but silently, and if you cannot be silent, well then stay down there."

She had no intention of remaining at the bottom of the stairs.

He walked with a slight hesitance to his steps. He needed the security of the bannister rail, but did not reach out for it. The extra drugs that she had given him would be working, and he was clearly fighting their effects. For a man so ill, he had strength that came from some hidden place.

They reached the top of the flight and he stopped to listen and gain his breath back. He pointed down the corridor, towards Price's business room and she nodded. She understood.

The door was closed, but they both pressed their ears to it, assuming that Monahan would be within. If he was, he was moving stealthily, as they could hear nothing.

Russell waved her away from the door. He composed himself, and she saw that he was standing upright with difficulty. He sagged against the frame for a moment, and she reached out to him, but he frowned at her. Then with a deep breath, he grabbed the door handle and flung the door open. He leaped into the room, and she stepped in behind him.

Jack Monahan was standing behind Price's wide polished desk, looking down at a ledger that was spread open over the green leather top. He froze in horror.

Russell strode right up to him, closely followed by Marianne. He leaned over the desk, slamming his hands onto the cream pages. "Sir! Tell me, at once, without a lie, what you are doing here."

He blinked slowly, just once, and said in a calm tone, "Fear not. I have authority."

"You have no authority, you dog! What are you doing in this room? From where do you claim this authority comes?"

Monahan stepped back and smiled icily. Marianne remembered how he had told her that he was always prepared with at least a dozen cover stories to use for any occasion. "Father," she said. "You cannot trust any answer that he gives."

"I suspect you are correct. For shame, *sir*." In Russell's scathing tones, *sir* had more insult in it that *you dog*. "You are in a private house, and you are here at the request of my daughter. Do you seek to bring a tarnish upon her reputation? I will not have any association between her and you, sir, not any. Get yourself gone from here and we will not see or hear of you ever again."

"I have one more thing to inspect."

"You have not!" Russell launched himself around the desk, steadying himself against it as he went. She hoped that Monahan did not notice her father's lack of balance. "You have two choices here, and I would urge you to take the first one, for my daughter's sake. Leave now, silently and without being seen, and that will be the end of it."

"Or?"

"Or I raise the household, and we call the police."

He smiled smugly. "The police have no authority over me. I am connected."

"So you say, but I know your connections are tawdry and of no use here," Russell said. "Even if you could claim some help in lofty quarters, I do not think the police would care for it. They would arrest you, I would make sure of it! But that recourse would involve my daughter's name, at whose invitation you are here; and I do not wish that. Nor, if you have any scrap of finer feeling, do you."

Monahan shrugged, lifting one shoulder and letting it drop, while a smile tugged one corner of his mouth. "I have no finer feelings at all, old man; not a one. I care nothing for her reputation or your police or any such thing."

"Then I shall shoot you where you stand!"

"What with?"

"Damn you, sir."

Monahan sniggered, and Marianne hated every inch of him. He flipped over a few pages of the ledger, and then closed it. He looked up at Russell, who was glowering by his side, struck almost to stone by his fury and his impotence in the situation. "All done. Right; I shall leave, as quietly as you ask. Marianne, would you pass on my compliments to the cook? She is a true marvel. What do you pay her?"

"We pay her enough."

"I could pay her more."

"Get out!" snarled Marianne, shocking her father.

Monahan fled and they followed him out to make sure he left the premises.

Then Marianne helped Russell to bed and went back to the gathering with a grim feeling.

Twenty

Phoebe came into Marianne's room around midnight that night. She was dressed for bed, and her face was bare, with her hair tucked up under a cotton and silk cap. Marianne was sitting up in bed, nestling against cushions and pillows, and she had her notebook on her lap. She had done many angry scrawlings and crossings-out.

Phoebe slid under the covers alongside her, and peered at the words that Marianne had written.

"*Damn*," she read aloud. That was the only word on the page. "That sums it up. Dear cuz, I agree. What a night."

"You do not know the half of it." Marianne kept her fingers on the book in case Phoebe tried to flip the pages; she had more incriminating notes about her husband on the other pages. She had lied to everyone on her return to the drawing room but now she had to come clean to Phoebe, as much as she was able to.

"What, there is more? More than Monahan getting lost, and somehow passing out through drink, halfway up the stairs? And your father trying to carry him out – alone! – without calling for Barrington or Dry? And you there, too, assisting? Dumping the ridiculous man on the front steps? Your father going to bed, quite ill? When you came back into the drawing room to tell us this, I thought that Mrs Jenkins was going to faint! What a terrible man he was. But we were warned, were we not. And I do not blame you."

"I am so sorry that a hint of impropriety now attaches itself to your household." Marianne put her hand over Phoebe's.

"Oh, we shall weather this minor upset. The shame attaches to Monahan, not to us."

"Let me tell you the truth. None of that is as I said that it happened. Except father, who now lies in bed, muttering and twitching."

As Phoebe listened to the truth, she drew her knees up and hugged her legs, growing more and more alarmed with each revelation. By the end of Marianne's recount, she was ready to leap out of bed, grab a shotgun from the hunting room, and go in pursuit of Jack Monahan.

"The police should have been called at once!" she said. "He is nothing but a burglar."

"Here? The police, to one of your esteemed and famous dinner parties? You have that extravaganza planned for next month – would the good Lady Flowers still attend, do you think, if she knew?" There was more, of course. Marianne did not want the police asking questions about Price Claverdon and investigating why anyone might want to look at his business affairs. Far more would be revealed, and she had to protect Phoebe – and keep a roof over her own head.

Phoebe grumbled, but she accepted Marianne's logic. "Do you think he might have been responsible for the attempted break-in the other week?"

"I suspect it," Marianne said. "He had one aim, and that was to get access to the work that your husband does here and not at his office. What does he do here?"

"You know I do not know. Ha! For the first time I find that I am in agreement with your father, though. That Monahan man will never more even so much as *think* about us, and nor we of him. If our paths ever cross, I shall not be responsible for my actions. Do you hear me?"

"I do. And I quite agree."

"Good." Phoebe yawned. "At least he threatened us with no physical danger. Tomorrow, I shall do nothing but lounge, like a painting by Rossetti, on comfortable chairs in the rose garden. I might even mope, in a pretty way. But I certainly shall not do anything that involves effort. I shan't even talk."

"And all the household counts itself blessed," Marianne said.

Phoebe elbowed her, laughed, yawned again, and slid out of bed. "Barrington ought to be advised to take extra precautions locking up," she said as she left.

"I already have done so."

"Oh, you are so capable. You are a treasure. Good night."

***

She must have slept. When she woke, in a tumble of sheets and notebook pages, she had resolved to think no more of Monahan. He had concluded his business, and that was an end of him. She had nothing to occupy her mind but the investigation into Edgar Bartholomew, who was obviously a fake. She found a scribbled note on her dresser which had been left by her father at some point – she didn't know when.

Wade Walker's address in London.

She had evidence that Edgar was a fake, and now she had more of a lead to follow up.

But who was he really – was he Wade? – and why did George have to die?

He had to die because he knew that Edgar was a fake.

Something was still not right.

And so she set out to sort things.

Marianne now stood in a busy side-street where small businesses seemed to be thriving. The rain was pattering down, very lightly, and she tucked herself under the striped awning of a butcher's shop. She looked across the street to a tall thin house, crowded in among a row of others, which had been split into separate apartments and flats. This was her third appointment of the day, and so far the visits had not been going well.

She had changed her approach. She could not sneak into gentlemen's clubs and the search there seemed fruitless anyway. She would not ask her father to look into Edgar Bartholomew – he had done enough for her with Monahan, and now he needed to rest.

But she still needed to know what the man known as Edgar Bartholomew was doing when he was visiting mediums.

Therefore Marianne resolved that she, too, would visit these mediums.

Unfortunately her reputation preceded her, as she knew that it would. This was why she had not undertaken this course of action at the start. "Hello, I am Miss Starr, the well-known exposer of fake mediums, can I talk to you about a matter that is private between you and a client? You can trust me." It was not a conversation that could possibly go well.

And as predicted, it had not been going well at all.

She had lied about who she was to the first medium, who nevertheless recognised her immediately, and would not admit her, adding that "Had you not lied, I might have spoken with you." Marianne thought it was an infuriating jibe, calculated to annoy her, but she took it on board and when she called, unannounced, on the second medium, she declared exactly who she was.

That medium, a stout woman flanked by her equally stout husband-and-manager, gaped at her, and they both shook their heads. "Why on earth would I speak with you? You ruined Lollie Smith. She is working the streets now. Because of you!"

Marianne retreated hastily. She had heard that the fall of Lollie had been particularly bad. *But there had been nothing stopping the girl going into service,* she thought angrily. Except probably her lack of references and now her reputation for falsehood.

Marianne had walked away from that encounter with a very heavy heart, and had to tell herself, repeatedly, that Lollie was fallen the minute she had taken on the task of duping people for money and preying on their grief.

Now she stood opposite Miss Deirdre Connor's address, and she did not want to knock on the door. *What would that master of persuasion, that cad Jack Monahan do,* she wondered. She had agreed, with Phoebe, that the man would not even cross their thoughts never mind their paths again, but she had found it hard to push him out of her mind.

He would have a wonderful cover story prepared. One that

skirted close enough to the truth to be convincing. She would not risk pretending to be someone else – she had to be herself.

So, what might realistically bring Miss Marianne Starr, paranormal and scientific investigator, to the door of a middling sort of medium?

The answer came to her in a flash.

Miss Connor was known to be an understated and quiet medium. She did not go in for public spectacles. She hadn't crossed Marianne's path much, because she kept herself close, and only did small and private meetings with carefully chosen people. She had a reputation for honesty, and she did not promise results.

She might, Marianne thought, be one of those people who actually believed in her own powers.

That would be Marianne's way in.

Before she could talk herself out of it, she marched across the street and rapped on the door. It was opened, eventually, by a small girl who peered at her with suspicion.

"What?"

"I would like to see Miss Connor."

"No, she lives upstairs. We're downstairs."

The girl started to close the door, but Marianne forced her way in. "Ah, sorry, I'll just go up then." She ran up the bare wooden stairs. She would never get used to how these houses were all divided up. On the first floor, she found another set of stairs, and a door, with a nameplate screwed into the frame: Miss Connor.

So she lived alone, as a woman of her own modest means? Bold, but a growing trend, Marianne knew and stifled her pang of jealousy. She rapped again, and tried to prepare her opening statement while she waited.

"Miss Connor? Good day. I am sorry to disturb you. I'm Miss Marianne Starr and I was hoping that you would be able to help me."

The dark-haired woman, as petite and finely boned as a sparrow, folded her arms and kept her face blank. "Oh? But you are the one who goes around trying to trick people like me, aren't you?"

Marianne nodded. "It is true that my work involves exposing those mediums who are falsely preying on people. And you must admit that there *are* those who do so. And don't you think that they bring your profession into disrepute, and must be stopped?"

Miss Connor's eyes narrowed with suspicion. "Yes, I would agree with that."

"Then you can help me! Please, do let me in. Have you heard of Mrs Sidgwick and her work?"

"The Census of Hallucinations? Of course." Miss Connor still looked unsure, but she stepped back, and allowed Marianne into the room.

It was a small and cosy place, with a folding screen across one corner. There were two doors, which she guessed would lead to a bedroom and some other room – she wasn't sure if this place would have a kitchen, as most people in London who crammed into small accommodation would brew up their tea on the fire, and purchase hot food from the many cheap street vendors all around, available any time of the day or night. Chop houses and eating places abounded, and a hot pie could be had for a few

221

pennies. Muffin sellers would come door to door, and the markets were always teeming with bargains. For someone with a few shillings to their name, they could dine well. For the poorest, they could at least survive, if they didn't mind oysters and mystery sausages.

There was a small and well-blackened open fire on one wall, and a tea-kettle was nestled near the corner of it, near a shiny orange pan that hung from a nail. Miss Connor, however, did not offer Marianne any refreshment. She waved her to a wooden chair by a circular table in the middle of the room. It was plain, and devoid of ornaments.

"Miss Starr, do you believe any of us are genuine?" Miss Connor asked directly as she took her own seat.

Marianne sighed. "I am a woman who has been trained in rigorous scientific investigation, and thus far, I have not been presented with any evidence. Should any proof come to light, I would of course change my views and accept the existence of spirits with all my heart."

"But what about the testimony of thousands of people, good, solid, reliable and honest people? Your Mrs Sidgwick must have some faith in their accounts, or she would not be collecting them so diligently."

"She collects them with an open mind, and it is an attitude I am striving to emulate."

Miss Connor knitted her fingers together. "So why are you here, and why me? Am I to be your next target for a public unmasking? Do I need to look for alternative employment already? Should I leave town now, before you humiliate me?"

This was going to be difficult. Marianne did not want to

compromise her own integrity, but she said, "I will make you this promise, if you can believe my word, that I have no intention of investigating you in any way. If, that is, you can answer some questions for me."

"That sounds like a threat!" She unlocked her fingers and sat up straight.

"No, no, I did not mean it to sound that way. Let me put my questions to you, and then you can decide. I will not ask for a promise or commitment from you until you have heard the reason for my questions." Marianne took a deep breath. "I have been engaged, by a man who is now dead, to look into the background of one particular man and I understand that this man has been to see you. He is called Edgar Bartholomew."

Miss Connor nodded slightly. "My discussions with my clients are as sacred as those between a priest and his flock."

"Of course and I respect your privacy. However..." Marianne licked her lips. She took a risk, and began to explain a little more. "I have made a promise to the dead man, and he is your client's son."

Miss Connor's eyebrows shot up. "His son? No, that cannot be right. Has he recently passed over?"

"Yes. Within the week, and under terrible circumstances – and the police are involved." That last part was not entirely true.

But it was enough to trigger something in Miss Connor. She said, "I cannot break the confidences of what has passed between us. But I can perhaps say that he seeks to contact his best friend."

"And his name, the name of the best friend?"

She shook her head. "I do not know. I ask my clients to withhold all information from me. I cannot afford to be compromised."

She did seem to be genuine – at least, to think that she was genuine. Marianne felt sorry for her. And also curious. What experiences had the woman had, to lead her to believe so fervently? Those were questions for another time. She had a feeling she might revisit Miss Connor in the future. But for now, she focused on Edgar Bartholomew. "Is there anything at all you might tell me? The dead man must be honoured," she added, hoping to appeal to Miss Connor's apparent sense of duty and morals.

"I agree," Miss Connor said. She half-closed her eyes. Marianne watched with curiosity in case the woman was about to slip into a trance. She said, "You might be wrong."

"I'm sorry?" Marianne asked.

"You have come here asking about Edgar Bartholomew. But I feel there is something that is not quite right. Something here does not fit, that is all."

"Oh. Anything else?"

Miss Connor opened her eyes and shook her head. "No, sorry." She got to her feet, and extended her hand, and signalled that the interview was over.

"I suppose this best friend is definitely dead then," Marianne said, thinking about Wade Walker.

"Oh no, that's not certain at all," Miss Connor replied. "You are the one who mentioned Mrs Sidgwick. Don't you recall that a large proportion of the ghosts that have been recorded are those of the living?"

Twenty-one

"I am telling you, Simeon, I honestly believe that the man who calls himself Edgar Bartholomew is actually his friend Wade Walker."

Simeon was lounging in his favourite easy chair, and eating a pie that was probably mostly mutton, or so one could hope. His lips glistened with fat and grease. "I don't understand why he'd do it. What does he gain?"

"I just don't know. But look at the evidence which we have. He dyes his hair. Wade was blond. Wade has not been seen for weeks. Even for a couple of reclusive gentlemen, this is strange."

"Have you been to this Wade Walker's house? Have you spoken with his staff?"

"Yes, and yes. This morning, actually. It took some time to discover his address, but my father found it out. The house is a small but wealthy one, and it is empty save for the staff, who are confused and scared, because their master has not been seen for a while, and the police are ignoring their concerns. Which is no surprise to me," she added bitterly.

"They should move on and get new positions."

"They should – that is what the police told them – but it is not so easy, without references and the wages that they are owed. It is a wonder that they are so honest, and have not looted the house for all of its goods."

"I suppose they expect that he will return, then, and is not dead at all. I still do not fathom why one of them would impersonate the other. And then, you say, he is visiting a medium to try to speak with the dead friend? Why impersonate one and then try to call him up? It makes no sense at all. And his son? The son of one of them, at any rate – he is also dead. The whole thing is a mess, Marianne. You should go back to the police of course. Or ask your father to go instead. They will listen to a man."

"I know it, but if we can gather more evidence they will have to listen to *me*." Marianne got up and prowled around the messy workshop. "The son, and Anna, are also involved. But Anna is involved with my own cousin-in-law, and he has attracted the interest of Jack Monahan. I am starting to understand that we are standing in the centre of a very tangled web, Simeon, and there is one link."

"That link is you," he said, his eyes opening wide. "Oh!"

"It could be co-incidence."

"Hardly. So what have you been up to, Marianne?"

She flapped her arms against her sides in frustration. "Nothing. I don't know! It all centres around me and it's a mystery. I am nobody."

"No – wait," Simeon said. He wiped his mouth and sat forward. "You are not the link. Price Claverdon is."

"Really?"

"He was the one to invite George to your house for dinner

in the first place, do you remember? And he invited him because of the business links, and they were both in Prussia, though at different times."

"Yes, that's true. It was only after that when George asked me for help. He said he had not expected to see me at the dinner."

"And Monahan has used you to gain access to your house, so that he could get into the study, to look at Price Claverdon. You were useful to him."

"The scoundrel. He tried to break in. Then he tried to flatter me. Then he said to his friend that he would get to me through my mind. In the end, I allowed him in because I had used him. But he has used me more. Simeon, I fully intend to shoot him the next time that I see him."

"You will hang."

"I will lightly wound him, that is all, just to make a point. And I will cry a little and claim it was an accident due to a feminine issue. Green sickness, perhaps. Hysteria. Something plausible."

"You've never been hysterical in your life."

"No, but if society says that I am, then so I shall be."

"Marianne, please don't shoot anyone." He sounded worried, as if he had realised that she really did have it in her. She was pleased.

"What triggered this chain of events?" she mused. "Was it George's return from the continent, do you think? He came back and Anna followed."

"Something must have happened before then."

Marianne cast her mind back. "I spoke with the gatekeeper. Two men came to the house, the Bartholomew's old and empty place. One remained, and claimed to be Edgar Bartholomew. A week later, George turns up, and gets a frosty reception and decides the man is an imposter. So let us say that in the week between the two men arriving, and George coming home, one man kills the other. And it is Wade Walker who kills Edgar Bartholomew, and takes his place. He did not expect Edgar's son to turn up."

"But luckily, his son was long unknown to him, and so does not recognise the difference. He must have hidden his hair under a hat until he could dye it," Simeon said, eagerly taking up the narrative. "The son begins to ask questions, and he comes to you for advice and help."

"Which I dismissed," she injected gloomily. "I should have listened from the beginning!"

"You weren't to know. And then the son is ejected from the house, and dies a painful death the next day. Poisoned, we know, by phosphorus."

"That is the strangest way to kill someone," she said. "It is not the poison that I would choose."

"First you are to shoot men, and now you intend to poison them. Marianne, have a care. I am a sensitive man."

"Oh, you are safe. Also, I think it unfair to have the poison be so painful. Poor George; he died hard. Now, why would someone, and I think it likely to be this imposter, this Wade Walker, use such a specific poison?"

Simeon ticked off the reasons on his long fingers. "One, it could be that it was the only thing he had to hand. Two, perhaps he did not know it was poisonous and it was some kind of accident. Three, that he chose it deliberately as he wanted to cause confusion. An unusual poison is more easily overlooked. Any half-witted coroner can spot arsenic these days, but no one is looking for phosphorus."

"I am going with your first one. It was all that was to hand. Now we must ask why. And I know. It is used by false and fake mediums to cause things to glow in the dark. Do you remember the girl that I ... er ... stabbed in the face? She had phosphorus on her cheeks."

"Shooting, poisoning and stabbing. And yet you are still unwed? It is a mystery to me."

"Shut up, Simeon. He might not have fully realised what it was that he was using. He was inviting mediums to the house, if you remember. One might have left it behind. If he did recognise it, perhaps he decided to use it and not be aware of its fatal effects. He could have been trying to warn George, you know, scare him." She stopped and thought about it. "No, that doesn't work. He already knew that George was dead. He *did* intend to kill him."

"And he believes in the mediums. Would not the phosphorus, the fake stuff left in his house, have shaken his conviction?"

"He does, but even the most ardent believers know that some of the mediums are false. And so he trawls from place to place, looking for a real medium, seeking connection with his dead best friend."

"If he is dead."

"I think that he is."

"But," said Simeon, "did you not posit that Wade has killed Edgar? Why, then, would he now seek out his spirit?"

Marianne ceased her circuits of the workshop and flung herself into an armchair. "To say sorry?"

"You mean, it was an accident?"

She closed her eyes. "It could be. And so he would cover it up … try to look for a way forward to evade the law … and his plans would be thrown into confusion by the arrival of the dead man's son. To avoid raising suspicion, then, Wade takes the place of Edgar." Her voice got faster and faster as she imagined the chain of events. "Yes, does that not make sense? It does make sense to me. He never intended to impersonate the man he has killed. But George's arrival complicated everything! He panicked and reacted."

"And George came back in disgrace. He was not likely to go away again quickly."

She nodded. "And he came back pursued by the other party in that disgrace, Anna. Or whoever she is. But now this all falls apart. For Anna appears to be engaged in immoral activities with Claverdon, and I wonder how long that has been going on? And, given that she is young and beautiful, and he is not, why? Did Anna perhaps come here before George? Or did she follow him, as we are suggesting? If so, she has not had much time to get her hooks into Claverdon. She moves fast."

"What about the blackmail?"

"It is linked. She is probably blackmailing him about the affair. I doubt she has true feelings for him."

"How do you know?"

"I just do. I am a woman."

"You'll be having hysterics next. What about science?"

"Shut up again, Simeon."

230

He pouted in mock indignation. "So what do you intend to do about Claverdon and Anna?"

"I don't know. I have given him the money and he should have paid her off. Perhaps we ought to pay her a visit and give her a stern warning."

"Do you think she will still be there after that foreign man burst in like that?"

"If she has any sense, no, she will have gone," Marianne said. "I'll call at the hotel on my way home and double-check, though."

They lapsed into silence, their rush of energy depleted by the unknowns and the unanswerable questions. Marianne began to feel quite gloomy about the whole affair, and she realised she hadn't eaten for some time. "Have you another pie?"

"No, sorry. Would you like some bread and butter?"

"How mouldy is the bread?"

"It's trimmable."

"I think not. Perhaps I will head out to find some food. I cannot think on an empty stomach."

"I will accompany you. You need to eat to think, and I need to move to think." He leaped up and began to hunt around for a decent outdoor coat and hat.

"I do not need to eat to think," she complained, almost automatically, as she pulled on her gloves and got ready to leave.

He ignored her routine comments. "Oh, now, look at this – I had forgotten I'd been working on this."

"A new trick?"

"Oh, no, simply a new device for a very old trick." He shrugged into an ordinary-looking jacket. It was cut quite long, and had a slight bagginess to the arms, but was presentable enough and would not have attracted comment.

That was, until he raised up one arm and a bunch of flowers shot up out of the cuff, arranging itself around his hand. They were silk and wire, but nicely made and convincing enough from a distance if you were on a gas-lit stage.

"Oh, pretty. But now what?" she said, clapping her hands.

"This is the extra part; I can reverse it just as easily." He brought his arm down in a steady manner, the elbow first, and the flowers slid back into their hidden housing, the petals folding in neat and symmetrical ways. "I pulled it out on a seller of muffins and she let me have one half-price as I had charmed her."

"Try that charm when you are on stage. Come on," she said, and they left the workshop, Simeon still fiddling with the sleeve.

***

The streets were as busy as ever. London never slept. It slumbered at night, in places, while other areas kept the beating heart of the city alive, albeit in a tawdry manner. Still, business was business, and at any time of day or night, there would be a business transaction taking place somewhere in London. Marianne felt proud of her capital as they pushed through the crowds, heading for a street seller of hot food that Simeon particularly recommended.

She was not too high up in society that she could not purchase food on the street, but still Marianne baulked at eating it there, standing up on a corner like a fishwife. They ducked into a narrower side street which was more residential than trade, with

232

a maze of narrow alleys and courts running off to either side. Here she was still watched, but she didn't think the ragged children and dirty animals counted as "being in public" quite so much. They wandered, feeling perfectly safe in the daylight. A few urchins came to beg for a penny, but they were astute children, and could see that this pair was not a wealthy church mission couple come on a sight-seeing and charity tour. Marianne's habitual dress was plain, and Simeon was ever so slightly crumpled.

So the children begged a little, for form's sake, and left them alone as they passed along the street.

"Are we being followed?" Simeon said suddenly, and drew to one side.

"Oh, not again," she said. "If we are – and I am not indulging your paranoia, because we are probably not – but *if* we are, then it will only be Jack Monahan, I would think. And I have something to say to him."

"Marianne, no, we talked about this! You are not to shoot him."

But when she turned around, she could see no one. Monahan would have revealed himself by now; he would be lounging against a wall and grinning at her. She shook her head, and they went on.

They turned a corner into an alley that led along the back of a row of houses as a short cut to Simeon's workshop. They were only fifty feet from sanctuary. They didn't run but they went along a little more briskly. The alley was deserted and suddenly she longed for the children to be following them and plaguing them for money. It was narrow, cold and dark, with the windowless brick buildings either side seeming to lean over as they rose, making it feel more like a tunnel. At the end, the alley stopped abruptly, but there was a door to the right which would open into another narrow passage and lead them to the stairs at the bottom of the building where Simeon lived. It looked as if they were heading into a dead end, if you did not know the place well.

The hairs on her neck prickled when she heard a noise behind them, a rustle and a crack. *It will be a rat in the rubbish*, she told herself, well used to such things in London.

But she turned around anyway.

Of all the people she thought she might see there, holding out a tarnished and heavy pistol, it was not Anna Jones.

Marianne blinked. Or was it? The woman looked like Anna, with her high cheekbones and curious almond eyes, and some golden locks escaped the dirty length of cloth she had wrapped around her head, like a lopsided turban. She wore seven shades of brown and dirt, and a shapeless dress. Could this be some evil twin? Or, well, an even-more-evil twin?

Anna kept walking towards them, and she was frowning and laughing at the same time, a twisted and triumphant glee of madness. "I have you now, don't I? Clever science woman. And some fancy-man too, well, that is a shame."

"What has happened to you, Anna?" They had not parted as friends, but this current incarnation was a terrifying vision and Marianne could not work out why.

"This? Oh, this is a disguise. This is not *me*," she spat. "This is necessary because of *you*."

"I doubt it. I have done nothing to you. Can I help you,

Anna?" In spite of it all, Marianne felt an affinity with the woman.

She laughed. "Help me? After all the trouble you have caused? No, no. And I do not see why you are so cool. You have walked into a place where there is no escape. See, I have a gun. And I will have revenge."

"But I threw that man out of your hotel room," Marianne said. "I do not understand! Perhaps you cannot thank me, but you surely cannot blame me." Simeon and Marianne backed up the alley until they were against the wall, with the door now to their left, hidden in shadows. Anna came up close until she was only four feet away. A shot at this distance, Marianne thought with bile in her throat, would do a great deal of mess.

"You did, yes," Anna said. "But you know about me, and Price, and George, and you have exposed me here, to them, you see. I do not think you even realise what you have done! Now I must start again. I have some money, still, but I wanted to stay in London. London is freedom for me. But now *they* have found me, and I must go, before they make me go back. Hence I wear the disguise. But before I leave, I want you to die. I am not as cool as you English women. I have a *heart*. And it is broken."

"If you wanted us to die, you would have done it by now," Marianne said. "You're talking so that you don't have to act. You've never shot a person in your life." She hoped she was right. Anna had a determined glint in her eye and a desperate person was an unpredictable one. And Marianne realised that if Anna pulled the trigger, she would not have time to dive sideways through the door.

She'd be dead.

She needed a distraction.

Anna provided the opportunity. Marianne let her hand twitch toward her handbag. "Put your hands in the air," Anna shouted, remembering suddenly what Marianne kept in there. Marianne put her hands up high.

"But I…" said Simeon.

"Do it," Marianne said firmly. "Do exactly as she says." She shifted her weight. She called to mind everything that the old gardener had ever taught her, in those summer days, tumbling on the lawn with Phoebe like a couple of reckless tearaway boys.

Hesitantly, Simeon began to raise his hands.

"All the way up," Marianne said.

"Whose side are you on?" he muttered, and even Anna gave her a curious look, her attention already wavering. She took one step back, readying herself to shoot, although the muzzle of the pistol swung from one to the other. She obviously couldn't decide who to kill first.

There was the tiniest of clicks, and the bunch of flowers shot up from Simeon's cuff. The moment of surprise was all Marianne needed. She dived forward, not sideways, with no time to grab her own gun. She went in under Anna's upraised arm and slid around her, so that she was clasping Anna from behind. Marianne's right arm grabbed Anna's, and hauled her hand down, digging her fingers into the soft space between the tendons on the inside of Anna's wrist. It worked better with nails exposed, not gloved hands, but the pressure was enough to make Anna drop the gun.

Anna struggled and squirmed and screamed as Marianne rocked backwards and then went forwards, the same direction that Anna was trying to go in, adding her own force to Anna's.

They fell forward to the ground in a tangle, a classic move, and Marianne squashed down with all her weight.

Simeon had recovered the pistol from the ground and now he held it, his hands shaking, pointing at Anna. She twisted her head and stared up at him. Her head cloth was shaken loose and her blonde curls tumbled around her dirty, scuffed face.

"Shoot me then! Shoot me! For what else do I have to live for?"

"Go and call for the police," Marianne said. "He won't shoot you."

"I know that he won't – look at him! I bet he cannot kill a beetle." And while Anna spoke, she took Marianne by surprise, spinning over beneath her. Marianne lost her balance and went to the right, and Anna jumped up to her feet, hunching like a spider, before running off down the alley and her freedom.

She knew that Simeon could not shoot her in the back.

They watched Anna go.

"She is injured," Marianne said. "Injured and angry. What do we do about her now?"

"We have her gun. And are you injured?"

"No, just shaken." Marianne felt icy-cold all over, and when she looked down, she was surprised to see that her hands were trembling. "I'm just realising what happened," she said, "and I think I need to sit down."

"Let's get back to mine. I have gin," he said. "I find that it makes everything all right."

Twenty-two

Marianne was only slightly tipsy when she got back to Woodfurlong. First she checked on her father. Mrs Crouch assured her that he had slept well, and was relatively lucid in his waking moments. She peeped in on him, and could not see anything but a huge pile of blankets, slowly rising and falling in time with gentle snores. She retreated quietly.

Then she went to find Phoebe.

She found her cousin in the drawing room, taking tea with the local vicar's wife, and agreeing to help out at all manner of upcoming events and charity drives. Mrs Forster was a force of nature in the unswaying service of the Lord, and tended not to hear the word "no." Phoebe looked relieved when Marianne entered, and she sprang to her feet.

"Ah! Marianne! How is Gertie?"

Gertrude was perfectly fine, as far as Marianne knew. She raised her eyebrows. "Er – do you want me to go and check on her?"

"I thought that you had been in the nursery. You know, what with her *fever* and *everything* this morning. I ought to go and see myself, but as I have company..."

"Oh!" cried Mrs Forster. "The poor lamb. You should have said. Might we say a little prayer for the innocent mite?"

The three of them bowed their heads and Mrs Forster kept it mercifully short before apologising again and retreating from the room.

"Why didn't you use that excuse at the start?" Marianne said as Phoebe flung herself back into the chair with a sigh.

"I didn't think of it until I saw you. Your face reminded me of séances and fake mediums and lies, and it just came to me. Huh. Maybe you are a bad moral influence after all."

"I am not! Who says that?"

"Oh, no one, no one. Don't worry about it. If anyone did say it, which they don't, they would be wrong, but of course it doesn't matter, because no one does say it. What's that in your hands?"

"Letters." Marianne collapsed into the other armchair.

"You smell of gin."

"Yes. I have been drinking gin. So would you, if you had had the morning that I have had."

"What, worse than conversation with Mrs Forster? I am to do the flowers for the third Sunday next month. I can't think why I agreed to that. You must help me."

"Unless Mrs Forster has taken to waving a gun at you, I have decidedly had the worst morning." Marianne told her cousin everything, and Phoebe grew more and more alarmed.

"I have a feeling that I want some gin myself," she said. "Oh my goodness. She will come back for you, you know, this Anna. She sounds unhinged. She will soon discover where you live. This is what Price was so worried about, you know."

"I beg your pardon? He was worried about random foreign women attempting to shoot me?"

"No, I mean, he thought that once your business became known, people might come to the house. We had a discussion about it. I took your side, of course, but he was not happy. I hate to say it, but perhaps you ought to think of taking premises in London?"

"My finances hardly run to that. Not yet."

"But George Bartholomew gave you a great deal of money, didn't he?" Phoebe said. "I know that you chafe being here – don't deny it to spare my feelings! You insult me to suggest that I don't notice. You will leave, one day. I am surprised that you haven't already. I'll miss you, of course. And don't you have more money to come once you give that evidence to his solicitor? When do you plan on doing that? Why have you not done so already? I should love to come along when you do it."

"Tomorrow, I think." It was always tomorrow. She'd promised herself that for a few days now, but circumstances kept intervening. "I want to get it over with, it is true. I fear I will be mocked and disbelieved, though." She wanted to sidestep the question of where all her money had gone. It was only a loan to Price, but she wondered, now, if she would ever see it again.

To further distract Phoebe, she fanned the half-dozen letters out. "Anyway," she went on, "Look here. These are all for you."

"Oh! When did they come?"

"They have been appearing, by first and second post, over the past few days. But not here at Woodfurlong. They are actually addressed to the famous and talented medium, Mrs Algernon Carter, and have been delivered to the rented rooms where we

241

performed the séance. The landlord passed them to Simeon, and so I convey them to you. I can guess who sent them even without psychic powers."

Phoebe took the thick folded envelopes and looked at them. "I can also guess. The man calling himself Edgar Bartholomew."

"Wade Walker himself, I am sure of it. Open them."

Every letter was a variation of the same – a plea to Mrs Carter to afford him a private sitting. He heaped praises upon her, calling her an inestimable talent of unique skill. Her privileged position with the spirits, he said, must not be wasted or ignored.

Phoebe read them in growing horror. "Oh the man is obsessed, Marianne! What do we do?"

Marianne smiled. "The thing about gin is this: a certain amount of it can lead to some marvellous ideas. Simeon and I have a plan, Phoebe."

"Oh … let me guess. We will hold another séance?"

"Exactly right!"

"And I didn't even need gin to think it up," Phoebe said. She bit at her lip. "Excited as I am by the prospect of a little more adventure, what exactly is the aim of this?"

"We will work on the assumption that he is Wade Walker, who has killed Edgar Bartholomew and taken his place. And so, by careful revelations, we intend to force him to confess."

"But will this confession have any weight in law? You will have to make him say it all before a policeman or magistrate."

"Ah, as to that, we have not yet worked out the final details," Marianne said airily. "We thought maybe you could do some spirit writing that he could sign, perhaps. We need as much evidence as possible for the police. I am starting to think we need to take out a newspaper advertisement just to make them listen to me. The most important thing at the moment is that you agree. Do you?"

After a fractional hesitation, Phoebe said yes.

"Then you must reply to him, and we will set a date." Marianne clapped her hands. "At once!"

***

There followed a flurry of activity over the next few days. Marianne spent her time shuttling between Simeon's workshop and Woodfurlong, all the time looking over her shoulder, expecting Jack Monahan to appear out of one direction and Anna Jones to descend upon her, fully armed, from another.

She considered – and immediately dismissed – the idea of going to the police about Anna. She wouldn't be believed, of course, and she was concerned that she would get a reputation as a delusional woman. If that happened, they would not believe her when they absolutely had to.

But she was also still concerned for Anna. She wanted to help her, as much as she wanted to avoid being shot by her. She didn't know enough about her past in Prussia, but she was a clever woman in a new city and she clearly wanted to start a new life.

Marianne had to put Anna out of her mind. She was unlikely to ever see her again.

Russell was awake and active once more, and spending much of his time in town, visiting old friends. He had revived some acquaintances when he was engaged in the quests on her

243

behalf to find out about Monahan and Wade Walker, and now he was accepting invitations again. She wondered how long it would last – invariably he would say something to upset someone influential, and there would be a public spat, and he would retreat to lick his wounds.

But while he was up and about, she took the chance wherever possible to travel with him, minimising the time that she was alone, just in case Anna did reappear. At other times, she was accompanied by Emilia, who welcomed the excursions into London. One day, she took Mr Dry, who was the valet to Mr Claverdon but as part of his usual duties he tended to escort Phoebe on her shopping trips if she were heading into London alone. He was a silent and watchful man, and she wondered how much the servants knew about what was going on. Probably more than she or Phoebe realised.

She wanted to ask what they knew about Price Claverdon and Anna, but she didn't dare, in case she put ideas into their heads and started rumours she would not be able to quash.

Marianne had spent most of the few days before the planned escapade away from Woodfurlong. It reminded her a little of her time away up at the college. All her life she'd longed to be somewhere else, away from her father and the fading childhood memories of her mother; away from her glamorous and beautiful cousin; away from the tedious and predictable run of everyday life.

Phoebe, being older, had had her season while Marianne was only just starting college, and was then caught up in a whirl of balls and parties. She had, for a time, forgotten Marianne, and their letters to one another had dwindled. And why not?

244

Marianne would not have such a coming-out, and nor did she want one, or so she assured her father when, from time to time, it occurred to him to ask.

She wanted, she had told him, only a good education and the chance to make her own way in life.

She was not quite of the same class as Phoebe, although it seemed to be more a matter of presentation than blood and birth these days. Marianne went away, into a world of small rooms and gossip and heady excitement and plans for the remaking of society. She went to lectures and talks, to secret meetings and public ones, and thought that perhaps the world with women in it could be different.

Until she had come back to London, and to her shabby childhood home, and hit reality with a thump. Her father was ill. He'd not bothered to hide it from her – what would be the point? He was not one for unnecessary drama. "I shall die," he told her. "Slowly, and in agony. But you know enough now to ease my passing, and I expect you to honour that."

It was a grim request but she promised that she would. She would not watch him suffer.

"Anyway," he had added, "it won't be for a while. And what shall we do while we wait for my death, my learned daughter?"

"Well," she had replied, looking around the room, "we can't stay here."

Her childhood home had fallen into disrepair and neglect while she had been away. Most of the staff had run off, or been dismissed. The old building was too close to the rookeries in London which had all been pulled down. Only a few twisted filthy streets remained, and their family home was not far from the planned redevelopments. It made sense to sell up and get gone.

Phoebe, by this time, had had her whirlwind romance, and fallen in love with Price Claverdon – a much older man, a sedate man, a respectable man of business.

Marianne laughed at the memory. So he had seemed to her – back then!

And now what was he to do? He was all tied up with Anna and the blackmail, and respectable no more – at least under the surface. Marianne thought that there was one consolation in that Anna would not be demanding any more money from him. That was a comfort.

A chill ran down Marianne's spine, then.

She had missed something very obvious. She was sure of it.

She stood in the centre of her day room at Woodfurlong, and it seemed to darken all around her. She had come back late in the evening, and it was the day before the planned escapade. She had intended to have a quiet night, skipping the evening meal in public, and spending it instead privately in her room. She'd already spoken with Mrs Cogwell who promised her "an internal picnic."

Anna wanted to harm Marianne. Maybe she would stop her mission, and flee London – that would be the sensible option, especially now that she had revealed her intentions to Marianne. She must know, Marianne thought, that now Anna had shown her hand, Marianne would be on guard. Marianne had ensured she had taken precautions by not being alone, and always being armed, and surely Anna would expect that. A second attempt on her life would be difficult, if not impossible. It would certainly be ill-advised.

There was another thing that was only just occurring to her. Anna's source of income was through Price. Perhaps it was an affair and perhaps it was blackmail. Marianne could see that it was likely to be a mixture of both. So what would Anna do now?

She might go back to Price for one last meeting.

And then?

She could try to tell Price about Marianne but there was nothing there that could be used as a threat. She could demand more money. She could threaten to expose Price, of course.

And that would be the act of a spiteful woman who was leaving London. She could expose Price, and so ruin Phoebe, and by association Marianne and her father. The scandal would see him dismissed. He had debts, run up from small and shady banks – he had told her so. What would happen to Woodfurlong? It would be sold. Where would they go? They would be broken up.

If Marianne had no one to look after but herself, she knew that she would survive. She could turn her hand, she thought, to anything. But she had been in this house for so long, that it wasn't just her father that she felt a responsibility for. What about Phoebe's children? Gertie had been promised a pony. Charlie would be ready for school soon. And the staff, too – dear, honest, lively Emilia, where would she go? Mrs Cogwell and many of the others would find good positions, but they had been together for years.

Marianne clenched her fists. Anna Jones was out there, and she was planning something.

She wished she could ask Jack Monahan for help. He was rough, rude and immoral. Someone like him would know exactly what to do.

Twenty-three

But there was no Jack, and she could not confide in Phoebe, so she resolved to face this alone. Simeon was hard at work preparing for the next day. No doubt he'd work the night through in a frenzy, and then sleep until midday.

She took up her large notebook and sat at her desk. Her priority had to be the upcoming fake séance to entrap Wade Walker and force him to confess to killing Edgar Bartholomew. She had to admit that she was far more interested in why he had done it, and where the body was now. If they could unearth those facts, then they didn't need to reveal themselves at all. They could continue the pretence, and then take the knowledge to the police. A body and a timeline would have to be enough to convict him, she was sure. But if they ignored her? Well, at least she would know the truth and she would have to be happy with that.

After that, she would take the evidence to the solicitor and collect the rest of the money.

Then she would speak to Price Claverdon, and inform him that no more money would be coming to him, and ask him what he was intending to do. If Anna had fled, she would not be asking him for anything else, anyway. No more blackmail. That would be an end to that, and Marianne barely need do anything. It should resolve itself.

Marianne tapped the pen on the paper and left a smudge. If. *If* Anna had fled.

If Anna returned to Claverdon, there was nothing Marianne could do about that.

If Anna came after Marianne – she would have to be on her guard. She would need to be prepared to shoot her, just lightly, enough to wound her and keep her down while she was arrested.

And that would be an end of *that*.

She drew a line across the cream paper.

But there was one more untied end. This was the matter of Jack Monahan, and his apparent investigation into her cousin-in-law. He was not working for anyone, unless he really was telling the truth about his employment with the government.

Would his probing cease with the disappearance of Anna? What did Monahan really know about Anna? Was Monahan interested in the affair and blackmail, or something else?

Was he really on the side of the government or was he an independent agent ... or a foreign spy?

Prussia, she wrote. Junkers. Trade.

She drew a large question mark, and then scribbled it out, angrily.

She closed the book and sighed. She knew already that she was in for a sleepless night.

***

They had planned for everything. The next morning, at breakfast, as Claverdon rustled his papers and sucked his kedgeree down slowly, Phoebe began the first attack.

"Price, darling, don't forget that I won't be dining at home tonight."

"Mmph?" He barely looked up.

"Don't you remember? Marianne has invited me to that talk about birds."

"Birds?"

"By the Fur and Feather League. Eliza Phillips is lecturing against the importation of exotic plumages. Have you read her pamphlets? She is most convincing."

"No, I have not. I thought they were only for women."

"It is not women who are shooting these birds, though it is us women who are wearing them."

"Well, I am not shooting nor wearing them." Claverdon flicked to the next page of the large and unwieldy newspaper. "I shan't be coming."

"You can't, anyway. It is not open to men."

"Huh."

He seemed completely unconcerned, and that was exactly what they wanted. "So I shall be out all evening, and we will not return until late. Marianne will be with me the whole time. I shall ask Mr Barrington to arrange for someone to meet us at the station when we return. Perhaps Wright will wait for us."

"Good, good. You do as you wish, my dear." He was absorbed in the financial section of the paper, and he was frowning. Phoebe and Marianne fell into silence, their work done for the moment.

***

251

"I cannot settle," Phoebe complained.

She was pacing around in the fern-filled glass-walled room on the south side of the house. All the large windows had been opened, but it was still humid and cloying. She prowled among the fronds, peering at the exotic blooms without really seeing them.

Marianne stood by the open door, looking over the patio. It had a low stone wall and was ranged along with urns that had cascading purple and blue flowers – lobelia, campanula, and periwinkle. Fletcher the gardener might not allow roses into his garden but he had a fine eye for flowers.

"We will leave soon. We cannot go too early and arouse your husband's suspicion."

"Oh, nonsense! He will not notice a thing. I don't understand why he is hanging around at home, anyway. He ought to be in London, doing … whatever it is that he does. Making money. But have you noticed, Marianne, he is at home an awful lot these days?"

"I think he concentrates better in his quiet study."

"Do you think so?" Phoebe turned a corner and came up alongside Marianne. "No, that is not it. He must have been dismissed from his job, and simply cannot find the courage to tell me."

"Oh Phoebe, you cannot think that. Your imagination is wild."

"Well, what else could it be, then? It is that or … or … the unthinkable."

"Which is?"

"You know. Do not make me spell it out. I have spoken

with Emilia about this and asked her to look for evidence. I think that Price might be ... he might have fallen out of love with me."

Marianne put her arm around Phoebe. "I am sure that he is as devoted to you as he has ever been, and he is simply tied up with difficult business decisions at the moment. If I suspected anything different, dear cuz, I would tell you immediately."

Phoebe squeezed her back, and Marianne vowed to confront Claverdon the very next day, and wave a gun in his face if she had to.

"Come on. Let us go. It will be better if we are active and Simeon will need our help," Marianne said. "And we mustn't forget to buy that tambourine on the way."

***

They walked to the station in the pleasant early afternoon, carrying bags containing clothes for the evening, and took the train – first class this time, of course – to London. From there it was a short walk to Simeon's workshop, but they had to detour to take in a music shop.

"I'll wait out here with the bags," Marianne said. Phoebe dropped her large carpet bag on the cleanest section of pavement that she could see, and Marianne put hers on top. Phoebe disappeared into the busy shop, and Marianne put her back to the wall, looking around, on guard for pickpockets, and she immediately felt uneasy.

Anna could not possibly try anything out here, in the open, on such a crowded street, she told herself. She was safer here than almost anywhere else, really.

But it was not the presence of Anna Jones which had raised

up the hairs on the back of her neck. The mass of men, in their checks and their tweeds and their plaids, their bright dandy jackets and the ones in their workmen's browns, and the sober men in black and grey, parted. A dark blue top hat was heading her way.

"Mr Monahan," she said, and felt for her handbag swinging from her arm.

"Miss Starr. I appreciate that we may have parted under uncertain terms…"

"I was fairly certain that you were ransacking my cousin's house, so no, it was not uncertain. I *certainly* do not wish to ever speak to you again."

"Oh, come now, don't be so petulant about it. It was not a ransacking. How you exaggerate! I did not disturb a thing. I was merely investigating, and you cannot be sniffy about that. It's your job, too. If you spent a little more time investigating what was right under your nose, and less time worrying about dead men, you'd understand."

"Who are you really, Jack Monahan?"

He folded his arms and grinned down at her. "Who do you want me to me, Miss Starr? I'll be whoever takes your fancy."

"Nothing about you takes my fancy and I don't appreciate these crude attempts at flirting. It makes me feel quite ill. What do you want? No, why am I even asking you that? We have nothing to do or say to one another."

"Are you sure?"

"Yes. You wanted to use me to gain access to the house, and nothing more. The rest was a ruse. You used me. You got what you wanted. There is no partnership, nothing, and I for one am glad about that. I do not care that you have taken me in, sir, and hoodwinked me. I only care that it is over, and I should not be so careless again. I have learned my lesson."

"You are a hard woman to crack, Miss Starr."

"I have no intention of being cracked." Such an unfortunate phrase sounded dreadfully impolite to her. He was jesting with her, and she did not like it. "What do you want with me now? Why are you still following me? You cannot deny it. There is too much coincidence with your presence here."

He let his grin fade, and he nodded. "I was hoping to have a gentle and civil conversation with you, but I can see that it won't do. Well, then, I have come to give you a warning."

She rolled her eyes at him, as dramatically as she could. It was rude and uncouth of her. She did not care; he did not deserve anything more.

"I cannot think what you are warning me of now, unless it is to avoid footpads and rakes."

"Of course you must avoid such people. I do. No, I am come to warn you to keep your father clear of me."

"My father?"

"Yes. Your daft old sod of a father is running around London in a frenzy, digging up my name in every corner that he can, and he has roped in some old friends of his, too, who still seem to think that he means something. They are, apparently, tasked with 'putting the frighteners' on me, though how they intend to do that, I do not know – they cannot even find me."

Marianne hoped that her shock did not show on her face. She had no idea that her father was doing such a thing. "What my father does is up to him," she said. "And I would suggest that if you have nothing to hide, then you have nothing to fear."

"No one ever believe that old lie. I won't discuss this with you, Miss Starr. There is nothing to debate. Simply inform your old man that he needs to be careful. He has literally no idea what he is messing with."

"I shall let him know. Thank you, and good day." She could not walk off, but she could turn away. She pointedly presented her shoulder to him, and gazed off across the street, tilting her chin to the sky.

He grabbed her elbow and bent low to hiss in her ear. "Listen, you idiot. I will do whatever I need to do to protect my reputation. I have some issues to address in my personal employment, I will admit. No doubt your father has dug up all that gossip. But I will not let anyone jeopardise my position and my future positions. Do you know what I am investigating at the moment?"

"Mr Claverdon?"

"You pretty fool. Him? I am on the trail of the Junkers. With Bismarck gone, we have a new opportunity to trade more freely in Prussia but the gentry out there aren't having it, not one bit. They'll do anything to keep a tight hold on their peasants and their estates."

"That has nothing to do with me, nor with Claverdon." *But it was, wasn't it*, she thought. *The link has been Price Claverdon, all along.*

"What do you think his company does? They are an import and export business. They have negotiated, on behalf of the Crown, some new deals. Von Caprivi is reducing the tariffs for trade, and while that is splendid news for us here, the old guard over there are having fits about it."

"Fits?"

"And by fits, I mean, some of them are angry enough to be moved to violence."

"Junkers," she said slowly. "Prussia. Oh." *Anna Jones*, she thought. *And there was that man in the unfamiliar uniform, and the strange language that they had spoken.* "Oh," she said again. "But my cousin-in-law is not a spy."

"Of course he isn't. But he's got himself tangled up with one."

"Anna Jones."

"That will not be her real name."

"But what would that be to you?" she asked. "You work for no one and don't give me that nonsense about working for the government for we got no whiff of that at all."

"I do."

"You do not."

He stared at her. She stared back, defiant. He would not take her for a fool. She had had enough.

Finally, he said, "Well, then. I promise you that when I worked for Lord Hazelstone, I was indeed on the government's business, indirectly, in hunting out the leaks from Harker and Bow to the more militant Junkers. I had to get into your house. But that went wrong and my methods were clumsy. And Lord Hazelstone is a proud man and we had words, and I did not hold my tongue as I ought to have done, and I was dismissed. I know that he is too proud to apologise and I do not wish it. But if I can continue with my task and bring him the information that he wanted, he is sure to give me my old position back."

"That's it?" she said, incredulous.

"I have told you the truth, and still you want more?" he snapped, and she could see that he was very irritated.

"Why not get employment elsewhere?" she said. "Why put yourself through all this?"

"What else am I to do?"

He looked like a lost boy. She did not laugh but she wanted to. He had struck her before as an odd mix of confidence and awkwardness, and now she saw all the confidence was an act. He was like a slightly more successful version of Simeon. Were all men just pretending to be confident and in charge, she wondered. What does that bode for us? They may as well allow women into power, if it's all a façade anyway.

Then she thought of other men, who were so confident in their own abilities that they couldn't imagine ever being unsure of something. That was how Monahan wanted to be. Poor man, she thought. He just wants someone to tell him what to do. He's running along in the same groove like an automaton because yes – as he says – what else is he to do?

"So you are seeking out Anna Jones," she said.

"Yes. I am on her trail, though it seems to have gone recently cold. You brought her to my attention. Do you know anything about where she might be?"

"Yes, she … she is probably injured," Marianne said with an awkward laugh.

"What? What happened?" There was a note of concern in his voice. She flattered herself that it might be for her.

"She is somewhat upset with me. She came at me with a gun, but we – ah, I was with my friend – we evaded her and she was injured in the fracas. She fled, and if she has any sense, she will have left London by now. And it is not only yourself who is pursuing her. There are rough men, soldiers, who speak her language, who also seek her out."

"They are not rough men at all. Those are the younger sons of the landed gentry in Prussia, who end up as officers, just as they do here."

"Like you?"

"My past is blissfully straightforward, and nothing to do with you nor our current situation. So, the Junkers want her too, do they?"

"Yes. I chased one of them off. Listen, will you tell me a little more about something else? Will you be honest?"

He winced briefly. "I shall try. It depends on what it is."

She glared at him. "Other people don't need to concentrate when they are trying to be honest, you know. Anyway my question is not about you. Were Claverdon and Anna engaged in ... criminal conversation?"

He blurted out a laugh. "Good heavens, those two? Can you really think that? Of course not. He's a silly fool and his head was turned by that pretty face but it only went as far as giving her business secrets – business secrets that not only have the potential to damage Harker and Bow, but the government too, and that is why I was initially involved. Her Majesty and the Prime Minister are very keen to make the most of potential new trade deals in Prussia. He has put that in jeopardy. She was blackmailing him, of course. But that is all."

She lapsed into a thoughtful silence. She was relieved. She wanted to tell herself that she'd known it all along.

"Has Anna approached Claverdon again, do you know?" he asked, out of the blue.

She felt an uncomfortable prickling on her skin. The street noise rose and fell, like waves, obscuring and revealing. "I don't think so. I hope that it's the last we've seen of her. She's brought too much strife to the household. Poor Phoebe…"

"Does she know about Anna?"

"She knows nothing. And I will ensure that it stays that way."

Jack sighed. He looked around, and said, "What do you intend to do now?"

"Apart from intending to avoid you, and also to avoid being shot again by Anna, and get my money from Bartholomew's solicitor, and rebuild my good name and my business? Oh, I imagine I shall have leisurely afternoons of high tea in the sun, and spend all my evening playing cards and the piano."

He grunted, and didn't even bother to bid her good day. He stepped out into the swirl of the passing crowd and was soon lost to view.

"Who has approached my husband? Who is Anna? Who has brought strife to the household? Poor Phoebe? *Poor Phoebe*?"

Marianne went utterly cold, and then hot. She took a deep breath and turned around to face her cousin.

Phoebe stood behind her, clutching a brown paper bag, and her face was white and pinched. "I don't care that you were talking to Monahan even after we agreed he was to be avoided. I am not sure that I care that Price is having a clandestine relationship with another woman. I had suspected as much. Did I not say? Did I not *ask you* about it?" She drew herself up stiffly and seemed to grow another two inches. "But you lied to me! I asked you and you lied to me, Marianne! You denied it – and yet here you are, speaking to that man about it!"

"Phoebe, not here – let's not make a scene. I can explain everything, but you won't like it. It is not quite what you think it is. Mr Claverdon is not unfaithful. Come – let us step into a tea shop, or even better, wait until we get to Simeon's where I can…"

Phoebe thrust the wrapped tambourine at Marianne, catching her hard in the belly. "Do you really think I am going to Simeon's, now, after this? I need to go home! I need to sort this out."

"There is nothing to sort out – please, don't go to your husband until I've told you what's going on. You will make things worse."

"The time for you to tell me anything has passed. You have had your chance. And his name is Price. Price! You can say Price, can't you? Not Mr Claverdon, not your husband. For god's sake, Marianne, we have lived under the same roof for years! Are you really so bitter and dried-up and spiteful that you can't even accept him? You have hidden this, to destroy our happiness! I have nothing more to say to you. Nothing."

She spun around and half-ran away. People looked at them, without disguising their amusement and curiosity. Marianne stretched up on her tip-toes and called, "Phoebe! Come back!"

But she did not come back and Marianne had known, before she shouted, that she wouldn't.

Twenty-four

There were four hours before the séance was supposed to begin. She could follow Phoebe, waste time persuading her to carry on with the deception, drag her back to Simeon's workshop, go over to the rented rooms ... yes, there was time to do all that.

If Marianne could convince Phoebe, that was.

Of course I can, she thought crossly. *But honestly – do I need her? I've always coped.*

She tossed her head to no one in particular, and set out at a very brisk pace in the opposite direction to the way Phoebe had gone.

Simeon, naturally, was horrified when Marianne arrived alone, and told him what was happening.

"That's it!" he said. He stood in the middle of his workshop, dressed in the sober black and white of a middle-ranking house servant, and flung his hat dramatically across the room. It landed on a cage and made a bird flutter and squawk in protest. "The séance is cancelled. It cannot go on tonight."

"Nonsense," said Marianne. "Look, we still bought the tambourine." She shook it at him. "*I* shall dress as Mrs Carter. I watched what Emilia did to make Phoebe look older. Anyway, it will be dark! Even you could play the part, Simeon."

"And who will hide and perform the tricks? I am to wait at the door; I'm the loyal servant."

"I can perform the tricks as well. It does not take two. Look, this is just how the fakers do it, isn't it? I can slip off my shoes – watch." She sat down and pulled off her shoe, and tried to pick up the tambourine from the floor. Her stockings prevented her toes from curling around the edge. "Well, you can see how it would work if I divest myself of a few more layers," she said, and shoved her shoe back onto her foot. "The tambourine is only for atmosphere, anyway. I can tip the table a little, moan, that sort of thing. If you are inside the room, and we have the room completely dark, you can do a little too. Aren't you the expert in cunning? Treat it like a stage show. Let us make a wax hand!"

"He will meet you in the light, first, and he will not be convinced by your disguise."

"Hush. Where is the black gown that Phoebe wore? Ah, I see it." She picked it up from the back of a chair and slipped into the workshop's other room. She continued to talk as she struggled out of her own clothes and into the plain and dusty cotton and linen that "Mrs Carter" had worn.

"Anyway, this is just like it is at Woodfurlong. Everyone thinks that Phoebe is essential to the running of things. She gathers all the praise at dinner parties for being the most excellent hostess. But it is I who manages things. Oh, she chooses the menu with Mrs Cogwell, and she meets with the housekeeper every day, but who is it that the servants come to when there is a problem? Who knows more about the children – she, or I? I do. You shall see, Simeon, that I can cope with anything, and I keep things running just so. Ah! Here we are. Thank goodness this fastens at the front. I will need a shawl this time, I think…"

She re-emerged into the main workshop again, and Simeon started to laugh, with a slither of panic running through his giggles. "You need more than a shawl. I have a burlap sack you might use. For your face."

She pulled at the badly-closed front of the gown. "Nonsense. This is fine. It will not show. Alas, I am taller than my cousin."

"And stouter."

"I think not! Now, on to the face paint. A white base, and then powder, greyish, for the creases and the shadows. I will need a looking-glass."

He sighed and brought a large mirror on a swinging stand, setting it on a table opposite a chair. He folded his arms and stepped back, and watched her.

"You are waiting for me to fail," she said, keeping up her litany to stave away her doubts. She perched on the edge of the chair and looked at herself in the mirror, but took care not to meet her own eyes. "I can feel it rolling off you. You think I cannot do this." She stabbed a sponge into a small jar and smeared the sticky stuff over her cheeks. "Do you have a cloth? I might have put a little too much on for the first layer. Emilia has such a light hand."

Wordlessly, he threw a rag over to her, and she caught it. She dabbed at her cheeks, and then started to apply some powder. "I can even do her voice," she said. "I have known her all my life. She is easy enough to copy. Why, once, when we were

265

children, I hid in a corner of the library and when I spoke, pretending to be her, even her own father was convinced!"

"All children sound the same," Simeon said at last. "And all women look different. Oh, Marianne."

She pressed a little more powder into the crease of her eyelids, and sat back. "I shall also wear a veil. I can make up some excuse as to why. Come on. Let us get to the rooms, and get set up."

***

The room was ready. They were planning to keep the whole event very simple. They knew that Wade was there to contact his dead friend. And he was a fervent believer in the spiritual world, so they didn't need the bells and whistles to convince him. There was no need for a show, just a few standard events to reassure him that he was still in the presence of a true medium.

Marianne sat at the table, and spread her fingers over the polished top. It had a thick central pillar and by pressing down at certain places, she could cause it to rock and shift. With her bare foot, she practised picking up the tambourine. "We are early in our preparations," she said. "We still have at least two hours to wait yet." She shook the tambourine and it tumbled from her foot, hitting the floor with a thump. "Oh, the spirits are clumsy. Perhaps I can say a child has thrown it."

"Why? He is not here about a child."

"I could have a child controlling me, a child spirit."

He stared at her.

She had run out of things to say.

She slid her foot back into her shoe.

"I am noticeably taller than Phoebe, aren't I?" she said in an unhappy voice.

He nodded.

"And my voice must be very different as an adult."

He nodded again, sadly.

She put her face into her hands, and spent a moment decidedly refusing to cry. This was all a terrible mess, but it could still, yet, be redeemed.

"Why am I sitting here when my best friend of all time is at home, distraught and upset about her marriage?" she cried at last, feeling sick and ashamed. She jumped up. Her right foot, stockingless in the shoe, was cold. Her whole body was hot, then freezing.

"We can cancel it. I will stay here, and tell him that you were taken ill, suddenly, but we can reschedule the séance. I will send a note," Simeon said.

"No, wait. Don't send a note. I have time to get to Woodfurlong and bring her back. I will! But yes, if we are not back before he arrives, then tell him of Mrs Carter's sudden illness."

She ran out of the room, holding onto her shawl with one hand, ignoring her horribly cold ankle, and headed for the nearest railway station.

***

She knew that she looked quite a sight as she fled down the street. Her painted face would look dreadful out in the fading afternoon light, and her rough black dress would mark her as some kind of poor widow. She resolutely did not look at anyone,

267

though she could feel the curious eyes of onlookers on her.

She did not look behind herself, either. She had the feeling, as usual, that she was being followed, but she was almost used to it, now. If it were Monahan, up to some nefarious purpose that he'd only ever half-tell her, she didn't care. She knew that he would not harm her. If it were Anna, then good luck to her if she wanted to take a shot at Marianne in public. Anna was a clever woman and Marianne did not think that she'd risk her freedom in such a way. Did she not say she loved London? She would find a way to stay, Marianne thought. She couldn't do that if she were swinging from the end of a rope.

The Prussian woman's urge for revenge would surely abate in time.

Marianne shouldered a young woman out of the way and muttered an apology as she passed, shocked at her own actions, but she had no time to lose and certainly no time for social niceties. She joined a queue at the ticket office, jumping from foot to foot in frustration as every single person in front of her seemed to have a complicated travel query. She took the time, here, to look around, hunting for the familiar faces of Anna or Monahan in the crowds in the ticket office, or through the glass doors into the waiting rooms.

There was one person looking towards her, intently, but it was a thickset man who ducked immediately behind a pillar. It was not either of the people she expected to see.

No doubt he was simply startled by her flight through the town, and her rough, scruffy mode of dress. She bought a third-class ticket, and flung herself into the carriage.

She would be at Woodfurlong within twenty minutes, if she

ran when she reached the other end, and then she'd have to convince Phoebe that it had all been a dreadful misunderstanding.

Marianne let her head hang, and it bobbed with the motion of the coach over the track, jumping the points and clattering along the rails. Marianne believed that she could do anything she set her mind to.

But this was going to be a challenge indeed.

***

Marianne slid into the hallway of the house very carefully. She had caught sight of herself in the train windows when it passed by some dark houses, and she now realised why Simeon had been so horrified. She could not explain herself to Mr Barrington or anyone else who might be lurking in the public spaces downstairs. She pressed herself behind a large fern in a Chinese vase that stood nearly as high as she did, and when she caught a glimpse of Emilia passing along the back corridor, she shot out and waylaid her by the green baize door.

Emilia took two seconds to recognise her. "Oh my!"

"Hush. Let us go somewhere private."

Emilia pulled her through the door and into a storeroom near to the housekeeper's day room. She stayed by the door, and Marianne kept her voice low. "First of all, has your mistress come home?"

"Yes, and she is locked in her bedroom, crying. I have been unable to gain entry. What has happened? I was on my way to speak to Mrs Kenwigs about what to do."

"Don't trouble the housekeeper with this. What about Mr Claverdon? Is he at home?"

"No, miss. He has not been seen since mid-afternoon. After you and Mrs Claverdon left, he put his outside coat on, and went into town himself."

"Who else has seen Mrs Claverdon come home?"

"I don't know. Possibly only me. What is the matter with her? What can we do?"

"Just leave it to me," Marianne said. "I can tell you that she is not hurt, and that Mr Claverdon is definitely not having an affair. Come on, let's go up to her room. Go ahead of me. I cannot be seen like this."

"Why are you like this? You are wearing her fake outfit."

"I was trying to copy your art of disguise."

"Oh! Oh," Emilia said. "Oh dear."

They made it to the corridor of bedrooms without incident. Marianne rattled the door handle. "Phoebe! Let me in. I will tell you everything, and I have proof, too!"

Something hit the back of the door and broke.

"Phoebe! Please. You will understand, I promise…"

Something else hit the door, with a dull thud this time.

"I shall come in regardless," she warned.

A glass shattered.

"Right. Watch the corridor, Emilia." Marianne fished the lock-picking set out of her bag, and pulled out a ring of skeleton keys. Emilia's mouth dropped open.

"But how?"

"Oh, that's easy. Domestic doors don't need to be very complicated, as they are more for privacy than security. So they use warded locks, which are the easiest to pick. As long as my master key has the right shape at the very end, it will open. No,

270

not this one. Nor this. Ah! You see? There are only so many shapes it could be."

"No, I meant, how do you know how to do this?"

"Ah. Simeon taught me." Marianne stood up and put the keys back into her bag. She knocked again, and said loudly, "Phoebe, I have picked your lock and I'm coming in — please don't throw anything sharp or heavy at my head."

She inched the door open and was smacked, instead, by a satin-covered bolster. Marianne fended it off with her forearms. "All right! Yes, I deserve a beating, but hold your fire for a few minutes…"

Phoebe was sitting on her bed, clutching another pillow. Her face was stained and streaked with tears. "How could you?"

"He is not having an affair. He is not."

"Why did you lie to me?"

"I … didn't want to hurt you."

"Well done. What an excellent job you have made of it."

"Oh, Phoebe." Marianne approached her carefully, like she was a nervous young horse. "I will start at the beginning and tell you absolutely everything, although it won't paint your husband … sorry, Price … in a very good light. He has been foolish, and easily led, but he has not been unfaithful. And I will have to speak quickly so we can get back and do the séance."

Phoebe snorted, but she did at least listen to everything that Marianne had to say. Her face crumpled when Marianne first mentioned his weakness in giving business secrets to Anna, and she cried when she heard about the blackmail.

But she had dried her face and was sitting upright by the time that Marianne had finished.

271

"So, doesn't that sound more like the Price Claverdon that you know and love?" Marianne said.

"Have you a shred of proof for any of this?"

"Yes. Come to my room and I'll show you my notebooks."

"You could have doctored them and amended the dates."

Marianne sighed. "Come and see."

When confronted with the handwritten notes that Marianne had made over the past few weeks, Phoebe's acceptance grew.

Their final stop was Claverdon's study. They looked at the ledger on his desk. Neither of them could understand most of it, written as it was in abbreviations and shorthand. But some payments stood out – the ones made to "AJ".

"Anna Jones," Marianne said. "You see? And she was linked to George Bartholomew, too, and now she has vowed revenge upon me."

Phoebe looked around the room. "This has always been a secret, private sanctuary for Price," she said. "I feel like I ought not to be here. But … look. He has been drinking."

"Is that not what men do in their studies?" But Marianne understood Phoebe's concern. There were half a dozen empty bottles of whisky and brandy, and torn-up papers, and broken cigars strewn over the table by the dead fire. Books were piled haphazardly on the floor. This was not the calm, peaceful abode of a man happy with his lot.

"This is the room of a man who is having trouble with his business," Marianne said firmly. "It is certainly not the room of a man having an affair."

Phoebe nodded. "I could never really believe it," she said. "And I do not know if I can ever truly forgive you for lying."

272

"You have half-forgiven me," Marianne said, "for you have stopped throwing things at me. And I can accept a half-forgiveness. I don't deserve a full one."

"No, you don't. Right. You look terrible. Do we have time to get back to the rooms where Simeon is waiting for us?"

"We might. It will be down to the luck of the trains. Shall we try it?"

"Let's."

They ran. Marianne felt more confident with Phoebe by her side. They leaped onto a train, and Phoebe muscled them into first class, in spite of Marianne's poor state. "Let a woman mourn!" Phoebe snapped at a man who looked askance at them, and he scurried away, shame-faced.

Then it was a mad dash at the other end, through the streets of London, and Marianne looked behind only once.

A small, stout man turned away and she did not see his face.

Twenty-five

Simeon met them in the hallway, alerted by the clatter of the door. He hustled them upstairs and said, "He will be here within fifteen minutes! And he was early last time."

"Then leave the room so that we might change," Phoebe instructed.

His face flushed red, and he left. Marianne ripped a seam in her efforts to get out of the dress, and then realised she had forgotten to bring the plain white dress to wear in the cupboard. She only had her own gown to get back into, which was pale pink and done about with ribbons, one of Emilia's indulgences. "This will be ruined when I get into the cupboard!"

"Then you will have to buy a new dress. Hurry! Can you do my face? I mean to say – can you do it better than you have done your own?"

"Yes, for now I have had practise."

Marianne made a reasonable job of it, but not as expertly as Emilia had done. "We should have asked her," she grumbled.

"I have exposed her to compromise once, but that is well enough," Phoebe said. "Let me see." Marianne passed her a glass. "Oh. Well, I shall say that I have had the influenza."

"Was that a knock?"

They froze.

Simeon rapped on the door and called through, "He is here. Are you ready?"

"We are."

"To your places! I shall bring him up directly."

Marianne squeezed into the sideboard. She had to fold herself down, and shuffle in backwards. The voluminous dresses and skirts hampered her, and she had to drag in the fabric bit by bit. She did not wear the huge bustle favoured by fashionable ladies, but she was surprised at how much she had to fold around herself. "I should take this off and squat here in my underclothes," she muttered.

"You will do no such thing!" Phoebe said in horror as she took her place at the table. "What would people say?"

"Because hiding in a cupboard is perfectly fine as long as you are dressed correctly?"

"Close the door behind you."

Marianne did. She sank into the fusty darkness, and stuck her tongue out in the direction of Phoebe.

"I know that you are pulling faces at me, even if I cannot see you."

Marianne did not dare to mutter a reply back. She could hear the distant voices of Simeon and Wade – who, in her head, was still Edgar Bartholomew. He would remain so, she thought, until they had actual clear proof. There was still a chance this was all a dreadful mistake. Dyed grey hair and a mad son dead of oysters – it could be so.

She strained her ears to here. Someone had raised their

voice. She thought it was Simeon, but it was difficult to tell. Was he shouting? Then the voices faded. She held her breath.

The door opened and she heard the scrape of a chair. Phoebe must have stood up. There were the usual greetings. Phoebe addressed him as "Mr Bartholomew", and invited him to take a seat.

"Would you like any refreshments?"

"No, no. I would like to get straight on with things, if I may. Thank you once again, Mrs Carter. I have high hopes for this."

So do we, thought Marianne.

"Simeon, would you dim the lights, please?"

There was a rustling, and footsteps. The tiny strip of light that marked a gap between the door and the cupboard's side went out. He would have lit a candle, but that was all.

"Take my hands, please. Simeon, will you wait outside? Thank you."

There followed a period of silence. Phoebe had been told to wait until the candle blew out. They had rigged it, of course. The candle had been put on a small table by the far wall, near to a large and ugly oil painting. The painting concealed a hole in the wall which had been made for the purposes of a gas pipe during the renovations to the building. No pipe had yet been fitted, and it was easy work for Simeon to stand on the other side of the wall, poke his finger through to shift the painting to the side, and blow the candle out.

She heard Bartholomew mutter in surprise, and she guessed that it had happened.

Phoebe said, "Sometimes the spirits prefer darkness. Let us wait to see who might appear before we ask our questions."

It was the sign for Marianne to carefully open the door and extend the stick which had the tambourine tied to the end. Everything felt different in the dark. She held it at arm's length, the thin pole waving, and hoped that she had cleared their heads. She didn't want to bop anyone in the dark. Once she judged it to be above the table, she began to rattle it gently.

She heard Bartholomew hiss and draw in a breath.

That was good. Their intention was to unsettle him, and convince him that he really was in the presence of the spirits, without going too far and putting on a show.

She carefully retracted the pole, trying to stop the tambourine from shaking again, and did not dare to breathe again until her hand closed over it, and she was able to silently draw it back into the cupboard.

Phoebe then went into her prepared script. "Ah ... yes. Yes, my control is here." She began to drop her voice and alter the timbre of it. "A man wishes to speak to you."

"Who is it?"

"Wait ... oh. There is something strange. He is unsure. He is confused. He thought that he had come to speak to you but he might have mistaken your identity. He is sorry but he is in the wrong place. He is not here asking to speak to Mr Edgar Bartholomew..." And she fell into silence, and they waited.

Marianne had inched her way back into the cupboard, pausing every other second to try to hold the fabric of her gown so that it didn't make a sound. She was conscious even of her own silent breathing as she waited for someone to speak.

Finally, Bartholomew said, "Edgar? Is that you?"

In a very low voice, Phoebe said, "I cannot tell you until

you confirm who you are. The spirit world is like a mist all around me. I cannot see. Oh, how cold it is here! I am alone and I am scared … who is it that calls me? Who is it that is *using my name?*"

Even Marianne felt the hairs go up on her arms, and she knew that Phoebe was faking it. How much more effective it was, then, for people who expected to hear this sort of thing.

And Bartholomew cried out, "You know me! It is I, Wade, your friend! I have ever been your friend! Do you not know my voice? Oh, Edgar! Oh, God. It wasn't supposed to have happened, not like it did. Tell me, tell me, tell me that you forgive me. It was an accident, by God! And if anyone should have died, then it should have been me – believe me when I say that every day since then has been a torture to me. Oh God! Edgar! Do you forgive me?"

"What happened?" Phoebe blurted out in her normal voice, forgetting in her horror that she was supposed to be speaking as the control spirit, or as the dead man. She hastily dropped her voice again and continued, "What happened? It is a blur. My memories are all mixed together. I was at my house and then I was … lost. I was here. What did you do to me, Wade?"

"Tell me that you are all right! I have been hunting for you all over London. I only want to know that you forgive me." Bartholomew – *no,* Marianne corrected herself, *this really is Wade Walker, just as I suspected* – sounded broken.

"What did you do to me, Wade?" Phoebe repeated.

"Our experiment. You must remember, Edgar, as we had been planning it for so long. It was that experiment to cheat death and discover what really lies beyond the veil. But now you are here, you can tell me! At last we have proof. I will write for the journals! Everything is proved" But it wasn't supposed to be like this. We gave up so much. We gave up society and everything. For it to end in both failure – and yet success! Oh, Wade, have you found your Molly again? Is she there, too?"

"What did you *do*, Wade?"

The silence stretched out. Marianne perched in her cupboard, the door still open, but her hand on the handle ready to retreat. She heard a snapping sound, and thought it might be Wade licking his lips.

But before he could speak, there came a furious banging on the door, and shouting, from two voices – one was Simeon, calling "You cannot enter, sir!"

"By God I shall break down this door. Step aside, you weasel. You're all in it together. Snakes, the lot of you!"

The door was slammed open and light flooded in. Marianne squirmed backwards, and dropped the tambourine as she tried to close the door, trapping her skirts. She had a glimpse of a small, squat man outlined in the doorway, and Simeon launching himself at the man's back as if he were a monkey.

"This is a private séance!" Simeon yelled, trying to strangle the man.

Wade Walker leaped to his feet in alarm, and his first instinct was to rush to Phoebe's side to protect her. "Mrs Carter, have no fear, I shall – wait. Who are you and what the devil are you doing?"

Marianne looked up at him from her tight spot in the cupboard. "Good evening. I'm the maid, doing some cleaning…?"

He grabbed her arm and hauled her out. Her monstrous skirts popped and unfurled at the back like one of Simeon's flower tricks. He held her and said, "Oh – it is you, that dreadful meddler, Miss Starr. Did I not say that you should stay well away from me?"

"I was trying to, but you pulled me out of the cupboard."

"And you're damned cheeky, too!" snarled the stout interloper, still trying to prise Simeon from his back. He was currently smashing him against the wall, and Simeon was crying out with each blow.

This would *not* do. For the umpteenth time in as many days, Marianne pulled her gun from her handbag, and waved it at the intruder. She was getting quite good at it, now. She hoped that she would never have to fire it.

"Simeon! Get off that man. You, sir. Stand still. Who are you?"

Simeon relinquished his grip and slithered to the floor. The man shook himself and put his pudgy hands on his hips. He was dressed very smartly as a man of taste and wealth. He had young, twinkly pale eyes in a pink and white face, and was clean-shaven. And he was looking at Marianne with pure disgust. "Are you really Miss Starr?"

"I am, sir! Who are you?" she asked again.

"I see before me everything that is wrong with the so-called New Woman," he spat out. "There is nothing more ugly than a woman threatening violence. Except perhaps a woman burdened with an education more befitted to a man. This makes you doubly ugly, Miss Starr."

Even Wade Walker protested at the insult, and he had no reason to be kind to Marianne. And she felt sorry for him. She was going to take another scrap of comfort away from the man, and he was a murderer and a fool but he was a decent one for all that, she thought.

She kept her attention, for the moment, on the man in front of her. "Who are you?" she insisted. "This is loaded, and you are an intruder, and I can happily shoot you for burglary."

"I know you. I didn't, at first sight, but I do now. Everyone knows you, Miss Starr, yet you don't know me? You will. My name has been in the press more than yours has, this last month or so. Your star – ha ha! – will fade but mine is rising, and I shall take your place. I am Mr Harry Vane."

She lowered the pistol. "The psychic investigator? Late of Vienna and Paris? *The* Mr Vane? Oh! I have been wishing that we might meet…"

"So that you might learn from a master? That, my dear, can never happen. It is time to clear the arena of silly women playing at science, and put the business of psychic investigation back firmly in the hands of rational men once more."

She brought the gun back up level again, although her arm was getting tired and she could feel a tremor rippling through it. He laughed. "You cannot aim straight," he said. "You have held it out, for too long, too stiffly." He shook his head and looked at Wade Walker. "You see?" He didn't need to add "silly women" but it was there, hanging in the air.

The attention on Wade seemed to wake him from his trance. He looked around at Marianne, at Phoebe, and at Simeon who was standing by the door and rubbing his wrist. "What is going on here? Why were you in the cupboard?" And then he looked back at Phoebe, at her inexpertly painted face, and at the matching paint and powder still smeared over Marianne. He saw the tambourine on the floor, and the pole. "It was all a trick, wasn't it?" His lip twitched.

Marianne lowered the gun again. "Oh, Mr Walker – that is who you are, isn't it? – Mr Walker, I am so sorry. But we needed to get at the truth. And that is the truth. You are Wade Walker, and you killed your best friend Edgar Bartholomew."

"No, no, no," he was saying in a miserable, heart-breaking stream of words. "I am Edgar, I am Edgar…"

"Simeon heard your confession," she said, knowing that his testimony would count for more than hers or Phoebe's. "And we also have scientific proof that you have been dyeing your hair." She shot a dark glance at Vane. "My father did the tests," she added with a sneer. "If that is any help."

Walker hung his head and did not speak.

"We need the police here," she said.

"I have done nothing wrong!" Vane said with a bark.

"This is not about you," Marianne shot back. "For goodness sake, why are you here? Phoebe, would you go and find a policeman?" She did not want to be alone without Simeon present. Phoebe nodded and slipped past them all, and they heard her run down the steps and out into the street. It was not yet very late, and they all walked regular beats. She would find one quickly enough.

"I am here because I have been interested in the reports I heard of a certain Mrs Carter, new to the town," Harry Vane said. "I thought she would be a good person to expose. However my initial observations of her premises revealed certain irregularities, and I grew even more suspicious today when there was a flurry of activity. I followed the mysterious persons and knew that something was amiss. And here I am, and I was right!"

"Ugh," Marianne said. It was all she could think of. What a terrible way to meet one of her heroes, and what a terrible let-down too. She turned away from Vane again. Walker was looking dejected. He had sat down on a chair and slumped forward, broken.

"It is all over, isn't it?" he said in a small voice.

"Yes," she said, as kindly as she could. And then the police arrived.

Twenty-six

Phoebe had used her family name and connections to persuade a higher rank than a mere constable or even Sergeant Giles to come out. Inspector Gladstone was lean, lithe, young and personable. He spoke with a rough Cockney accent. Like so many of the up-and-coming police force, he had clearly been recruited from the streets, and had shown promise which had been rewarded with promotion.

He was assisted by an older constable who was not introduced to them. The constable took notes while Inspector Gladstone addressed Wade Walker first.

Wade hung his head. He muttered, "It is as you have been told."

"No, sir, I need to hear this from your own lips."

"I cannot. I cannot speak of it. But just come along with me, and I shall show you."

"What do you intend to show us, sir?"

"The body of my friend Edgar Bartholomew, which is the man whom I have killed."

Inspector Gladstone nodded as if it were a perfectly normal sentence to hear someone utter. Harry Vane, on the other hand, exploded into a barrage of questions.

"Hold on one minute!" he cried. "This woman here is a fake – a fraud – she is no medium at all! And she is being assisted by someone who claims to expose mediums. There is a crime happening here, right before our eyes!"

"Mrs Claverdon has explained her situation while we came from the stationhouse," the inspector said. "I am aware of the business in which she and her cousin Miss Starr were engaged here and while I do not condone their methods, I am grateful to them and their efforts. Have you any business here at all, sir? Are you a witness?"

"To what? This travesty?"

"No, the murder."

"What murder?"

"Constable, take his details. We will be in touch. Now, Mr …"

"Walker. Wade Walker."

"Mr Walker, will you please lead us on?"

"Certainly."

Harry Vane stared after them in frustration and Marianne knew that she hadn't seen the last of him.

***

"Where is Simeon?" Phoebe hissed to Marianne as they walked, arm in arm, behind Wade Walker. He was flanked by the constable, who was ready at any moment to grab him should he try to flee. Behind them came Inspector Gladstone.

"I was going to ask you that."

"He must have slipped away when the police turned up."

"Silly man. He has nothing to hide, has he?"

"No, not at all. He just gets scared about things. He doesn't like authority."

Phoebe sighed. "He has some demons chasing him, doesn't he? Does he indulge in laudanum?"

"No."

"Maybe he should. Your father does all right by it, doesn't he?"

"Hmm."

It was fully night by now and the air was growing chilly. They began to walk more briskly by a mutual and unspoken agreement.

As soon as a vacant cab of a suitable size passed them, Inspector Gladstone flagged it down and commandeered it for official police use, and their journey passed quickly once they had all wedged themselves together within. It was slightly smelly, but a good deal warmer.

There was a light on in the window of the gatehouse but the cab driver took them right past it and up the driveway. He was ordered to wait while they entered the dark house. The constable accompanied Wade to the back of the house, disappearing down a corridor which seemed to swallow them in shadows while Phoebe, Marianne and Inspector Gladstone stayed by the open door, where at least a little light was provided by the grey clouds and the moon behind them.

The constable returned, carrying a lantern aloft, which filled the hall with shifting yellow and black shapes. All eyes were now on Wade.

"Show us what you need to show us," the inspector ordered.

He hesitated. "No, I cannot – it is not for ladies. They should not have come. I did not think clearly. I feel as if I am in a dream. You know those dreams where you fall and fall and any minute, you expect to hit the ground?"

"Well, they are here now, and they are witnesses, of a sort. Bert, did you see any candles back there? We cannot leave them here in the dark."

"You will not leave us here at all," Marianne said. "I have seen dead bodies, and in some terrible states, too." She thought of George Bartholomew, then, and the sympathy that she had been feeling for Wade evaporated. She pointed a finger at him. "I found your best friend's son, sir, who died in agony at your hand."

"What's this? Another victim? Is this true?"

Wade nodded. "It is true. Oh, I am sorry."

"How did this other man die?"

"By poisoning. White phosphorus, in fact," Marianne said. "And I found the body. So I have no fear of what I am about to see. I am a woman of science," she added. "I have a professional curiosity which overrides my natural feminine instincts and sensitivities."

"I don't," Phoebe muttered, but she followed along anyway.

The constable kept even closer now to Wade as they ascended the main wide staircase. Their footsteps echoed on the uncarpeted floor. The air inside was even colder than it had been outside. Phoebe leaned on Marianne's arm, and she was shivering. "I might wait at a distance," she whispered to Marianne.

Marianne patted her arm.

They passed along a dizzy and disorientating series of

288

corridors, and one narrow flight of stairs at the back of the house, until they were walking along a long gallery with a sloping ceiling. At the far end stood a door that was not quite the height of a fully grown man.

"In there," Wade said in a croak.

"What will we find? Do we need to be prepared?"

"You will find a dead body. There is nothing to harm you – there are no traps, no tricks, no poisons. It is only the final resting place of my dearest friend, and the scene of all our folly."

The constable and the inspector exchanged glances. Then, to the surprise of the constable, the inspector addressed Marianne. "Miss Starr, you seem to have uncommon knowledge about this whole affair. Can we believe what he says, do you think?"

"I think that you can." She dropped Phoebe's arm, and stepped forward along the corridor with Wade and the two policemen, leaving her cousin behind in the gathering shadow. "I have been piecing things together as we drove over here. Mr Walker, you only intended to half-kill Mr Bartholomew, didn't you?"

"Yes, and it was with his consent. We thought that we could trick death, you see, and peek beyond the veil."

"But it went wrong."

"It … did."

"Why did you not report this terrible accident at once?" Inspector Gladstone said. They reached the door, and no one seemed willing to touch the handle.

"I would have done, but I was submerged in grief. And panic. For I had killed him. There is no escaping that fact," Wade

289

said. "But yes, I knew what I had to do. Except … there was another part to our plan."

"Whichever one of you were to die first, then they would contact the other, is that right?" Marianne said. It was a common enough pact among the spiritual crowd.

He nodded, still staring at the door. "This was his house, you know. And he died here. So I knew that he was going to manifest here. That was what we agreed. I had to stay, to wait for his spirit."

"But you didn't expect his son to turn up, did you?" she said. "That changed everything."

"Oh!" said the inspector. "This George Bartholomew that was spoken of?"

"Indeed, the very same," Wade went on with a heavy sigh. "He came in darkness, suddenly, one night, without even sending word. I hid myself in my room and heard him tramping around. I called out, saying that I was sick, and I spent the night sleepless and wondering how to go on."

"A good man would have gone on by telling the truth," the inspector said. "I reckon, however, you did not choose that option."

"I did not. I had to stay here, you see. I had to wait for Edgar to contact me, and I could not let George know what had happened to his father. They were long estranged, anyway, and so as dawn broke I went into town and bought the hair dye. I thought that I might be able to pass myself off as his father, but… he suspected."

"Of course he would!" the inspector scoffed. "Oh, this is a sorry tale. And we are all avoiding the main thing – we must enter this room. Mr Walker, you will go first."

"I?"

"Yes," Inspector Gladstone said very firmly. "Go on with you."

The constable held the lantern high. Wade Walker closed his eyes, and opened the door, but did not proceed over the threshold until the inspector jabbed him roughly between the shoulder-blades.

Walker stepped in, and the constable went in beside him. Marianne and Gladstone followed closely, as much to stay in the lantern's safe embrace as anything else.

"What do you see?" Phoebe called in a small voice from the now-dark corridor.

Marianne looked around. They were in a small room with a sloping ceiling and the windows were papered over. In the middle of the room was a circular table familiar to a thousand séance rooms. There was a curtain across one corner of the room. Two chairs stood either side of the table.

Neither contained a dead body.

"I brought the mediums here, at first," Wade explained. "I thought perhaps he needed an intermediary to make contact with me. But every attempt failed. Until I met Mrs Carter. She, too … oh, Edgar!"

Marianne stepped towards the curtain. The pole passed from wall to wall, making a triangular space behind it. She steeled herself, and took hold of the right hand edge of the curtain.

"Miss Starr…"

She dragged the curtain across.

There was nothing but a very large trunk there.

291

"I assume that he lies within," she said, trying to keep her voice steady as a prickle of cold sweat trickled down her spine.

"He does."

"How did he die?"

"Asphyxiation. We thought that we could stop his breathing for long enough that he was dead, but that I would be able to bring him back again before it was too late and he fully crossed over. But I miscalculated."

"So he is not mutilated or damaged in any way?"

"No, but he has been there now for at least three weeks."

She stepped backwards. "It is a well-sealed trunk."

"Yes, I took care to use bandages soaked in camphor and strong scents. But I would not recommend that the trunk is opened until it is in a safe laboratory space."

She turned to face the others. "I would agree."

"Is that your professional opinion, Miss Starr?" Inspector Gladstone asked.

"Yes."

"Wade Walker, I am arresting you on the suspicion of murder by two counts. One, the murder of Edgar Bartholomew and two, the murder of George Bartholomew." He began to run through some cautions to Wade, regarding what he should or should not say. Wade hung his head, and she could tell that he was crying.

Again she quashed the sympathy that threatened her. He was guilty. The first murder might be accidental, but his killing of George was premeditated and awful. That reminded her of one more thing.

"Why did you poison George with white phosphorus?" she

asked. "You knew what you were doing, didn't you?"

He hung his head. "I did know. I had found it in a jar of water, left behind by one medium who had thought to trick me, and I knew what it was. I was going to throw it away but George was becoming increasingly troublesome. I used it to spike everything he might eat or drink in the kitchen, and then I threw him out."

"You monster."

"You don't understand. I had to ... I still have to ... make contact with Edgar. It was our life's work and I couldn't allow George to ruin it all!"

Marianne shook her head in disgust. He might plead that he was of unsound mind, but if he didn't hang for these offences, he was surely going to Bedlam for the rest of his life.

As if reading her thoughts, he said, "Will I swing for this?"

"It is likely."

"Good," he said. "I deserve it. And my friend will be waiting for me. I welcome peace, and death, and I look forward to being reunited with Edgar and all the others I have lost."

"Well," Marianne snapped, "let us hope, then, that you are right and there is someone else waiting for you too – George Bartholomew, who might have made mistakes in his life, but he didn't deserve to die. He will be wanting to be reunited with you, too."

Wade shuddered, and the constable put the lantern on the floor so that he could fit the handcuffs to the arrested man. Their shadows flared up around them on the walls, and Marianne tried not to look at them, because she was sure she could count more than four.

Twenty-seven

"Let me speak to Price before you do," Marianne said as they walked wearily up the steps to the front door of Woodfurlong. It was nearly midnight. Inspector Gladstone had sent a younger constable with them to see them home safely, and he promised to call upon them in the morning. Wade had been taken into custody, and would be up before the police court magistrates in the morning. The police would need to build a case if they were to do the prosecution, which seemed likely, and they would need to talk to Marianne and Phoebe again.

About *everything*, Gladstone had warned.

That was complicated.

"He is my husband," Phoebe complained. "I am so tired, Marianne. Just let's go to bed, and we can approach all this over breakfast."

Mr Barrington opened the door, and hustled them into the hallway. He looked at Phoebe's unfamiliar and unbecoming dress, and their smeared painted faces, but he didn't make a comment beyond enquiring as to anything they needed.

"No, thank you, Barrington. You may close up for the night."

"Very good, madam."

At the bottom of the stairs, they stopped to embrace. Marianne would be going along the ground floor to the garden wing, and Phoebe would creep upstairs to her rooms.

"Phoebe?"

They remained holding one another's arms, and looked up to see Price standing at the top of the stairs, illuminated by one gas light on the wall behind him. He was in his silk dressing gown, and his face was unreadable in the shadows.

"Price! I am sorry we are so late."

Marianne cursed. Price would have questions if he saw their faces or studied their clothing.

But maybe it was time to answer those questions.

"Come on," she said to her cousin. "Let us go up, and find some brandy, and settle this whole matter. Then I think we will find that sleep comes easily."

***

Price's study seemed the natural place to go. He poured himself a large glass and fixed Marianne with a glare. She ignored it. The truth was going to come out, and he needed to be grateful that it was not as bad as it could have been.

He tried to take control from the start. It was his private space, after all, and he was used to being in charge from his work life. "I don't know what is going on here, but Miss Starr, you are a bad influence. I do not want to be the cruel or heavy-handed man but I must warn you that changes will have to be made." He stared and stared, willing her to keep silent.

"More has been happening than you know about," Marianne said. "I beg you to listen to everything and not to speak

296

until I am quite done." Then she turned to Phoebe. "And the same goes for you, dear cuz. Please. Nothing I say will harm either of you, really, in the long term. Please just listen to the very end."

She paced around while they sat on comfortably scuffed leather wing-back chairs. Phoebe nestled herself in a blanket and Price just sat, his back straight and his hands on his knees. She started at the beginning, telling them things that they already knew and things that were new to them.

She explained how she had initially been approached by the shady Jack Monahan, and how her refusal to help had triggered some reaction in him. "He did not like being told no," she said, "and it all became personal." She told them about George, and his suspicions, which was a shock to Price. She then told them about Price's appeal to her for money, and Phoebe clutched her knees and laid her head on her forearms, all bunched up like a little girl, and didn't speak at all. And Price was gazing intently at Phoebe, watching for a reaction, any reaction, and Marianne could feel the love between them that was desperately stretching, growing thin, but still there like a thread that connected them. They *wanted* it to be all right, and so it would be.

Price was shocked that Marianne had found the dead body, and intrigued by the experiments she had done with her father. He was shocked all over again as she told him about the fake séances.

"You did this twice?" he spluttered. "Sorry, sorry, carry on."

At the end, there was silence.

Price got up, and refilled his brandy glass. As he crossed the rug on the way back to his seat, he detoured to go alongside

Phoebe. As he passed her, he bent and kissed the top of her head. She put up her hand and caught his, and squeezed it. He nodded, and went back to his chair.

"I think I might fill in one or two gaps which remain," he said, in a rough and low voice, quite unlike his usual self. "It is true that I have been a weak and foolish man, but I have always been utterly faithful to you, Phoebe, and it hasn't been any kind of effort on my part – it is easy to stay your devoted husband, my dear, for you are my world, my everything. Everything. Do you believe me?"

"Yes."

"Well, then. What I did was show weakness for my country, not for a woman. Is patriotism a weakness? Perhaps I was blinded, more, by my own puffed up sense of importance. I truly thought that the authorities had chosen me to help them in their investigations! I was excited. I liked the secrecy. It was like living in a book. Can you imagine?"

Phoebe and Marianne both nodded. It made more sense to Marianne than she would ever admit.

"Anna was charming, but I thought of her like she was a clever daughter."

Phoebe narrowed her eyes. But Marianne stepped in. "She really was, Phoebe. I liked her a lot. She was clever, witty and had a way with her. We should have been friends," she added wistfully.

"Where is she now?"

"We believe she has fled," Marianne said.

"Good. Shoot her if you see her again."

Price nearly smiled at that. He said, "Anyway, it soon

298

became apparent to me that she was not who she claimed to be, and I was ... I was, to my eternal and undying shame, caught fast in a blackmailer's plot. She was one of them – one of the Prussians. I made Marianne promise not to tell you, Phoebe. Don't blame her."

Phoebe met Marianne's eyes. She would always blame her a little bit, Marianne knew, but it didn't matter.

"But at least she has gone," Price said. "And that is an end to that, or so I hope."

"But your company's information is now in the hands of these foreigners, these Junkers," Phoebe said. "What happens now?"

"I do not know," he said. "But I have been scouring the newspapers every day for news from Prussia. The new chancellor's attempts to open up trade and drop the tariffs – which we were primed to capitalise upon – are being thwarted at every turn. The ruling landowners in the east really won't give up their monopolies without a fight. It might be that she didn't need to take that information about the deals from me at all. Perhaps we won't be expanding operations there, not as we planned, at any rate. Maybe she did not manage to pass the information on."

"Do you think you ought to tell the management at your company?"

Price jiggled his knee nervously. "I will watch and wait, at this stage," he said. "The main thing is that she is gone, and I will be able to pay off the loans – and what I owe you, Marianne."

When had he started using her first name? She smiled. "Take your time," she said. "After all, I live here under your sufferance and generosity."

"Nonsense, nonsense." He waved at her and turned his head away slightly, embarrassed. "You are family. What matters more than this?"

"Well, there is a question that Wade Walker needs to consider," Marianne said.

They fell into silence, and this time it deepened. No doubt there would be a dozen conversations over the next few days, rehashing the same events over and over, but for now, everything had been said.

It was time for bed at last.

Twenty-eight

Marianne was shocked when she awoke the next day. It was already past midday. She could not remember ever having slept so long before. She rolled over and stared blankly at the heavy curtains at the window. Bright light shone down one edge where the fabric had not been pulled across tightly enough. Usually, that would have annoyed her and she would not have been able to sleep.

But she had fallen into bed and barely moved.

Now she was stiff and foggy-headed. She sat up slowly, and remained there on the edge of the bed, hunched forward, trying to work out why she felt as if she had been hit by an omnibus.

That was how her father found her. He was dressed in a perfectly smart and respectable suit as if he were going out for luncheon. He was carrying a tray of food which he put on her bed, and she finally stirred.

"The maids will be furious – father, put it on the table."

"Nonsense. You need to eat. You're in bed during the day, which makes you an invalid, which means normal rules do not apply."

"I'm not in bed."

"You're on bed. It is the same. Now, eat. I command it."

It was not worth arguing about and anyway, her stomach had started to rumble. So she did eat, and gratefully too.

"Do you know how Phoebe and her husband are?" Marianne asked.

"Sickening."

"I'm sorry?"

Russell stood up and picked up the empty tray. "I went to join them for breakfast. But no place had been laid for me!"

"Because you never come for breakfast."

"Well, it didn't matter, because I took your place."

"Oh, I bet they were delighted."

He shrugged. "They were mostly focused on one another, simpering and cooing and *looking* at each other. You know. *Looking*. I expect Gertie and Charlie will have a new sister or brother next year."

"Father! Get out of my room. I need to dress."

He retreated, and Marianne sighed, but she smiled. At least the Claverdons were safe once more in their relationship.

***

Phoebe was in her morning room, reading her correspondence and looking at her diary for upcoming events. She rose when Marianne entered and they embraced.

"You look pale," Phoebe said. "Do not read the papers."

"Well, that just ensures that I will do that first. Which paper and what am I supposed to avoid?"

"Oh, Marianne, you will get yourself worked up. It's the top one on the table. I've opened it at the right page."

302

Marianne saw it immediately. There was a long thin column written by Harry Vane, the "celebrated and distinguished investigator of the science of the paranormal" accompanied by a flattering print showing him to be a proud but benevolent man. Marianne took up a pencil as she read, and shaded in some devil's horns.

The article alluded to her, of course, and took a swipe at all women who dared to unbalance God's own order of things, bringing down certain calamity and ruin upon society.

He drew a parallel between women becoming educated, and the women who were performing séances, using both as an example of the degradation of the feminine.

By the time she had got to the end of the article, she had stabbed right through the paper.

"I am taking this," she said, folding the newspaper up. "I shall write a rebuttal this very afternoon."

"Leave it until tomorrow," Phoebe said. "Today we should go and check on Simeon."

Marianne remembered that he had left the scene yesterday, and felt like a bad friend for not thinking of him. "At once," she said. "Let us go. And after that, we will call on the solicitor and I shall have the balance of payments that is owing to me."

***

"I am sure that we are being followed," Marianne said to Phoebe as they walked from the railway station. Marianne had suggested they catch an omnibus and Phoebe had insisted on a cab and neither had prevailed, so they walked like any commoner.

Luckily it was a chilly day so the streets did not smell as bad

303

as they might have done.

"Who do you think it is?" Phoebe asked, walking closer to Marianne.

"Oh … it is probably nothing. I am on edge, and feel unsettled, that's all."

They carried on through the usual everyday throng of London with its noise and its bustle and its rush. Everything was faster here, louder, more colourful and more exciting. It could quite drain a person and Marianne was not feeling particularly resilient.

"I should feel very happy that it's all over," she complained to Phoebe.

"You need a little time to catch up with yourself. Oh!" Phoebe grabbed Marianne's arm and dragged her to the side but she was too late.

Jack Monahan materialised behind them and doffed his hat, sweeping them a low bow. "Ladies."

"Are you following us?" Marianne demanded.

"Yes I am."

"Don't!"

He smiled. "I was rather hoping that someone else would be following you."

"Anna Jones," Marianne said. "I don't believe that is even her real name."

"Anna is correct. Her other names change with the wind."

"Were you hoping she would make another attempt on my life, so you could swoop in and save me, and become a hero?" Marianne asked.

He was still grinning. "Oh yes, that would be rather good."

"I don't think she's still in London."

"Where else would she go? She is an outcast."

"She could go home to Prussia."

Monahan shook his head and lowered his voice, edging closer to them when he spoke again. "She cannot. I have unearthed a little more information about this woman."

"Tell me!" Marianne said. "It could help Mr Claverdon…" She shot a glance at Phoebe, who was pale and biting her lip. His future at the company was certainly in doubt if things became known.

"Your Mr Claverdon need have no worries at all." He hesitated.

"You are thinking how you might hold on to this information to make it work for you, aren't you?" Marianne said. "Listen to me. I am tired, and unhappy, and out of sorts. I have a gun and a great deal of feminine irrationality. I will shoot you. Right now. Unless you speak."

"Well, then. I have pieced it together from what you have told me, and my own sources. You know that she and George did have an affair in Prussia?"

"Yes. And he came home, and was dismissed. She followed. Did she truly love him, then?"

"Did, and probably still does. I do not know if she thought she could continue her liaison with him here, but anyway, she came."

"She loves London," Marianne said. "She simply wants to be here."

"Well, she came, and she needed money, and then various men found her. Men from Prussia, old money and aristocrats, the ones in power, the ones seeing their power slip away."

"The Junkers."

"Those very same, and the more violent and desperate end of them, too. They instructed her to get company secrets from Mr Claverdon."

Phoebe broke in. "Why? What would he know?"

Monahan sighed with a condescending edge. "He spent years out there and he knows all the best trading spots and landing areas for ships; he knows men who can be paid off and men who cannot. He has contacts out there. He has been drafting legal documents, and writing letters detailing expected shipments, all under a cloak of secrecy to avoid attracting the attention of those who would sabotage this expansion of free trade."

"Oh."

"And he passed some of this to her, and she expected to give it to the Junkers in exchange for money."

"Then why did she blackmail him?"

"Because by the time she had the information, her husband, in his fury, had sent word to all of the spies in London that he knew of, that she was not to be trusted. The Junkers in London would not take her secrets. She was contaminated, corrupt and her information was false. She found that she could not sell it. So all she could do was to blackmail Claverdon instead."

Phoebe gasped, shocked. Marianne thought, *how clever! Oh, the silly woman.*

"So you see," Monahan went on. "She is quite friendless here, and alone, and without money. She is desperate and you, Miss Starr, are the cause of her undoing."

"Do you really think she will come after me?"

306

"I am convinced of it. She thinks that you will expose her."

"I have no desire to do so," she said. "But you will, won't you?"

Again he hesitated before saying, "Actually, what would be the point? No harm has been caused by her actions – I mean, no political harm. No secrets have been sold. No one at Harker and Bow know about this. They suspected a mole, but with George Bartholomew's death, they believe it to be all over. And so it is."

"Then why are you here, following us, to find her?"

"Just that," he said. "I want to speak to her and tell her that she is, in a sense, free. Certainly she is free of persecution from me. What her countrymen do is up to them. But she should not fear us, and perhaps … well."

He didn't need to say it. If Anna felt more safe, perhaps she would not pursue Marianne for revenge. Perhaps.

"She can still be convicted of blackmail," Phoebe put in.

"Yes. And that would drag your husband's name into the public eye. Shall I?"

"No! No, please don't," Phoebe said.

He looked at Marianne. She nodded. "Please don't. Thank you."

He grinned again, and bowed to them once more, breaking the mood. "You owe me a favour for this!" he said. "Good day to you both."

As he backed away, Marianne called out, "And what of you? Have you gained your position of employment once more?"

His face clouded momentarily but he covered it up with a boyish laugh. "Oh, I have decided to move on to new projects. Goodbye!"

Phoebe took hold of Marianne's arm. "He is a menace."

"He is a menace and a liar," Marianne said. "But I do hope that life treats him kindly."

Phoebe snorted. "Put him very far from your mind," she said. "If you feel at all tempted to fall in love with a rogue, let me know, and I shall find you one with a fortune and a short expected life span."

"How mercenary!"

"I am practical, that is all. Come along. We are but one street from Simeon's."

***

They were welcomed into his workshop and had barely sat down with tea and cakes when someone else knocked at his door – Inspector Gladstone entered, and made everyone feel supremely awkward.

No one knew how he had discovered that Simeon had been part of the previous night's escapade.

Gladstone smiled amiably and waited to be offered a cup of tea, which fell in the end to Marianne, as Simeon was standing by a chair and looking to be struck dumb with fear.

"Oh, don't worry," Gladstone said, sitting down with his fresh brew. "I'm not here to arrest you, lad."

"Why? I mean, I know."

"How did you know we were here?" Marianne asked.

"I didn't know you and Mrs Claverdon would be here. That is a most pleasant surprise. It will save me a journey to your house. I came only to call upon Mr Stainwright."

"But why?" Simeon almost wailed.

Marianne winced. Poor Simeon's fears and frets would be working overtime.

But Gladstone spoke reassuringly. "I knew who owned the house where last night's alarums took place, and I spoke to him, who let me know that it was you who rented the room. I came here only to get a statement from you about what happened. We are building a case, that is all."

"Against Wade Walker?"

"Yes."

"Has he not confessed?"

"He has confessed all. He seems rather mad, if I am honest. He may not hang for this, if his insanity is fully revealed."

"I think he'd rather hang."

"So he says, and that in itself is the mark of insanity. Anyway, that is not my concern." Gladstone flipped open his notebook and looked expectantly at Simeon. "From the beginning, if you please."

Simeon spoke haltingly, looking frequently to Marianne for confirmation of his words, and she bit her tongue but nodded encouragingly. When he had done, Gladstone flapped his notebook shut and thanked him.

"And now us?" Phoebe said. "You said it has saved you a visit to our house."

"Ah, yes, yes," he said, "all in good time. I was actually going to call on you with another matter." He was looking at Marianne. He pulled out a piece of paper from an inside pocket of his jacket. "We received this letter and I was rather hoping you might give me some of your insight."

He passed it to her and she read it three times with growing interest.

She gave it back to him. "Ghostly screaming in the night, sir, certainly has a very human explanation. Has the house been searched?"

"Many times."

"Have your officers heard this screaming?"

"Yes, and it has almost unhinged one of our younger constables. We simply need you to visit and find the mechanical means by which this infernal noise is made, and we shall pay you for it, for I confess that we are all mystified."

"It sounds very straightforward." Marianne felt her oppressive mood lifting almost instantly. "Thank you sir – I shall be delighted to assist."

They shook hands, and when Marianne set out to Mr Harcourt's office, even Phoebe remarked on her lighter step.

"I have a very good feeling about the future, Phoebe," Marianne said.

"The future appears to involve devilish screaming."

"I know. Isn't it fun?"

"It is. It is, indeed."

The End

If you have enjoyed this book, please leave a review where you bought it!

If you have really, really enjoyed this book, why not sign up to my New Releases Newsletter? I don't share your email with anyone, and I don't spam. Here is the link:
http://www.subscribepage.com/o5y2q0

I am also on Facebook.
https://www.facebook.com/issy.brooke